EB

Redemption's Whisper

Kathleen E. Friesen

Redemption's Whisper

Contact Information: titleadmin@pelicanbookgroup.com

Cover Art by *Nicola Martinez*

White Rose Publishing, a division of Pelican Ventures, LLC
www.pelicanbookgroup.com PO Box 1738 *Aztec, NM * 87410

Publishing History
First White Rose Edition, 2017
Paperback Edition ISBN 978-1-61116-971-3
Electronic Edition ISBN 978-1-61116-972-0
Published in the United States of America

Acknowledgements

Writing is a solitary occupation for the most part, but without my support groups, this book would still be stuck in my imagination.

A huge thank-you goes to my fantastic online critique partners, the ACFW Scribes 202 group and Rhonda Starnes. You not only found typos, you all helped me develop as a writer.

My dear pen pals, Gerry Meggait, Robin Flaten, Virginia Fairbrother, and Anne Lockhart continually encourage me not only in writing but in faith. I love you.

Fylis Edwards, thank you for answering my medical questions. Your nursing experience is expansive, and your friendship is precious.

Thanks goes to my editor, Jamie West, and Pelican Book Group's publisher, Nicola Martinez, for seeing something special in this story.

Last, but definitely not least, thank you to my husband, Ron Friesen, for your patience, your understanding, and your wacky sense of humor that keeps me somewhat sane. You're my hero.

May the God of hope fill you with all joy and peace as you trust in Him, so that you may overflow with hope by the power of the Holy Spirit. (Romans 15:13).

1

A gust of wind shook the narrow, sloped jet bridge as Hayley Blankenship dragged her carry-on toward the jumbo jet. Fear lodged in her throat, and her footsteps faltered.

People surged past. "Excuse me."

She swallowed hard and lifted her trembling chin. Not now. She would not give in to fear today. "You are strong," she whispered. The floor trembled, and Hayley stumbled as the moveable passageway adjusted itself. She clutched the handle of her bag, inhaled sharply, and trudged on. Almost there. She stalled at the entrance to the airplane. Her nerves vibrated. The narrow opening seemed to close around her. The air felt too thick to breathe. Her shoulders curled forward, and her head lowered. This was a mistake. She wasn't ready, not yet. She turned, but a long line of passengers stood behind her. Could she push past all those staring faces? Her knees threatened to buckle.

The flight attendant reached out and touched Hayley's arm, startling her. "Is there a problem, miss?"

Hayley shook her head and stiffened her resolve. She'd made the decision to go to Saskatoon. This might be her last chance. She inhaled through her nose and forced her shoulders back, her head up.

The flight attendant said something as she entered the plane, but it didn't register.

Hayley needed to concentrate. She glanced at the boarding pass in her hand. Seat 20A. The rear of the plane, out of sight of most of the other passengers. A window seat, so she could watch her past disappear. She walked by people already seated, avoiding their eyes, until she came to her assigned spot. Hayley shrugged out of her coat and stuffed it in the overhead compartment. She slid into her allotted place, stored her carry-on under the seat in front of her, and leaned against the window.

Various workers on the ground hurried to load luggage, refuel the plane, and do whatever else was needed to prepare for another flight.

As Hayley watched their purposeful strides, a twinge of envy twisted her lips. Self-pity and self-loathing reared their ugly heads. She closed her eyes in a futile attempt to block the terrible images racing through her mind. *Give up. You're not going to make it. You may as well take the pills—all of them.* She shook her head as though that would dislodge the negative thoughts. She sensed someone settle into the aisle seat but didn't bother looking. She didn't want to talk to anyone. Casual conversation was pointless. If only she could curl into a ball and block out the world, at least for a while.

~*~

Trevor Hiebert ran down the empty passageway to the plane's doorway. As he ran, he muttered a rant against Toronto traffic and cabbies who seemed more interested in conversing on their radios than getting him to Pearson International on time. He couldn't afford to miss this flight.

If only he'd pre-booked a seat. Now he was stuck with a center spot, and he knew from experience how uncomfortable it would be. Maybe the plane would be nearly empty so he could have a row to himself. He ducked around the smiling flight attendant and groaned. So much for that wish. He dragged his wheeled carry-on down the aisle as he scanned the numbers above the rows. Finally, he spotted it: 20B. He glanced at his row mates, a young woman leaning against the cabin wall with her eyes closed and an older woman who looked like a sweet grandmotherly type in the aisle seat.

"Excuse me, ma'am. I'm in 20B."

The old woman looked beside her at the narrow seat and back up at him. Her attention settled on his broad shoulders, and her mouth compressed into a flat line. "Good luck."

Trevor shifted his weight and pulled his leather bag closer. "Would you mind trading spots with me? Then I won't have to climb over you." And he'd have a little more breathing room.

"I certainly would mind. I want this seat." She jutted her chin and glared at him. "You young punks are used to getting your way, but you won't bully me."

The attendant moved to the front of the cabin, ready to begin her safety speech.

His temper surged, but Trevor clamped a lid on it. The woman wasn't worth the regret he'd feel later. He shrugged out of his well-worn leather jacket, lifted it and his bag into the overhead compartment, and tried to maneuver over the woman's legs in the cramped space to his assigned spot. Her leg jolted against the back of his knee, and he lost his balance. He caught himself against the window so he wouldn't land in the young woman's lap.

The girl's eyes snapped open as he turned to apologize. She gave a sharp intake of breath and tried to ease away, but Trevor's power to move deserted him. Her mesmerizing green eyes widened as shock turned to fear.

"What are you doing?" Her shrill voice broke the spell.

"So sorry," he mumbled. He pushed off from the window and plunked into his chair. "I tripped." He looked sideways at the old woman, who smirked as she smoothed her pant legs.

It was going to be a long flight.

He glanced back at the young woman and wondered at his desire to see her face again. But she had turned away and sat huddled against the wall. Her sharp-angled shoulder blades and the back of her spiky auburn hair made an effective barrier. Kind of looked like a hedgehog. Trevor snorted. He was stuck between a prickly old grouch and a hedgehog. For three and a half hours.

~*~

Hayley pressed against the wall of the aircraft as chills raced through her limbs. Her legs trembled and her heart raced. She'd made it onto the plane. Would she fall apart now? That man had nearly landed on top of her. It happened so fast, she hadn't had time to react. There was no room to move, anyway. But he'd caught himself and apologized. She wasn't hurt, just scared. Her breathing evened out. She'd survived worse. She silently repeated her psychiatrist's prescribed refrain. *I am OK. I am strong. The past is gone. The future is God's.*

Over and over, until her body began to relax. Just like in Dr. Freemont's office.

She'd heard the brief exchange between her seatmates. The man's voice would have excited her in the past. She would have smiled at him and flirted with him. But that was the old Hayley. She was dead.

When she'd looked up and stared into his rugged face, all her senses had sharpened. He smelled like pine forest mixed with motor oil, a strangely tantalizing combination. His tanned skin indicated time spent outdoors. And his dark-lashed gray eyes, like a stormy Lake Ontario, invited her to sink into them. For one brief moment, she had the strangest sensation she could see her future in those eyes. And that terrified her.

~*~

Trevor jerked when the woman he'd first pegged as a sweet grandmother jabbed his arm with her elbow. "Pardon me?"

She already had the aisle seat. Did he have to give up the shared armrest, too? She pushed against his arm. Apparently.

"I need the armrest." She dug into her oversized purse and pulled out a paperback book with a suggestive picture on its cover. "Now leave me alone and let me read my story."

Trevor bit back a retort. He exhaled slowly to cool his frustration. Maybe if he concentrated on work, he could ignore both seatmates, one a royal pain and the other too intriguing. He reached for his phone, leaning to the left so he wouldn't incur the old woman's wrath again. But the space allotted wasn't enough for his wide shoulders. His left shoulder pressed against the young woman's back and elicited a gasp.

She uncurled and seemed as though she was trying to merge with the wall of the plane. She looked sideways at him, eyes wide and lips clenched.

"Sorry, I didn't mean to disturb you. I don't think the airplane designers made these seats for people my size."

Shadows flitted over her pale face and disappeared. A tentative smile softened her lips. "You may be right." She hesitated for several heartbeats, and then turned and held out a slender hand. "I'm Hayley. Hayley Blankenship."

That little smile was like a rainbow during a storm, offering promises of spectacular beauty. Stunned by his reaction, he stared at her mouth until her smile disappeared and she started to pull her hand back. He took her hand in his. It felt fragile, cool, and…a zap of electricity shot up his arm, and she snatched her hand back.

Their eyes connected, and he was lost again until she blinked.

He gave himself a mental shake. "I'm…Trevor Hiebert. Nice to meet you."

She lowered her long lashes. "You too."

"Are you from Saskatoon?"

A shadow returned to her beautiful face. "No, I'm visiting friends there. I...I've been…sick, and my doctor suggested a change of scenery."

That explained the pallor, shadows under the eyes, and fragile appearance. He'd never been good with sickness. He stumbled over what to say. "I hope it helps." That was the best he could do.

She ducked her head, her hands clenched so

tightly her knuckles turned white.

He waited, but she didn't speak. Obviously his best wasn't very good.

~*~

Hayley could hear Dr. Freemont's voice. *"You need to make new friends. Open yourself to positive relationships. Start living again."* But she didn't know how. She carried too many secrets, too much sorrow to ever be a party girl again. That life no longer appealed. She wished she could at least carry on a normal conversation, though.

Especially since this intriguing man would be crammed next to her for more than three hours. She studied him with sideways glances. He'd apparently given up on her and was frowning at the screen of his phone. The lines on his forehead invited her fingers to smooth them. Where had that thought come from? She tucked her hands under her thighs and turned enough to see him more clearly.

There was something familiar about his face. They'd never met before, she was certain. His nose looked like it had been broken more than once, but something about his face reminded her of…The name wouldn't come.

The inflight movie started, one she'd seen many times, and a dashing, dark-haired cowboy appeared onscreen. An older, smoother version of her companion. Not identical, but the resemblance was remarkable.

She couldn't hold back a gasp, and he glanced at her. She looked at him, at the movie screen, and back at him with her eyebrows raised.

He sighed. "Yeah, it's been mentioned a time or two."

His rueful expression brought a long-lost grin to her face. Part of her mind registered wonder that her face didn't crack. She gave herself a mental shake. She needed to concentrate on the here and now. She glanced at the screen again and murmured, "Well, it could be worse."

He cocked his head as though deep in thought and then nodded. "I guess you're right." He didn't break a smile. "I could have looked like his horse."

Laughter bubbled up, surprising her. She touched her lips and watched as his gaze followed her fingers. She dropped her hands and clasped them in her lap, but his eyes didn't move.

He seemed to be a gentleman in spite of his intimidating size and biker-rough appearance. Maybe Dr. Freemont was right. Maybe this was her chance to chip away at her shell of isolation. She should try, at least. Besides, Saskatoon—if it was his destination—was large enough, they would probably never see each other again. So if she messed up, it wouldn't matter. She took a deep breath. "I'm glad I met you today, Trevor."

His answering smile warmed her. "Likewise, Hayley. I thought this flight was going to be miserable." He tilted his head toward the old woman.

Hayley rolled her eyes and whispered, "She can't be happy."

"You're probably right," he whispered back.

An angry retort came from the aisle seat. "I can hear you two. Mind your own bleepin' business and leave me out of it."

Trevor winked at her, and Hayley covered her

mouth with her hand to stifle a giggle.

She lowered her fingers. "Oops," she mouthed. She sat up straighter and tilted her head. "So, Trevor, tell me about yourself. Do you live in Saskatoon, or are you continuing on? What kind of work do you do?" She paused, her chin lowered. "Or am I being too nosy?"

He angled his body toward her. "The answer to your last question is 'no.' I live and work in Saskatoon, for now, anyway. I work at motorcycle shop there, but I may be moving to Toronto to work at Lowrider Cycles. Ever heard of it?"

She shook her head more to tame her emotions than to answer. His mention of motorcycles swept her back to the year she'd dated a young biker wannabe. She hadn't thought about that summer for years, couldn't even remember his name. Matt? Mark? Didn't matter. But she could feel the heat of the exhaust pipes by her legs, hear the wind shrieking past her helmet and the roar of the powerful engine. Such a long time ago, when she was still a teenager. Longing filled her—and shocked her. She hadn't experienced such a rush of yearning for months. Even as she wondered, the feeling faded, leaving a familiar, heavy emptiness.

"You OK?"

She felt her face warm. "Sorry, I got a little lost there." She replayed his question. "Yes, I've heard of it. They specialize in custom bikes, right?"

His smile brightened. "Right. That's what I do. When I can." His smile dimmed. "But I haven't accepted yet. My folks are getting on in years, and they still farm out near Langham. Do you know the area?"

Hayley shook her head. "I went to university in Saskatoon for one term a couple years ago, but I never got outside the city."

"Just one term? Why? What were you studying?"

"Um…yeah. I'd planned to go into accounting, but things didn't work out." She couldn't go there. Would she ever be allowed to forget? She fought tears as she glanced at her seat-mate. His expression held curiosity mixed with kindness, and Hayley lowered her head. Dr. Freemont was wrong. She couldn't socialize. That part of her was dead, or at least damaged beyond repair. Her shoulders hunched, and she turned toward the window, seeing only her failures.

~*~

It was none of his business. He didn't know this woman and would probably never see her again. But Hayley Blankenship's reaction troubled him, stirred his protectiveness. He'd seen it too many times, that tentative connection so easily broken.

Trevor glanced at his watch. It was almost three hours until they'd land in Saskatoon. He would give her some time and space to work through whatever had triggered her withdrawal. His mouth twisted as he touched the screen on his phone. He was no superhero. He couldn't protect everyone, no matter how much he wanted to.

He turned his attention to the notes he'd jotted yesterday, and his gut churned at the questions he'd written to himself. He had a decision to make, and no matter which option he chose, people's lives would change. People he cared about.

List the pros and cons. Trevor began with his first option, the one he'd gone to Toronto to investigate, and listed everything positive and negative he could imagine from its outcome. Including the faint uneasiness he'd felt during his interview. Too bad he couldn't have stayed longer, checked it out more thoroughly. But it seemed to be the job of his dreams. He listed several impressions of Lowrider Cycles and the positives and negatives of moving. Then the second scenario, the one involving his parents. That took longer, and he soon lost awareness of everything around him. Sometime later, movement from the left alerted him.

Hayley was trying to stand in the cramped space. "Excuse me, please. My leg…I need to get out."

What little color she'd had was gone. Her shadowed eyes appeared even brighter against the whiteness of her face. Lines had appeared beside her mouth.

"Sure. Of course. Let me get out of your way."

The old woman was snoring, her racy novel open on her chest, but when Trevor tried to step over her, she jerked awake.

"What do you think you're doing? Get off of me!"

He ignored her outburst and moved into the aisle. He offered his hand to Hayley, and she grasped it without hesitation. She seemed to stumble a bit as she joined him in the aisle. She grabbed the back of the old woman's seat with her other hand, and the woman glared at her.

"You two want to play games, go do it somewhere else."

"Just give me a minute, please." Hayley's voice quavered.

The other woman's fierceness dissipated. "You hurtin', girl?" The gruff voice was much softer now.

"I'll be fine. Thank you." Hayley offered a shaky

smile.

A glimmer of compassion softened the old woman's face.

"I know about pain. What happened to you?"

Hayley shook her head and closed her eyes. The plane shifted, and she wobbled.

Acting on instinct, Trevor snagged her around the waist and pulled her closer. She clung to him for a moment, long enough for him to inhale the scent of her hair. Peaches, or maybe strawberries. Something fruity. His arm tightened around her.

At that moment the flight attendant's voice came over the loudspeaker. "May I have your attention? We are flying into some turbulence, so please be seated and fasten your seatbelts. Thank you."

Hayley gasped and pulled away from him. "Excuse me again," she said breathlessly as she stepped over the older woman and back to her seat.

The old woman patted Hayley's back as she passed.

Trevor's eyebrows lifted. People certainly were complicated. He nodded to the woman as he carefully moved back to his seat and fastened his seatbelt. He glanced to his left. Hayley's belt was snugged tight, almost as tight as the lines around her mouth. He leaned closer to her and kept his voice low. "Do you have something you can take for the pain?"

She didn't look at him. "I'm trying to stay away from them. Too easy to get hooked."

Sounded like narcotics. It must have been bad, then. "Would ibuprofen help? I have some in my bag."

"I took some just before boarding, but it doesn't do much." She gripped the armrest as the plane bucked.

"How about a distraction? Give me your hand."

He'd asked without thinking and felt pleasantly surprised when Hayley held out her hand, palm up. He turned it over, found the spot above her wrist bone, and pressed his thumb against it, gently and then more deeply.

At first she watched his fingers on her hand as though hypnotized. After several moments her wide, green eyes lifted and connected with his. "Where did you learn to do that? It's actually helping."

"Something my mom taught me."

When she leaned back and closed her eyes, Trevor eased the pressure of his thumb and began slow, gentle circles on the palm of her hand. He watched as her lips lifted. Nice. He'd only tried acupressure on himself before, and it certainly hadn't been this pleasurable. Her slender hand had been cold when she'd offered it to him, but now its warmth radiated up his arm. It fit in his as though it had been designed for him. Shock halted his movements. What was he thinking?

2

The airplane seemed to have flown into an obstacle course. It jolted and bumped as the pilots guided it through the turbulence. Hayley concentrated on the rough texture of Trevor's thumb as it massaged her hand. It felt so soothing, so relaxing. She sank into the comfort, hardly noticing the pain in her leg or the plane's uneven flight. A tremor passed through his thumb to her hand, and the movement stopped. Hayley opened her eyes. Trevor stared straight ahead, his brow furrowed.

"Something wrong?"

He turned to her, his face flushed. "No. It's nothing."

The plane bucked, and Hayley's left leg banged against the wall. She groaned and tightened her grip on his hand.

"That was a bad one," Trevor said. "How can I help?"

The low rumble of his voice felt like a balm. She spoke through clenched teeth. "Talk to me. About anything." Hayley just wanted to hear his voice. Its bass resonance was an audio massage; she wished she could drown in its depths. It was better than those narcotics hidden in her bag. Perhaps as addictive, but she'd bet not as deadly.

As the plane bounced, Hayley's willpower ebbed. The pain was too much. The rod in her leg seemed to be reacting to the turbulence. Maybe one pill would help. Just one. Or two. She could handle that, couldn't she? Or would she be hooked again? She slumped in her seat and grabbed the armrest with her free hand. "Tell me a story. Maybe about your farm? I've never been on a farm."

~*~

Shadows flitted across her face as she fought some kind of inner battle. Trevor wondered if it concerned whatever had injured her. She obviously wasn't ready to talk. Tell a story. Didn't seem like much. Maybe it would help, though. He'd do it—as long as he avoided the reality of his childhood. He leaned back against the headrest and closed his eyes.

"Farm life is a pretty broad subject. Basically, it's a lot of hard work with a special kind of freedom. But I don't think we have time for everything involved. Let's see…I could tell you about my dog. He was a mutt, but he was my best friend."

"Sounds good."

The plane bucked again, and Hayley clutched his hand. He resumed the circular massage of her palm and tried to ignore the pleasure zinging up his arm.

"My folks let me choose one of the neighbor's pups soon after I got to the farm. He was the runt of the litter, not even cute, but when he climbed on my lap, I had to take him home. He looked like a mixture of German Shepherd, Rottweiler, and Border Collie. Short snout, floppy ears, black legs and brown and white body." His thumb's circular motion lightened to more of a caress. "I named him Hugo. Kind of as a joke, since he was so tiny, but it turned out to suit him.

He grew up fast. Didn't look like a runt for long."

He glanced at Hayley. Her eyes were closed again, but the lines by her mouth had relaxed a bit. Good. "Ever have a dog?"

She shook her head. "No animals allowed."

He was thankful his parents had seen the value in pets. And in him. He turned back to his memories. "Hugo taught me more than I taught him. Mom showed me how to teach him to do tricks once he'd learned the basics. He caught on pretty quick. Helped with the cattle and loved to play catch. I'd throw a tennis ball as far as I could, and Hugo could catch it before it hit the ground. He'd bring it back, drop the slobbery mess at my feet, and bark at me until I threw it again." Trevor chuckled. "What a goof."

The lines around Hayley's mouth eased, and her lips curved upward in a hint of a smile. "Tell me more. I can almost picture him. And a little-boy version of you."

Her whisper created a strange twist somewhere around his heart and blanked out his memory. What had he been talking about? *Oh, right. Hugo.* "He and I had some great times together exploring the bush around the house and in the fields. Turned out to be a good watchdog too. He was such a friendly mutt most of the time, I figured he'd be useless as a guard dog. Until one day."

Hayley's eyes opened, and her emerald gaze held his. "What happened?"

What was it about this woman? Was it the pain she fought? Was that what created this strange feeling of kinship? Trevor tore his attention away from the wide, green depths and back to his past.

"My parents had gone to visit friends from church.

They hadn't been gone long when Hugo started barking and growling. Never heard those sounds from him before. Freaked me out, so I ran outside. He stood at the bottom of the front steps, legs stiff, and the hair on his back stood straight up. His teeth were bared as he barked at a truck driving up our long driveway."

Trevor looked at Hayley. Her face looked softer, almost wistful as she whispered, "Sounds as if he was like a guardian angel. I always imagined they'd look fierce."

"I don't think Hugo was an angel, but he certainly did protect me. Because I didn't recognize the truck or the driver. The guy rolled down his window and asked if my dog would bite. I looked at Hugo and back at the guy. 'Probably.' That's all I said. The guy stared at Hugo for a minute, then backed up and turned around. Don't know who he was or what he was up to, but Hugo sensed an enemy and protected me." Trevor exhaled a long breath. "He was a good dog. I still miss him."

Hayley's answering sigh seemed to disappear into a deep well. "I wish I'd had a dog like Hugo. Or maybe a guardian angel to watch over me."

"Want to talk about it?"

He could feel her withdraw even before she pulled her hand away from his.

"No." She shook her head and started to turn away, but hesitated. "Thank you for sharing your stories with me. And for the hand massage. It helped." Her smile faded before it fully materialized, and a moment later Hayley had resumed her hedgehog position.

The "Fasten Seatbelts" light blinked off, and Trevor realized they'd passed through the turbulence.

His help wasn't need anymore. He should feel relieved.

Hayley's breathing evened out. The girl was obviously in pain, and he'd guess it was more than physical. Too bad she'd refused to talk it out. Holding things in just made it worse. He knew that from experience. He shook his head. He was no trained counselor. He'd been around them often enough, but that didn't make him one. He'd done what he could for her. But he wished he could do more.

After several minutes, Hayley's stiff posture seemed to melt against the seat. She'd fallen asleep.

Trevor pulled out his notebook and turned to his calculations, but he couldn't concentrate. The numbers he'd so carefully written looked like hieroglyphics. He gave himself a mental shake. Hayley Blankenship was his seatmate for this flight. Nothing more. So why did he feel such a connection to this stranger with the haunted green eyes and spiky red hair?

~*~

As the plane taxied into place at the terminal and people gathered their belongings, Trevor felt a firm tap on his right arm.

The old woman peered up at him, a sly smile softening her wrinkled face. "I gotta say, sonny, you got a real nice voice. Helped your young lady through that rough spot. You take good care of her, y'hear?"

He reared back as heat crawled up his neck. "She's not…I mean…thank you." He glanced over at Hayley.

Her eyebrows nearly reached her hairline, and a blush bloomed on her face. Her gaze seemed to stall at his shoulder, and then she ducked her head and reached for her bag.

When he turned back to the old woman, she'd already merged into the crowded aisle, her over-sized purse clutched to her chest. She met his gaze, nodded once, and turned to face the still-closed door. She reminded him of the elementary school principal who had reprimanded him for acting up and then slipped him some money for the class pizza lunch. A soft center under a hard shell.

He started to push upward in the narrow space when he heard a soft sigh. He looked at Hayley. The lines had reappeared beside her mouth. Trevor sank back into his seat. "You OK?"

"Yes. Well, I will be." She looked at her lap. "I have a problem lately with crowds…being crowded. I'll just wait until everyone clears out."

"Then I'll wait with you. If you don't mind. Is someone meeting you?"

Hayley's lips lifted ever so slightly. "I don't mind. You're very kind. And yes, someone is meeting me."

He didn't think his desire to spend more time with her qualified as kindness. Trevor rubbed his chin as he considered who that someone might be. A boyfriend? Maybe even a husband, although she wasn't wearing a ring. Why did it matter? They would probably never see one another again. Before long, he would forget those sorrow-filled green eyes. He glanced at Hayley's profile. Forgetting might take a while.

The door at the front of the plane finally opened, and the line of passengers inched forward. When the crowd thinned out, Trevor stepped into the aisle and pulled his jacket from the overhead bin. A long, black, wool coat threatened to fall as if it didn't want to be left behind. He grabbed it and asked Hayley, "Is this yours?"

She reached for it. "Yes, thanks." She stood in the narrow space, wobbled, and dropped the garment. Her shoulders drooped.

Trevor held out his hand. "May I help you? Leave the coat. I'll get it and your bag."

She nodded, took his hand, stepped gingerly into the aisle, and balanced herself against the aisle seatback.

He scooped up her carry-on, set it on the seat, and held her coat open. Hayley slid one arm at a time into the silk-lined sleeves, and Trevor settled it onto her shoulders. His hands lingered there, and he felt her relax against them. Or was that his imagination? Impulse made him blurt, "Can I call you sometime?"

She turned slowly, her head tilted. "Yes, you may. You could phone me at my friends' house, if you'd like. Or use my cell number. But don't feel obligated."

She recited a local and a Toronto number, and Trevor recorded them in his phone. He tucked the phone into his jeans pocket and picked up her bag. "Looks like it's our turn. Ready?"

Hayley took a deep breath and nodded as he held out his free arm to her. She slipped her hand through the crook of his arm and seemed to lean against him as they walked down the aisle. It felt good. They made their way down the long hallway to the escalator descending to the arrival area of John G. Diefenbaker Airport. His companion hesitated. He looked down at her as she trembled. "Take your time," he murmured. "I've got you."

After a moment, Hayley took a tentative step onto the moving staircase, and within seconds they reached the bottom. She moved away from Trevor and reached for her carry-on just as a vibration on his hip alerted him to a phone message.

Hayley glanced up at him, a slight smile softening her features. "I really appreciate all your help today. I can take it from here." She adjusted her grip on the wheeled bag, took a deep breath, and straightened her shoulders.

Trevor watched until she'd pushed through the door to the airport's waiting area. Then he paused in the middle of the walkway and pulled out his phone. The text message hit him like a blow to the solar plexus.

Mom fell. Phone me. Love, Dad.

Trevor couldn't catch his breath. He coughed, and it came out like a sob. He found his dad's number while rushing toward the door and called him. "Dad, what happened?"

"We're at City Hospital. I found your mom unconscious on the kitchen floor. I don't know..."

"Hang in there, all right? I'm still at the airport, but I'll get there as soon as I can." He made a beeline for the door, shoved it open, and headed straight for the taxi stand. He had to get to the hospital. Now.

~*~

Dave and Lydia Harris wore wide smiles that welcomed Hayley as she leaned into their hugs. "Pastor Dave, Lydia, it's so good to see you. Thank you for meeting me."

"Glad you made it." Pastor Dave's voice boomed. "It's good to see you too, my dear."

Lydia patted Hayley's back "How was your flight?"

Hayley twisted around, trying to spot Trevor. "It was fine. I'd like you to meet…" She caught a glimpse of his broad back heading out the double doors. Her shoulders drooped. "Never mind." She turned back just in time to see a look pass between her hosts.

Lydia moved closer. "Let's go find your suitcases, shall we? It's late, and you must be tired."

Hayley accepted Lydia's outstretched hand, and they followed Dave to the luggage carousel. As they waited for the machine to disgorge her luggage, Hayley wrestled with her thoughts.

Trevor Hiebert had surprised her with his compassion. He'd managed to break through her barriers and make a connection in those three and a half hours. So why had he disappeared? Maybe he'd realized she was too damaged to bother with. Her heart sank a little lower. He was the first man in a long time to intrigue her, make her feel something other than despair. She'd hoped he would want to see her again.

The carousel clunked to life, and a small, flowered suitcase flew down the ramp. A little girl rushed forward, grabbed it, and was swept into the arms of her father.

"All right, sweetheart, let's get you home," the man said.

The little girl wrapped her arms around his neck as they pushed through the crowd. "Home, Daddy, home!"

Moisture filled Hayley's eyes. Memories and broken dreams pressed in, and her throat tightened.

"Do you see your luggage yet?" Lydia's soft voice brought her back to the present.

Hayley nodded and pointed, unable to speak past

the lump lodged in her throat.

Dave grabbed both large suitcases, pulled out their handles, and strode back to the two women. "Is this everything?"

Hayley swallowed hard. "Y-yes. Thanks."

"Then let's get you home. Our car is in the first row." Dave started toward the exterior door, dragging the suitcases.

"I hope you'll be comfortable in the basement bedroom," Lydia said as she matched her pace to Hayley's. "Nila helped design and build it and it seemed to work well for her. But if you'd rather be upstairs, that's easily done."

"Nila's old room will be perfect. I saw it when I was here before, and it's beautiful." Hayley shivered when the door opened and a cold wind sliced through her winter coat. "Brr! I'm glad you warned me about March weather in Saskatchewan. Spring came to Toronto several weeks ago."

Lydia chuckled. "This *is* spring here. It was warm this afternoon, but we'll dip well below freezing again tonight. But Easter is coming—just three more weeks. I'm so glad you'll be with us for my favorite holiday." Her smile warmed Hayley like a sunbeam. "Here we are."

They caught up to Dave as he slammed the trunk on the beige sedan. "Hayley, you're shivering." He and Lydia exchanged a look, and Lydia gave a slight nod. Dave took Hayley's arm and pulled her forward. "Let's get you into the front where the seats are heated."

She hesitated. "That's not necessary, really. I'll be fine." But Lydia had already slid into the back, so Hayley eased into the front seat of the idling car. Warmth caressed her as she leaned back. "Thank you.

This is nice."

Dave fastened his seatbelt. "All set? Let's go home."

Home. A place of refuge, love, and hope. A place where people shared the ups and downs of life without giving up. That had been her dream, now obliterated. At the home Pastor Dave and Lydia shared, the place filled with their love for God and one another, could her longings find life again?

Hayley stared at the dark streets punctuated by oncoming headlights. Her dreams seemed like those headlights, here for a moment and then vanished from sight. Hopefully, with the help of these friends and God, she'd be able to find her purpose, and maybe even joy. Because if she couldn't, she knew she'd give in to the voice that taunted her to finish the pills hidden in her suitcase.

3

A plump, blonde nurse wearing floral scrubs entered City Hospital's emergency waiting room. "Mr. Hiebert?"

Trevor jumped to his feet. "That's me. I mean, us."

His dad rose more slowly, worry creasing his brow. "How is she?"

The woman smiled, a smooth, professional assurance. "Mrs. Hiebert is back from radiology, and she's asking for you." She directed a pointed look at Trevor. "You're her son?"

"Yes."

"OK, both of you follow me, please." She pushed through the heavy doors and glanced back at them. "Her arm is broken, so we'll get a cast on it right away. And the doctor has ordered a few more tests, so we need to keep her here for a day or two." She stopped at a curtained cubicle, and pulled the fabric aside.

His mom lay on the narrow cot, her lined face awfully pale and her right arm wrapped.

"Laureen." His dad leaned down and kissed her brow, cradling her face between his rough hands.

The tender look that passed between his parents brought a lump to Trevor's throat. He moved to the other side of the bed. "Hey, Mom. How are you feeling?"

"Silly and frustrated." She lifted her head, closed her eyes, and lay flat again. "Still dizzy."

The nurse stepped forward. "I can raise the head of the bed for you, Mrs. Hiebert." She pushed a button. "Tell me if your dizziness gets worse."

"There, that's enough. Now I can see my men. Thank you, my dear."

"You're welcome." The nurse looked at his dad. "After we get the cast on her arm, we'll bring her back here. It could take some time to get a bed upstairs."

"We'll wait." Trevor sank onto the chair. His mother's hand patted his head and brushed a stray lock off his forehead. He looked at the woman he owed his life.

"Not the homecoming I'd planned." Her smile twisted. "Kind of messed things up, didn't I?"

"What happened, Mom? Dad said he came in from the barn and found you on the kitchen floor, out cold."

His dad sat in the other chair.

"I'm not really sure, son." She closed her eyes for a moment, her brow creased. "I'd climbed up on the step stool to get my fancy cake plate from the top shelf. I'd made your favorite chocolate cake. It's probably still on the counter. All of a sudden the room spun, and the next thing I knew, your dad was yelling into the phone for an ambulance. Must have fallen on my arm somehow. At least it was my right one, thank God."

Yeah, right. Thank the One who could have kept her from falling but didn't. He admired his parents' faith, but it didn't make sense to him. He took her free hand between his much larger ones and kissed her fingertips. "Good thing you're a lefty, like me."

Laureen pulled his hand to her lips and kissed it. "Like mother, like son."

"And you're tough. You'll be back to normal in no time. Right?" His throat tightened.

"*Humph*." Franklin's cough alerted Trevor.

He caught the warning look in his father's eyes and raised his eyebrows.

A male orderly stepped into the cubicle. "We're ready to take Mrs. Hiebert for her cast, then we'll move her upstairs. A bed opened up, and she'll be in room 322. Visiting hours ended at eight, but you can come back any time after two tomorrow afternoon."

Trevor glanced at his watch. It was after ten, and he'd been up since five. No wonder exhaustion threatened to buckle his knees. His dad looked old and beaten. "Hey, Dad, let's get you home. I'll drive."

Franklin nodded, leaned over, and kissed his wife tenderly. "See you tomorrow, sweetheart. God knows what He's doing."

Trevor stifled a snort. If this was how God treated people who'd loved and served Him all their lives, he wanted nothing to do with Him. He'd brave almost anything for his parents, but he drew the line at trusting God. He'd seen too much evil to believe in a loving God.

The drive to the farm was silent until they took the exit onto Highway 16. Questions built up tension, but his dad's eyes were closed, and Trevor didn't want to disturb him. A vehicle with its lights on high beam came toward them, nearly blinding Trevor. "Dang it!" He flashed his lights as he strained to see past the spots dancing in his vision.

His dad jolted upright.

"Sorry, Dad. Some jerk had his lights on high beam."

"Guess I dozed off." He looked out the window. "Almost home. You staying the night?"

"Sure, I can do that. It's late, and we're both beat."

"Good. Because this changes things, and we need to talk. But not now. Can't think straight. In the morning."

~*~

Hayley shut the closet doors in her basement room and sank onto the bed. The rod in her leg seemed to pulse with each heartbeat, so she manually lifted her leg onto the quilted bedcover and leaned against the headboard. She focused on each breath, just as she'd been taught. *In through the nose, out through the mouth, deep and slow.*

Her eyes popped open. She'd forgotten to call her parents, and she'd promised. She glanced at her watch. Almost eleven-thirty, Saskatchewan time, so nearly one-thirty back home. Better to send a message than to disturb their sleep—or maybe their social life. Were they happy to be rid of her and her troubles? Probably, and she couldn't blame them. She had interfered with their busy lives for too long. No wonder they'd supported her decision to come back to Saskatoon.

She rolled over, ignoring the throb of pain in her leg. A quick text message: *Got here OK.* Good enough. They could relax and enjoy life again, get back to normal. A deep sigh escaped, and Hayley recognized it as self-pity. She clenched her jaw and lifted her chin. She was finished feeling sorry for herself. Well, working on it, anyway.

"The past is over, the future is God's." Her voice faded on the last word. She'd told Dr. Freemont she believed in God. But what did that mean? Her therapist encouraged her belief in a higher power, and she'd urged Hayley to find answers to the questions she'd raised about God. Questions Dr. Freemont couldn't answer. Like how God could possibly care about her when she couldn't stand herself. How could she ever forgive herself and move on? She hoped Pastor Dave and Lydia could lead her to the truth. She'd come here to find out if God cared enough to forgive her. Because if He didn't, life wasn't worth living.

Hayley pulled her sweater over her head and pushed her jeans onto the floor. If only she could remove her guilt as easily. She'd been carrying her burden for fourteen months, and nothing she'd tried could get rid of it. The weight had only grown.

As she reached to turn off the bedside lamp, Hayley noticed a framed picture on the nightstand. A watercolour sunrise was overlaid with a verse. *May the God of hope fill you with all joy and peace as you trust in Him so that you may overflow with hope by the power of the Holy Spirit. Romans 15:13*

She whispered the words as her finger traced them. Then once more, "the God of hope." The God she'd always pictured was a stern judge, ready to punish, to crush. And she deserved punishment. So who was the God of hope?

One more thought hit as the light clicked off. Had Lydia put it there for her? How had she known how desperately hope was needed?

~*~

Sunlight peeked around the pulled blinds, stirring Hayley to open her eyes. Unfamiliar surroundings disoriented her, and her gaze swept the room. Maple desk and shelves, pale blue walls, dark wood floors, and sheer white curtains over blinds on a shallow window. Not her room. Her heart began to race. Where was she? Another hospital or rehab clinic? Memory returned in bits and pieces. Nila's room—no, not any more. Nila and Will had married two and a half years ago. This was Dave and Lydia's house

Hayley leaned against the headboard, waiting for her pulse to settle. The last time she'd been in this home, this was still Nila's room. She'd ignored warnings about Nila's ex-boyfriend, who'd beaten her and nearly killed Nila. The distressing memories brought even more guilt. Hayley accepted its pressure as it settled in with her constant remorse.

Nila had forgiven her and they'd promised to keep in touch after Hayley went back to Toronto to heal. But that promise had been broken. Not by Nila.

Hayley hung her head, tears leaking in spite of her effort to keep them at bay. Her self-absorption had ruined everything. Time fast-forwarded to the last eighteen months and her deepest pain. If only she hadn't been taken in by Blake Horner's smooth words and flattering advances. He'd offered the attention she'd always craved. Now when she remembered his kisses, they left a bitter taste. Hayley wiped her mouth on her sleeve.

She'd had such high hopes, first when her dad offered her the clerk position at his accounting firm, and then when she'd met Blake from the law firm upstairs. Had her father known he was married? Was that why Blake had made her keep their relationship a secret? It didn't matter now.

She grabbed a tissue from the box on the nightstand and wiped her face. "The past is gone, the future is God's." Whatever future she had and whatever punishment God sentenced her to, she would accept. She'd certainly earned it.

The tantalizing aroma of fresh coffee wafted down the stairs. Hayley shoved aside the bedcovers and her memories, slipped into her housecoat, and climbed the stairs to begin this new phase of her life. The words on the bedside picture danced in her mind: "The God of hope." The words made her heart feel lighter. She'd always been afraid of God the judge. But the God of hope? She'd like to meet Him.

~*~

Trevor grabbed a brown ironstone mug from the cupboard, filled it with coffee, and joined his dad at the table. Dad's eyes were closed. Must be praying. Trevor patted Roscoe—by his dad's side, as usual—and was rewarded with a thump of the Border Collie's tail.

Dad's lined face lifted, and his dark brown eyes met Trevor's. "Hey, son."

"Morning, Dad. Hope I'm not interrupting."

Dad closed his Bible, and his mouth quirked upwards. "Just finished. How'd you sleep?"

Trevor took a sip of the hot, black brew. "Had to call Carlos about Mom, told him I wouldn't be in to work until later today if at all. Took a while, but I finally got some sleep. Chores done?"

"Not yet. Needed some coffee and encouragement first. Just have to check the cows, clean the troughs. You know the routine."

"I do, but it's been a while. Are my lined boots still around?"

"Should be in the back closet." His father leaned back and folded his arms over his stomach. "There's no rush. Want some breakfast first?"

"Not really. My gut's doing flip-flops."

"Mine, too. Been thinking about our situation—and yours." Franklin clasped his hands on the table and looked Trevor in the eye. "She didn't want to worry you, but your mom's had dizzy spells for a while."

Trevor set his mug down with a thump, echoing the plunging sensation in his heart. "How long, and how bad?"

"A few months. And not too bad until yesterday. I caught her grabbing hold of furniture or leaning against a wall a few times, but she waved me off and said she was fine. Said she was just getting old."

"That sounds like Mom." Trevor wiped a splash of coffee with his sleeve. "What did the doctor say?"

"Nothing. She wouldn't go."

Trevor leaned back in his chair and rubbed his bristly chin. He hadn't had time to shave for two days, and it itched. "So these dizzy spells were part of the 'slowing down' you told me about? Your reason for wanting to move to the city?"

"Yeah. Part of it." He shifted on his chair. "We *are* getting old, son, even though it's hard to admit. I'm seventy-two and your mom is seventy-three. Even with the fields rented, this home quarter is still a lot of work. We can't keep up any longer. And now with this..." Dad looked out the window toward the barn.

"I'm torn, Dad. I'd do anything for you guys, but I don't know if I can pass up the chance at my dream job."

His dad's question was silent, just a raised eyebrow.

"Yeah, I got the job offer." His words tumbled out.

"Better pay and a lot more freedom to design and build custom bikes. They'll even pay my moving expenses."

Franklin grinned. "Good for you. You've worked hard toward your goal." His grin faded to a soft smile. "Remember your first motorbike? I didn't know if it would ever run, but that box of bike parts turned out to be something special."

Years fled, and Trevor could feel the warmth of the summer sun on his bare, fourteen-year-old back. His habitual surly attitude had melted when Franklin Hiebert showed him the bike frame and cardboard box full of motorcycle components. His fingers itched to get started, but he had much to learn. Franklin's patience as he taught Trevor how to reassemble the ancient bike broke through his resistance. Until then, he'd survived by distrusting and fighting authority. Piece by piece, the project had forged a bond, a father/son relationship, something he'd never known could exist.

Trevor blinked away unexpected dampness. "That's what got me into motorcycles, reassembling that old Indian. You and me, working together. I still have it, you know. You and Mom gave me more than I can ever repay. Like building that bike. It gave me a goal." He shook his head, his smile gone. "How can I choose between my past and my future?"

"Rotten timing, eh?" Franklin got up and refilled his coffee mug. "We don't want to pressure you, son. The job in Toronto sounds too good to pass up, and we'd never ask you to give up your dreams. We'll figure out something, even sell this place if you don't want it, but we'd prefer to keep it in the family." He sat down with a sigh, coffee mug cradled in his hands.

Family. The term brought a surge of emotion Trevor couldn't name. Gratitude? Wonder? Maybe both. He looked at his father, the man who had changed his life, maybe even saved it. Deep lines etched Franklin's face, his once-dark, thick hair had become white and wispy, and the joints on his hands were swollen with arthritis. Trevor leaned back in his chair. Where had the time gone? When had his vibrant parents turned into old people?

"You know I love this place." Trevor gazed into the depths of his empty cup. "But now, with this chance in Toronto..." He clasped his hands as though in prayer and grimaced. "Tell me what to do, Dad. I can't figure it out."

A sparkle glimmered in his father's eyes. "That's what I was praying about. I might have a solution. Let's get those chores out of the way first, though."

~*~

Trevor zipped up his work coat, then bent over and tugged on his felt-lined rubber boots.

"Ready?" Franklin opened the back door against the wind, and with Roscoe at his heels, strode toward the barn.

Trevor had to hurry to keep up.

For someone who was slowing down, Dad moved pretty fast. But his shoulders weren't as straight as they used to be. His age was beginning to show.

They walked past the empty chicken coop and pen. His mother had quit raising chickens a couple years ago. She used to keep six hens for laying and raised fifty or more chicks for meat. His parents always took pride in raising as much of their own food as possible. Maybe she really was slowing down.

The first time he'd helped his mom collect eggs,

he'd dropped one when the hen pecked his hand. He'd been terrified, sure Laureen would yell at him or worse. But she'd laughed, her blue eyes sparkling, and told him it happened to everyone, and that he'd learn to avoid the beaks. Then when they'd gotten back into the house, her tender touch had shaken his damaged soul to the core as she'd cleaned and bandaged his hand.

"Coming?" Franklin opened the gate to the barnyard. But the morning seemed to be one for memories. They used to run at least forty cows with their calves. He gazed around the five-acre holding pen. Ten? No, twelve cows stood or lay on the frost-covered ground as several calves romped nearby. Trevor grinned as a couple calves kicked up their heels and head-butted each other. He'd done some head-butting of his own when he'd realized his adoptive home included hard manual labor.

They used to break open several bales of hay each morning for the cattle, but Franklin had switched to round bales last year. No more hands-on stacking or spreading bales. Trevor remembered how his muscles ached after a long day of haying. It had been a good ache, the kind earned by a job well done. Yes, the farm was a lot of work, but it was good work. He couldn't imagine letting strangers take it over.

Trevor clenched his jaw and followed his father as he checked cows, most with a brown and white calf close to her side. How had his father managed all these births? It used to be a team effort, especially when a cow had difficulties. Who would help now? Who would care about these animals if he took the Toronto job?

Franklin's voice interrupted his musings. "Look at

that heifer. She bred a little late, and now her udder's starting to fill. She'll probably need help." He whistled softly. "Roscoe, get me that one." He nodded toward the cow, and Roscoe ducked behind her and maneuvered the bulky, stubborn animal toward the barn.

Trevor ran ahead, opened the barn doors wide, and unlatched one of the stalls. Straw barely covered the floor, so he grabbed a pitchfork and spread several inches of bedding straw into what would be a birthing pen. He finished just as the small cow, with Roscoe still at her heels, lumbered into the barn. Within moments, she was safely enclosed in the stall.

"Good job, Trev. If you'd get her some hay, I'll fill the water bucket."

Dad bent over in the doorway with his hands on his knees. Was he panting? And why was his face so red? His dad whistled, and Roscoe raced to him and sat at his feet. Franklin rubbed the dog's ears. "Good boy."

Trevor's breath whooshed out in relief. False alarm, Dad was fine. Even if his face seemed redder than usual.

Dad straightened and joined Trevor at the stall. "Could be a few days, but I'll have to keep an eye on her. You know these first-timers."

Trevor's mind raced. With his mom out of commission, who would help his dad with the calving? And the rest of the chores? She'd filled in whenever Trevor couldn't be there. Which was most of the time, lately. Conflicting responsibilities bowed his head, until he felt his dad's gnarled hand on his shoulder.

"One way or another, God will work it out. Don't worry." Dad walked over to the spigot and filled a bucket for the cow, humming an old hymn Trevor used to know.

They finished the chores in silence, but Trevor wrestled with his desire to help his parents and the opportunity he'd been offered. It would take him two provinces away. His father had promised to tell him something. It had better include a time-warping miracle.

4

Hayley bit into the still-steaming muffin, and her eyes widened at the burst of berry goodness melded with tangy citrus. "Lydia, this is fantastic."

"I thought you deserved something special after your long day yesterday. Did you sleep OK?" Lydia sat next to her at the granite island.

Deserved? No, she didn't. As for sleeping, she had been awake much of the night, but that was normal. "The bed's comfy, thanks."

"I hope the doorbell didn't wake you." Lydia gestured to a large box on the table. "Your textbooks arrived early this morning. Dave offered to carry them downstairs when he gets back from the church. Have you always wanted to be an accountant?"

Accounting didn't thrill her, but numbers behaved. You could count on them. Her lips curved upward at her silent, unintentional pun. "Not always, but I enjoy working with numbers. And the bedroom's study area is perfect." She sipped her tea. Earl Grey, her favorite. "I can't thank you enough for letting me come here. I don't want to impose."

Lydia placed her mocha-coloured hand over Hayley's. "It's our pleasure to have you here, my dear. And our duty." Hayley's face must have shown her confusion because Lydia chuckled. "Enjoy your muffin, and I'll explain as soon as I get some more coffee. How's your tea? Did you want cream or sugar? Or maybe lemon?"

"No, thanks. This is fine." She took the last bite and savoured it. "That was the yummiest muffin ever. I can't believe I ate the whole thing."

"You haven't been eating much lately, have you?" Lydia's concerned look transformed into a confident smile. "We'll work on that."

Hayley looked at her scrawny wrists and hands. "I never thought I'd *want* to gain weight." She tugged her sleeves over her wrists and swiveled her stool towards her host. "So how is letting me live here your duty? Does it have anything to do with my parents? I know I've been a burden." Her lower lip trembled, but she compressed her mouth and lifted her chin. She would not break down.

Lydia closed her almond-shaped, brown eyes for a moment, and when she opened them, they shone. "No, Hayley. This isn't about your parents. This arrangement is between you and us. And God."

A jolt of surprise straightened Hayley's back. "What's that mean?"

"God loves you, and we believe He sent you here."

"I don't understand."

"When our youngest child left home, Dave and I considered selling this big house. But God showed us, through prayer and His word, that He wanted to use this house—and us—for His kingdom." She pulled her Bible between them and opened it. Her fingers flipped pages. "Look at this. 2 Corinthians 5. Paul talks about God's plan to reconcile people to Himself through Jesus. Here, read verses nineteen and twenty." Lydia pointed to the verses.

"God was reconciling the world to Himself in Christ, not counting men's sins against them. And He has committed to us the message of reconciliation. We are therefore Christ's ambassadors, as though God were making His appeal through us. We implore you on Christ's behalf: Be reconciled to God." Hayley lifted her gaze to Lydia's. "Oh, wow. So you and Dave are ambassadors? For God?"

Lydia beamed. "Exactly. And since we are Christ's ambassadors, this home is His embassy. We want our home to be a place of refuge and hope."

The picture on the nightstand appeared in Hayley's mind. "Like the verse in my room about the God of hope. Is that why you put it there? For anyone who comes here?"

"I put it there for you, dear. Everyone needs hope, but I sense that's especially true of you."

Unbidden tears tracked down Hayley's cheeks. She wiped them with the sleeve of her housecoat. Her throat tightened, squeezing her voice to a whisper. "How did you know?"

Instead of answering, Lydia slipped off the stool and opened her arms. Hayley leaned into the shorter woman's embrace. Lydia's arms tightened as Hayley's sorrow trickled down her face. She'd craved comfort without judgement for such a long time. She swiped at her eyes. Judgement was what she deserved. Hayley stiffened and pulled away, avoiding Lydia's warm brown eyes.

Lydia stepped back, accepting her withdrawal. Hayley carried her dishes to the sink and turned toward the stairs, but Lydia's voice halted her.

"I hope you don't mind, but I told Nila you were coming. She said to tell you she can't wait to see you and catch up. She's waiting for your call."

Catch up with Nila? Warmth filled her but was quickly replaced with cold regret. That would mean either pretending to be fine or confessing. She trudged down the stairs. No, she couldn't call. Not yet. She was too much of a coward to face the risk.

~*~

Trevor's father cracked eggs in to a bowl. "How many eggs you want?"

"With toast?" At his dad's nod, Trevor pulled the toaster out of the cupboard and plugged it in. "Two will do." He rummaged in the freezer. "Where's the homemade bread? All I can find is this store-bought stuff."

"That's all we've got. I should have known something was wrong when your mom quit making bread."As Dad poured the eggs into the hot pan, his shoulders drooped. "Said it wasn't worth the effort, but I know she enjoyed it. I sure did."

"Yeah, me too." Trevor got two plates from the cupboard and cutlery from the drawer. His mom would bounce back. She had to.

Dad scraped scrambled eggs onto the plates while Trevor buttered the toast. They sat at the table, and Dad held his hand out. "Pray with me."

The moisture in Dad's eyes turned it into a heart-felt request. He took his father's gnarled hand.

"Father God, we thank You for this day. Thank You for watching over Laureen and for giving the doctors wisdom. Thank You for Trevor, for his strength of character and compassion. Help him with the decisions he faces. And bless this food You have provided for the nourishment of our bodies. In Jesus' name. Amen."

Trevor ate quickly, barely tasting the food. He needed to get to the bike shop, but first he needed to hear what his father had in mind. He pushed his empty plate away and leaned back in the high-backed oak chair. His right knee began to jiggle. He stilled it and hoped his dad didn't notice. As soon as his dad swallowed the final bite, the question burst out. "So what's your plan? How can I take over this farm when I'm in Toronto? I don't have the money to buy you out yet, and I can't be in two places at once. No matter how I juggle things, I can't see a solution."

Dad's steady gaze was calm. "We don't expect you to buy the farm, son. It's your inheritance. Your mother and I talked to our accountant while you were in Toronto, and he suggested that at some point—not necessarily now, but whenever you can—you pay the original price we paid, $45,000. For tax purposes. Land was pretty cheap back then. Until then, you'd live here and do what you want with the place. No rent, just day to day costs. If you want it."

Trevor's mind spun. A lump had lodged in his throat. He'd never imagined such a scenario. Sure, Franklin and Laureen Hiebert had adopted him when he was fifteen, but to will him their farm? It didn't make sense. His eyes teared up. "I don't know what to say." He rubbed his jaw. He really needed to shave.

Dad placed his hand on Trevor's shoulder. "I have an idea that may help. If we can find someone to help Laureen until her arm heals and help a bit with the chores, we may be able to delay our move for a few more years and give you time to decide. Or if necessary, we can rent it out. But we won't sell unless you're sure you don't want it. Son, time has a way of slipping away. Don't let opportunities get away from you. The decisions you make now could change your life. Take my advice and pray about it."

Pray about it? He wished he could. "Can I have a few days to think about this? You've blown me away, you know. I asked for a week to make up my mind on Toronto, and now I'm more undecided than ever."

A slow smile softened the deep wrinkles on Dad's face. "We haven't even started the search for a home in town. You take all the time you need. Meanwhile, we'll manage here, but I'd sure welcome your help when you have time."

"Sure, Dad. Anything you need, call me, and I'll get here as soon as I can."

He got up, put the dirty dishes in the sink, and squirted dish soap under the spray of hot water. When washing dishes with his mom, she'd turned the chore into a splash-filled competition. Fear stilled his hands. "What about Mom? What if…"

His father pulled a towel out of the drawer. "God knows what's going on with your mom and this whole situation. Trust Him, son."

Trevor looked out the kitchen window, seeing only his memories. He envied his parents' faith. He wished he could experience the peace they got from trusting God. But as far as he was concerned, their God hadn't earned his trust.

~*~

Hayley removed her accounting books from the box and placed them in alphabetical order on the shelves above the built-in desk. When she lifted the last one, it uncovered a note in her father's familiar scrawl.

Hayley, work hard to finish this course in good time. Once you have your degree, I'll make an opening for you here. And if you earn your CPA certification, we can talk about a partnership. Don't waste this opportunity. Dad.

A pang of homesickness surprised her. Her father was always reserved, but he cared. That he was willing to look past her failures and offer her a position said a lot. Hayley hugged the note to her heart. She'd finish the online accounting program. She'd prove she could succeed and finally earn her parents' approval. But her heart sank a little as she pictured a desk in a cubicle or office, staring at numbers day after day.

She selected a textbook, found her calculator, pencil, and paper, and opened her laptop. Within minutes she was engrossed in the world of accounting principles. The light tapping on her door didn't register at first. She dragged her attention from the balance sheets to the present. "Come in."

Lydia poked her head into the room. "Are you ready for a break? Lunch is ready. If you're busy, I could bring it down."

Almost 12:30 PM according to her computer. Hayley pushed upright. "Sorry, Lydia, time got away from me. I should have helped you."

"That's not necessary. If you'd like to cook or help in the kitchen, fine, but we don't expect it."

"Then I'll be up as soon as I finish this page. I could use a break."

When she got to the kitchen, Dave was seated at the table, and Lydia was scooping a savory, thick soup into three bowls.

Hayley pulled out her chair and sat. The creamy soup held bits of carrot, peas, and some other chopped vegetables, with a sprinkling of cheese on top. Her stomach rumbled in anticipation. If Lydia kept tempting her with such tasty fare, she would regain weight in no time.

Lydia sat and held out a hand to Hayley.

Dave followed suit. "Father God," Dave prayed, "Thank You for this meal, for providing everything we need for life and godliness. Thank You for bringing Hayley to this home. Bless and guide her, in Jesus's name, amen."

"Thank you," Hayley whispered as she met Dave's tender look.

"You are most welcome. Try the soup. It's one of my favorites."

Her first taste brought a smile to her face. "Delicious. I wish I could learn how to make this."

Lydia patted her smiling mouth with her napkin. "We could arrange a cooking session. I love sharing recipes and my kitchen."

Hayley's face heated. "I'm afraid I'm no good in the kitchen. Toast and scrambled eggs is the best I can do from scratch."

"Then we'll have even more fun. When would you like to start? I'm baking chocolate chip cookies this afternoon around two. If you have time, we could make them together."

"I'd love that. I'll be finished with my homework by then." Hayley got up and impulsively hugged Lydia's shoulders. "Thank you. You're the best. I always wanted to learn to cook. Really cook, not just defrost and heat."

Lydia patted Hayley's arm. "It'll be my pleasure, sweetie."

Hayley gathered the lunch dishes, placed them in

the dishwasher, and headed back downstairs to her studies. For the first time in many months, a flutter of anticipation quickened her steps. But she faltered on the bottom step when she heard an echo of her mother's shrill voice. *"What are you doing?"*

Hayley's memory crystallized. She'd been fifteen and had wanted to impress a boyfriend by baking a treat for him. But the finished cookies didn't look anything like the picture in the cookbook. Her mother had stormed into the kitchen, grabbed a lumpy cookie, and popped it into her mouth. Hayley would never forget the look of disgust on her mother's face as she spat it into the garbage. Then she'd stalked out of the kitchen, but not before her words plunged deep into Hayley's heart.

"Dump that garbage, and clean up your mess. I'm showing a house in half an hour. I don't have time for this."

Hayley fought the dark memory. Lydia wouldn't respond like that. Would she?

~*~

"Good job." Lydia patted Hayley's back as she switched off the powerful mixer. "Do you want to fold in the chocolate chips and nuts? The batter is stiff, so this last part has to be done by hand."

Hayley reached for the wooden spoon Lydia offered. "Sure, I'll give it a try. This isn't as difficult as I'd thought." She moved the mixing bowl to the granite counter and plunged the spoon into the batter. "Oh, this part *is* hard."

Lydia dumped measured amounts of chips and nuts on top of the batter.

Hayley strained to push the spoon around and through the stiff mixture. "I never knew baking was such good exercise." She paused, breathing hard.

Lydia pulled baking sheets from above the refrigerator. "Do you want a break? You're doing fine, but I don't want to overtire you."

"No, thanks. I can finish it. I think I'm almost done." Push, stir, lift, repeat. Little by little, the chips and nuts melded into the mixture. "How does it look?"

Lydia peered into the bowl. "Perfect." She handed Hayley two teaspoons and pulled a baking sheet toward her. "These are drop cookies, so we scoop up a spoonful of batter with one spoon, and scrape it onto the sheet with the other. Like this. Try to keep them a consistent size."

"Looks simple enough. I wish you'd been my mother." Hayley cringed. "I didn't mean to say that."

Lydia slipped two filled trays into the oven. "Do you want to talk about it?" Her low voice pulled at Hayley's heart.

How could she explain her relationship with her mother? And what good could it possibly do? "No, but thanks anyway." She pulled another baking sheet over and began to fill it with precise, rounded blobs of cookie dough.

A few minutes later, the aroma of chocolate chip cookies filled the kitchen.

Hayley inhaled deeply. "Mm-mm. Those smell wonderful."

"Once they're cooled a bit, we'll have to sample them." Lydia winked. "Make sure they're as tasty as they smell."

Hayley's smile faded. What if they weren't? What if she'd messed up again? Then what would Lydia say?

"Coffee or tea?" Lydia's calm voice soothed Hayley's nerves.

"Tea, please. Coffee hasn't tasted right ever since the accident. Not sure why."

Moments later they sat at the counter with a steaming cup and still-warm cookie each. Hayley's first, tentative bite reassured her, and her smile returned. "It's good!"

Lydia tilted her head. "You sound surprised. We followed the directions, so why wouldn't they be good?"

Hayley's memory of her previous baking attempt poured out of her. Bitterness laced her words as she told the story to Lydia. "I never tried baking again. Until today."

Lydia didn't respond for several heartbeats, her eyes closed. When she looked at Hayley, the warmth in her expression and the touch of her hand brought a lump to Hayley's throat. "Thank you for sharing, my dear. May I ask you something?"

Hayley nodded.

"Was that typical of your interactions with your mother, or was it an isolated incident?"

Hayley's stomach clenched. The cookie she'd just enjoyed settled like lead. *"Open up to people who care for you. Take the risk. It's the only way to develop healthy relationships."* Her therapist's voice echoed inside her head. She didn't know Lydia well, but love radiated from the woman's face. Hayley would risk it. "Typical." She gulped. Her hands knotted into white-knuckled fists. "Lydia, my mother never wanted me. I was an accident."

Lydia gave a soft gasp.

"I heard her telling a friend. I was seven years old,

and she'd sent me to my room so she could visit in peace. But I sat at the top of the stairs and eavesdropped. I wish I hadn't." Tears plopped onto her fists.

Lydia's chair scraped as she scooted closer. Arms enveloped Hayley, and she leaned into the hug. "You are God's precious daughter," Lydia said. "He has always loved you, and He anticipated your birth and your life."

Tears ran down Hayley's cheeks as a slender root of hope penetrated her defenses. Was it possible? Could God love her even after what she'd done?

5

Odors of motor oil, leather, welding fumes, and the acrid tang of stale coffee enveloped Trevor as he strode through the back door of Easy Rider. He inhaled deeply, nostalgia already tugging at his heart. This shop had been his second home for more than ten years, ever since he'd ridden into town on his refurbished, antique Indian motorcycle and confronted the owner with his skills and dreams. His mouth twitched upward as memories rushed in.

Carlos Montana's long, black ponytail, graphic tattoos on his olive skin, and powerful physique had impressed his scrawny eighteen-year-old self, but as Trevor had grown in stature and skill, they'd become friends. Good friends, until recently. His smile faded.

"Hey, T-man, how's your mom?" The Latin-accented bass came from the far end of the workshop.

Speak of the devil. Not a devil, though, not anymore. He'd changed—one reason Trevor had jumped at the chance to interview for a job in Toronto. Trevor moved closer, shielding his eyes until the flare of the welder flicked off and Carlos lifted his visor. "Not sure. They're doing some more tests today." He leaned against a cluttered work bench. "I may need to take more time off."

His boss's dark brown gaze pinned him. "Just time off, or are you giving your notice?"

"I've got a week to decide about the move. But Dad needs help at the farm."

"OK, let me finish up here, and we'll talk." The visor snapped down.

The bell over the front door jingled, followed by two more alerts. Trevor paused in the doorway to the small showroom. Ryan chatted with an attractive young woman, while a well-dressed older gent perused the display of helmets. Another guy, probably in his forties, seemed to be admiring Trevor's latest creation.

Trevor angled toward the older man. "May I help you?"

"No, thanks. Just looking and checking prices. My grandson wants a new helmet for his birthday, but it's not until July."

Trevor asked a few questions and pointed out two of their most popular helmets in the preferred style. The man thanked him and headed toward the exit, so Trevor greeted the man at his customized 1982 Honda CX500. The guy was practically drooling as he ran a finger along the angular, indented gas tank and elongated seat. Trevor suppressed a grin as he greeted the man.

"Looking for a custom bike?"

"This one's a beaut. Who did the work?"

"I did. The bike was a mess when I bought it, perfect for a custom job. Kept the tank simple but angular, lowered the handlebars, and lengthened the seat. Now it's a great little café racer. Looking for something like this?"

"I wish I could afford it, but that's not why I'm here." Then the man pulled out a business card. "Greg Lewis, reporter for the *Star Phoenix*. I'm doing a story on custom motorcycles and their builders. Got a tip I could find a real talent here. Looks like you're it."

Trevor accepted the reporter's card and stuck it in his back pocket. "Trevor Hiebert. What can I do for you?"

Greg Lewis stepped closer, invading Trevor's space. "I plan to feature four or five guys who customize bikes—how you got started, that sort of thing. Each interview will showcase one of your creations, and readers will vote on their favorite. Great publicity for you and this shop."

Trevor moved back as the noose of stress tightened. Why now, when he might be leaving? What good would it do? "I don't know. Things are hectic right now…"

"Just think about it. You've got my card. Call me by Wednesday, and we'll make it work for you."

Trevor backed off another half step, his mind whirling. If he stayed, this could boost business for him and the shop. But the job in Toronto… His hand lifted as though to shield himself. "I'll let you know." He turned and fled to the office where Carlos waited. Trevor dropped into a dark green, vinyl-covered chair and released a sigh that ended as a moan.

Carlos raised his black coffee mug, along with an expressive eyebrow. "Want some? I made a fresh pot."

"Yeah, sure." Trevor, filled a mug and took a sip. "Good and strong." He sank back into the chair, frowning. "Did you know about the reporter?"

Carlos's smooth expression betrayed nothing. "Lewis? He called while you were away. Said he was writing a story about local customizers. Why?"

"He was just here. Offered to feature my work in a newspaper contest." His jaw clenched. He rubbed the back of his neck, but the knots stayed tight. "I don't need this right now. I can't handle any more pressure."

Carlos took a long swig of coffee without breaking eye contact. He set his mug on the desk and leaned forward. "You don't have to handle it alone."

Trevor leaned back, his chin jutted. "What do you mean?" He hoped this wouldn't launch another spiel about God. Ever since Carlos had "found Jesus" six months ago, he hadn't missed any opportunity to share his newfound joy. He grimaced.

"You know Who I mean, but I'm not gonna preach." Carlos stroked his black goatee. "I gotta admit, I'd hoped some good publicity might entice you to stay. Stoke those creative juices and ease your restlessness."

Trevor gulped, startled. He'd tried to keep it hidden.

One side of Carlos's mouth lifted, and he shook his head. "I've known you a long time, T-man. And while I'd prefer you to stay, you're no good for either of us if you feel stuck. That's why I mentioned you to Vince Starr."

"What?" His jaw dropped, and he forced it shut. It didn't make sense. Why would Carlos recommend him to the guy in Toronto? Nobody gave away his best employee. Or was something else going on here?

The phone rang, jarring Trevor's taut nerves.

Carlos glanced at the call display and held up his index finger. "Need to get this."

"No problem." Trevor stood and walked to the showroom door without a backward glance. But he could feel his boss's gaze boring into his back.

~*~

An hour later, Trevor slammed his sketch book shut. The gas tank design he'd drawn wouldn't work. This custom job might be his last one in Saskatoon, but at the rate he was going, it would take several months to finish. He propped his elbows on the counter and leaned his head on his hands. If he could just get the specs right, Carlos could fabricate the parts and assemble the bike. But then it would be a Montana bike, not a T. Hiebert creation. An annoying twinge of jealousy hit. Trevor's shoulders slumped forward. Why did life have to be so hard?

And why had his boss mentioned him to Vince Starr? He'd thought it was a lucky fluke when the ad for a bike customizer popped up on his website. Had Carlos planned the whole thing? Was he trying to get rid of him? But if Carlos wanted him to leave, why had he encouraged the reporter? He rubbed his tight neck muscles, stood, and stomped into the back room. "Carlos!"

His boss looked up from his paperwork, eyebrows raised as high as Trevor's decibel level. "Yeah?"

Trevor slammed the door shut behind him and stood with clenched fists. The twitch of his pulse throbbed a warning. "We need to talk."

"All right." Carlos leaned back in his swivel chair and swung his boots onto the paper-covered desk. "What can I do for you?"

Carlos's agreeable tone raised Trevor's irritation a couple notches. He plunked into the green chair and glared at his boss.

"Are you trying to get rid of me, keep me here, or what?" With effort he kept his voice low. "Is this your idea of a joke?"

Carlos shook his head. "No, no, my friend. I'm not playing games with you. You have ambitions and the talent to achieve them, but my shop is small. Maybe too small for you. So when I heard you were interested in a job in Toronto, I did some checking. Found out Vince Starr needed a good man, and I recommended you. I don't know much about him, but his business is big enough to give you the exposure you want. Now the ball's in your court." He shrugged. "Your decision."

Trevor frowned as he tried to make sense of this twist. "Why would you do that?"

"Creativity requires a certain amount of contentment. If you feel restless or stuck, your work will suffer." Carlos smiled, and his gold tooth twinkled. "I don't want to hold you back."

"Then why encourage the reporter?"

"To give you the publicity you deserve. Whether you stay or go, good press can make a difference."

The final dredges of outrage drained away, leaving Trevor numb. "I don't get it. Seems counterproductive for you."

"You're my right-hand man, and I don't want to lose you." Carlos turned his hands palm up, fingers splayed. "But if you stay here and regret it, we'll both suffer. You have to figure out what's most important to you." He paused and stroked his goatee. "And if I can help you achieve your life purpose? Bonus."

Life purpose? Who was this guy, and what had he done with his old boss? The one who preferred sexy pinups on his now-barren office walls. The guy who relished dirty jokes, the raunchier the better. The boss who'd always said this shop was his whole life, and hard work and hard play were all that mattered.

"What happened to you?" He squirmed, and the vinyl chair protested. "Yeah, I know, it's all about Jesus, but I don't get it. That whole God thing doesn't make sense to me."

One side of Carlos's mouth lifted. "You sure you want to hear?"

~*~

Butterflies fluttered in Hayley's stomach as Lydia drove her to Nila's house. No, not butterflies. Felt more like the bird that had flown into her apartment last summer. Its panicked, zigzag flight matched the sensation inside her. This was a mistake. She turned to Lydia. "I don't think…"

Curiosity overruled fear as the car slowed and pulled into a driveway of a charming blue bungalow.

"Here we are." Lydia patted Hayley's hand. "Enjoy your visit. I'm sure you girls have a lot of catching up to do. Give me a call when you're ready to be picked up. You have my cell number, right?"

Hayley nodded without speaking. The inviting front porch with its two cushioned, bent-twig chairs beckoned. A wreath of dried flowers decorated the front door. It looked homey, a safe place. She swallowed her anxiety. After a deep, shaky breath, Hayley unfastened her seat belt and opened the car door. "I'll call you. Thanks."

Lydia put the car in reverse and smiled. "Have fun. See you later."

Hayley reached to press the doorbell, but before she touched it, the door opened wide, framing a petite, smiling woman with short, brown hair. Nila, the friend she'd ignored for too long.

"Hayley, you're here! Please, come in. Welcome to our home." Nila's face glowed. "I'm so glad you came."

Hayley waved goodbye to Lydia, and then followed Nila inside.

"May I take your jacket?" Nila reached for a hanger from the coat closet. Her movement stretched her light blue sweater over her midsection, revealing a distinctive bulge.

Hayley forgot to breathe. Her knees buckled, and the room dimmed.

"Hayley?" Nila's voice penetrated the mist, and the smaller woman's arm around her waist kept her from falling.

Hayley forced her eyes open and pulled in a deep, shuddery breath. "S-sorry."

With Nila supporting her, Hayley staggered to the dark brown couch and sank into its comfort.

She couldn't look at her friend. She shouldn't have come. Her eyes filled.

A light touch on her arm penetrated the gloom. "Are you all right? Do you need a doctor?" Nila knelt at her feet.

"No, I don't need a doctor." She closed her eyes and allowed the tears to run down her face. "And no, I'm not all right." Hayley wiped her face on her sleeve and opened her eyes.

Nila's eyes mirrored Hayley's distress. "Talk to me. What's wrong? Are you in pain? What can I do?"

She gritted her teeth and shook her head. What would Dr. Freemont say? *You are strong. The past is gone; the future is God's. Open yourself to friendship, new relationships.* She slung her mental arm over her therapist's assurances as though onto a life preserver.

After several moments Hayley's breath evened out, and her heartbeat settled. She accepted the tissue Nila offered and dried her face. "Just be my friend."

Confusion showed on Nila's face as she pushed herself to her feet. "I *am* your friend." She paused, hand on hip. "And you know I understand heartaches."

Their friendship had been forged in trauma that had resulted in injuries to both of them and the death of Nila's ex-boyfriend. Hayley wondered at Nila's obvious health and joy. There was no trace of the desperation that had forced her to kill her ex in self defense. How had she come so far?

Nila interrupted her musing. "At least let me get you something to drink. Would you prefer hot or cold?"

"Um…cold, I guess. Water's fine, thanks."

"Coming right up." Nila paused. "Would you like to see the house? You've never been here, have you?"

A tentative smile warmed Hayley's face. "No, I haven't, and I'd love a tour. How long have you lived here?" She started to rise but was stopped by Nila's hand on her shoulder.

"Just wait here while I get our drinks. You still look pale." She tilted her head. "You've lost weight, haven't you? Good thing I made cookies yesterday."

By the time Nila returned with a tray bearing tall glasses of ice water and a plate of oatmeal cookies, Hayley had won the battle with her emotions by concentrating on her breathing. She accepted the offered snack with a smile and bit into a cookie. Her smile widened. "These are good. Thank you."

Nila put the tray onto the coffee table and sank into the overstuffed plaid chair opposite Hayley.

"You're welcome. They're Will's favorite."

The dreamy look in Nila's eyes when she mentioned her husband stirred a pang of longing in Hayley. She pushed it away. "He's a lucky man."

Nila grinned, her smile lighting her whole face. "No, I'm the one who's lucky." She shook her head. "Not lucky…blessed. God is *so* good." She caressed the gentle swell of her belly.

Regret surged, and Hayley stifled a moan. *You are strong. Think about something else.* She fixed her attention on the chrome and glass floor lamp beside Nila. It contrasted beautifully with the scraped oak hardwood floor. "Tell me about your home. I've been admiring your living room. Did you and Will do the updates?"

Nila smiled and set her glass on the half-wall beside her. "This was my first full reno as an apprentice carpenter, so it's extra special. The house belonged to Daniel—you remember Will's stepfather? When he married Will's mom, Melody, Will moved in here." She shifted, pulling her legs up onto the chair. "The plan had been for Daniel's sister, Hannah, and her husband to live here when they retired from the mission field, but they decided to move to France, instead. Where her husband's family lives." She shrugged. "And the climate's a lot milder, of course. Better for Hannah's arthritis. So Daniel offered us a super deal, and we jumped at it." She glanced at Hayley's empty glass. "Would you like more water or another cookie?"

"No thanks. I'm ready for your tour, though."

Hayley enjoyed Nila's nostalgic anecdotes as they inspected the kitchen, dining room and basement. She admired the wedding ring quilt Melody had stitched for them and the colors Nila had chosen. Hayley leaned in the doorway of the master bedroom, as an unfamiliar but welcome sense of peace enveloped her.

"This is lovely. Your whole house is beautiful, and it suits you."

"Thank you, but I saved the best for last." She pulled her into the last room, next to the master bedroom, and gestured grandly. "The nursery."

Hayley froze. The small bedroom had yellow walls, fluffy rag rugs on the hardwood floor, a glider chair in the corner, and a dark wood crib and change table. Pain lacerated her heart, and her face crumpled. She sank to the floor as shame and sorrow poured out of her.

Nila knelt beside her and rubbed her back. "Let it out, Hayley. Whatever it is, let it go. You're not alone. God is here, and so am I." Her words flowed like liquid honey, sweet and soothing.

When Hayley's sobs eased into shuddering gasps, Nila helped her up and half-carried her back to the couch.

Hayley hunched forward, her head in her hands, regret shaking her whole body. The couch depressed beside her as Nila sat and resumed her soothing back massage. Hayley pulled away. "Don't comfort me. I don't deserve it." The gloom of guilt pressed in hard. "I don't deserve your friendship. I don't even deserve to live."

Nila's hand stilled. "Why would you say that?"

The burden of guilt Hayley had carried for fourteen months ballooned and pressed against every pore until she couldn't hold it in any longer. Hayley lifted anguished eyes and sobbed. "I-I killed my baby."

6

Now she'd done it. The secret Hayley had so painstakingly buried had erupted, and its lava sizzled around her. Her chance at a new life hissed and vanished as despair enveloped her. Hayley wrapped her arms around her legs, but she couldn't stop shaking. She sensed Nila's withdrawal, even though she couldn't look at her former friend.

Nila would tell Will. He would hate her. They would tell Dave and Lydia. She couldn't bear their disgust. She'd have to leave. Where would she go?

An arm snaked around her shoulders, and a head leaned against her arm. "Oh, Hayley, I'm so sorry. Please forgive me." The quaver in Nila's voice penetrated Hayley's hysteria.

"Wh-what?"

Nila's words hiccupped. "Your baby…my baby…I didn't mean…God, help us."

Wait. *Nila* felt bad? Shock tranquilized Hayley's turmoil. Why was Nila crying and comforting her? Why wasn't she horrified, repulsed?

Time and place shifted, swinging Hayley back to the hospital in Toronto. Still groggy from anesthesia after surgery on her leg, her parents' raised voices sliced through the fog.

Her mother's strident voice vanquished the comfortable mists. "She was *pregnant*? Did you know about this?"

"Of course not." Her father sounded angry too.

Hayley cringed and reached for the button to dispense a dose of pain-numbing drugs.

Her mother's voice faded, but her words cut deeper than the surgeon's scalpel. "At least we don't have to deal with *that* now."

The baby? What happened to my baby? Sorrow and narcotics shrouded her as she sank into deep shadows.

"Hayley." Someone stroked her cheek. "Hayley, here, take this." A tissue pressed into her hand.

Where was she? Hayley lifted her head and looked into Nila's drawn face. She opened her mouth, but no words came.

Nila stood. "I'll get you something to drink. Then we'll talk." She disappeared.

Hayley fought the mists swirling in her head, her eyes closed. It didn't make sense. Her own parents had rejected her. Why hadn't Nila? Movement alerted her, and she glanced up.

Nila held out a glass of iced tea. "I thought this might go down better than plain water."

Hayley took a tentative sip, and the sweet drink soothed her raw throat. "Thank you. Feels good."

Nila settled in the chair across from her and folded her arms over her belly. Tears still glistened in her eyes. "I had no idea…I feel terrible. I let my happiness blind me to your pain."

Hayley shook her head, and the mists danced away. "You couldn't have known. I haven't told anyone. Except my therapist."

Nila's eyes widened. "Not even your parents?"

Hayley compressed her lips and shook her head slowly. "The doctor must have told them, and it didn't go so well." Understatement of the year. She took another sip of tea to force down the lump in her throat.

"Will you tell me about it? I've learned that sharing a burden is the first step to easing it."

Hayley considered that. Dr. Freemont had listened without judgement, and her acceptance had been Hayley's only refuge. For too long. She took a deep breath. "Maybe it's time…"

~*~

Trevor leaned back against the cool, green vinyl. Did he want another sermon? No, not even from Carlos. But he did want answers. He folded his arms across his chest and nodded. "All right, give it to me."

Carlos steepled his fingers and regarded Trevor without speaking for several long seconds.

Trevor squirmed and looked away. The man had been spouting words about how God had "saved" him for weeks. So get on with it. Not that it would make any difference to him.

"You're right, T-man."

Trevor's attention darted back to his boss.

"It *is* all about Jesus." Carlos smiled. "You know what I was like. On the surface, anyway. Good times—that's all I cared about. Always looking for the next piece of happiness I could grab. The next thrill. But it was hollow. I was empty." Carlos leaned forward. "But then I met Jesus."

Trevor rolled his eyes and groaned. More of the same. What had he expected? "Oh, yeah? Did He walk up to you and introduce Himself? Because I can't see you in a church. No offense."

"None taken. But you're right, in a way. Remember the old '71 Triumph that leaked oil so bad I had to fabricate a gasket for it?"

Trevor frowned and nodded.

"It still ran rough after the leak was fixed, so I gave it a tune-up and took it out for a spin to test the timing. Drove out Highway 12 a few miles past Martensville, and the stupid thing sputtered and stalled. I pulled off the road, reached into my pocket for my phone, and grabbed nothing but lint. Found it later on the floor by the helmets."

Trevor's memory latched onto that detail. He'd been dealing with a customer when Carlos had stormed into the shop pushing the bike. The look on his face could've branded leather.

"Anyway, I was stranded. Couldn't get the bike going again, so I figured I'd have to push it back to Martensville and phone from there. Just got it across the road when a guy in an old Dodge pickup pulled onto the shoulder ahead of me."

Trevor glanced at his watch. He wanted to get to the hospital to see his mom.

If Carlos noticed, he gave no indication. "Long story short, the guy introduced himself as Max and offered me and the bike a ride. There was something about him…looked real tough, except for his eyes." Carlos shook his head. "He knew stuff about me, things I'd never told anyone. I swore at him, but he didn't even react. Just kept going on about how much Jesus loves me, how He died to wash the mess that was me so God could wrap me in His arms and adopt me as His son."

Trevor sucked in a breath and narrowed his eyes. Adopt? That registered. Like a gut punch.

~*~

Trevor circled another level of the parking block. Why was there never a parking spot available at City Hospital? As he drove, Carlos's story continued to loop in his mind. His brain and stomach roiled as though in a churning contest. It couldn't be so simple. Or necessary, for him. He didn't need Jesus, no matter what Carlos said. And yet, the change in his boss couldn't be ignored. And if it didn't matter, why couldn't he quit thinking about it?

A car pulled out of a tight spot half a block ahead, and Trevor manoeuvred his Jeep against the curb. Finally. He grabbed the tissue-wrapped, potted miniature rose off the passenger seat and jogged to his mother's room. He shoved open the door and skidded to a stop.

The bed was empty.

~*~

Hayley shifted on the couch and hugged her knees. Should she tell Nila the whole, ugly story? Or just the part about the accident? *Might as well jump right in.* "A few weeks after I went home, my father had me fill in for his receptionist/file clerk while she was on maternity leave. I'd recovered physically from what Nick did, but not emotionally. I guess I kind of withdrew. Sitting at the front desk, answering phones, and greeting people forced me to interact with people, and before long, I was back to normal. At least on the outside."

Nila's wide eyes and a slight nod encouraged her.

"Then I met Blake, a lawyer from the offices upstairs." Hayley paused, remembering. "He was *so* hot—tall, blond, and blue-eyed, and dressed for success in a hand-tailored suit. Not my usual bad-boy type. More like someone my parents might approve. He walked up to my desk, leaned close, and asked me what I was doing for the rest of my life." Her lips twisted. "Yeah, I know it was corny, but it worked. On our first date, he told me his wife had died eight months earlier, and that's why he wore a wedding ring. His grief and my trauma drew us together, and before long, he was spending nights at my apartment."

Hayley couldn't look at Nila. She focused on the still-bare crab apple tree outside. "I know it was wrong, but he made me feel beautiful and loved, more than I'd ever known. When he said his place was still filled with his wife's things, and I'd feel uncomfortable there, I thought he was being considerate." She closed her eyes and groaned. "I was *so* stupid."

"Hayley…"

"Do you want me to stop?"

"No, I just want to encourage you. You're not the first woman to fall for a con man, you know."

Hayley refocused on the crab apple tree. "When I found out I was pregnant, I ran upstairs to Blake's office. I usually knocked, in case he was with a client. But I was too excited." She gulped and blinked rapidly as tears threatened. "Blake stood behind his desk, his arms wrapped around a blonde. Behind him were photos I'd never seen before. The same woman…with two kids…and Blake. His family."

The tree faded from sight as that day crystallized in shards of shattered dreams. Piercing pain, deep within. "I must have made a sound, because the woman turned and saw me. She asked Blake who I was, and he turned and barely glanced at me.

'Nobody,' he said. 'Just a chick from downstairs.'"

Hayley wiped tears from her cheeks with the backs of her hands as she continued in a monotone. "I ran all the way down to the parking garage, got in my car, and drove. I didn't care where. I had to get away. I got onto the 401 and floored it. I have no idea how fast I was going when I swerved around a minivan. I lost control. The car went over the guardrail, rolled into the ditch, and slammed into a signpost." She hugged her knees. "When I woke up in the hospital, I found out my baby was dead." Sobs broke through. "Because...of…me."

Nila knelt beside Hayley and stroked her arm. "It's OK to cry, Hayley. Let it all out. It's too heavy a burden for you to carry alone."

Hayley reached for a tissue and blew her nose. "My therapist, Dr. Freemont, said I needed to find the strength inside me to deal with it, but I'm too weak. I don't have any strength, and I *can't* deal with it." She dislodged Nila's hand when she planted her feet on the floor and started to stand. "I—I'm sorry. I shouldn't have come."

Nila stood to her full, petite height. "Not true. Sounds like you've needed a friend for some time, and I'm nominating myself." She gently touched Hayley's cheek. "I'm not a therapist, but I've suffered, too, many times because of my own decisions. So I can hear you with my heart. Listen to me now, Hayley."

Hayley sank back onto the couch. "All right, but even you can't relieve my guilt."

Nila sat beside her and took one of Hayley's hands in hers. "Of course I can't. But Jesus can."

"Jesus?"

"You know He died to pay for your sins, right?"

Hayley squirmed. "Yes, but God and I aren't exactly on speaking terms anymore."

Nila smiled gently. "Who walked away?"

Hayley couldn't answer past the lump in her throat. Her breath expelled in a deep sigh, and she tapped her chest.

Nila knelt again, so they were face-to-face. "He's waiting for you. Waiting to forgive you and take your burden."

Hayley stiffened. "He can't undo it. My baby is dead, and nothing will change that."

Nila sat back on her haunches, her head tilted. "Are you saying your baby's death is bigger than God's sacrifice of His Son?"

Truth slammed into Hayley's heart like a battering ram. She couldn't breathe. Tiny pieces of shame broke away, and a ray of hope warmed her soul. "I…I never thought of it that way."

Nila wiped her eyes on her sleeve and patted Hayley's leg. "I hope you will think about it. And accept God's forgiveness." Her lips lifted, and her face glowed. "It makes all the difference."

The rumble of a diesel truck drew near, and Nila pushed herself to her feet and looked out the window. "That's Will. He's home early."

Hayley cringed. She couldn't face Nila's husband—and her former crush. Not like this. She lunged to her feet. "May I use your bathroom?" Without waiting for a response, she dashed down the hallway and into the tiled room. Hayley splashed cold water on her face until her skin cooled. She reached blindly for a hand towel and pressed it to her eyes. Leaning against the counter, Hayley looked in the mirror. Puffy eyes stared back at her. She was used to that. But there was something different in their depths. Was that a glimmer of hope?

"Hayley?" Nila's voice came through the door. "Will's in the shop. He just needed another box of nails. I know he'd love to say hello to you, though, if you're up to it. How are you feeling?"

Hayley grimaced at her image in the mirror as she hung up the towel and opened the door. "I'm not sure. Like I've been through a war zone. And I look it. Maybe I'll take a rain check on seeing Will. In fact, I'll let Lydia know I'm ready to go."

"Of course." Nila led the way back to the living room. "Do you mind if I share your story with Will? I don't like to keep secrets from him, but I will, if you want."

Did she mind? How would Will react? Did she want to force Nila to keep secrets from her husband? Guilt stabbed at her. No, keeping her secret hidden inside hadn't done any good, only more harm. She couldn't do that to her friends. A deep sigh escaped. "Go ahead, but wait until I'm gone. OK?"

Nila turned and placed a hand on Hayley's arm. Her dark-lashed, brown eyes shone. "You took a huge step today by sharing your story with me. I hope you'll find that as you open up, your past will lose its power over you."

Hayley pondered Nila's remark. "I do feel lighter. Do you think I should tell Dave and Lydia?"

"Definitely." One side of Nila's mouth lifted. "Just prepare to be hugged."

Hayley smiled wistfully. No preparation needed. In fact, she'd been searching for love and approval all her life. She pulled out her cell to call Lydia. She couldn't wait.

7

Trevor dug into his pocket for his cell, pulled it out, and groaned. Dead. He'd forgotten to charge it. He rushed to the nurses' desk, but the attending nurse was on the phone. Trevor drummed his fingers on the counter. Where was his mom?

"May I help you?" The gray-haired nurse wearing purple scrubs spoke as she hung up the phone, her expression gentle yet alert.

Trevor glanced at her ID badge. "Yes, please, Ms. Jenkins." He straightened. "I'm looking for my mother, Laureen Hiebert. She was in room 322."

"You must be Trevor. She and your father were quite concerned when they couldn't reach you. She was discharged a couple hours ago and left for home."

"So she's OK?" He couldn't keep the worry and doubt from his voice.

"They asked me to give you this." Ms. Jenkins handed him a folded note.

Trevor tried to read her expression, but it held only professional compassion. "Thanks." He didn't open it until the elevator doors closed behind him. His fingers trembled as he unfolded the note.

Praise God, there's no tumor. Not sure yet what's causing the dizzy spells. More tests later. We're on our way home. Come out when you can. Love, Mom and Dad.

Relief wrestled with bitterness. No tumor? Great.

Praise God? Not a chance. He clenched his jaw as he retraced his steps to his truck.

His mom was still vulnerable, and God let people die.

~*~

"It's good to be home." His mother's voice sounded weak, but her face shone. "Have you made a decision yet about Toronto?"

Trevor perched on the edge of the afghan-covered couch. So typical of Mom, to be more concerned with others than herself. "No. I'm still on the fence. This opportunity is fantastic, something I've only dreamed about, but I don't want to leave you guys in the lurch." He looked from his mother to his father. "What would you do? If you were me?"

Dad cleared his throat and shifted in his big, black recliner. "Well, son, if fear for us is the only thing keeping you from your dreams, I'd say go for it. But if you're running from something or Someone, it won't work."

Stunned, Trevor couldn't formulate an answer. Was he running? Sure, he'd like to get away from the discomfort he felt whenever his folks or Carlos talked about God. But he couldn't ignore his family's needs. Or was it an excuse to avoid the challenges that such a big change would bring?

"We've been praying for you, son. Can we pray with you right now?" Dad leaned forward and clasped his hands as though already praying.

Trevor couldn't refuse, no matter how much he wanted to. "Yeah, OK." He closed his eyes and hoped his parents would do the same. He wasn't at all sure he could hide his discomfort.

"Father God, You know all things. You know our hearts, and You know our weaknesses. We praise You for the good news that Laureen does not have cancer. You are good, oh Lord, and what You do is good. Now we bring Trevor to You. Give him courage to follow Your leading, we pray. The opportunity offered by the shop in Toronto sounds fantastic, as he will have more freedom to use the gifts You have given him. You know what You have planned for him, and we know You will be with him, whatever he decides. Thank You, Father."

Trevor's mind churned. Dad's prayer seemed to pull him into the presence of God, and he didn't want to go there. He didn't dare. He opened his eyes. The expressions of peace on his parents' faces magnified his turmoil. He looked down and squirmed, and the couch protested.

Then his mom's soft voice soothed him, as it always could. "Dear Lord, thank You for Trevor, for bringing him into our home and making us a family. You trusted us with him, and now we entrust him to You. We love him dearly, and You love him even more. Give us all courage, I pray, in Jesus's name."

Did they expect him to pray too? He looked up. Both parents were looking at him with so much love, it made his heart ache. He should say something. He finally whispered, "Thanks."

"You'll stay for supper, won't you?" Mom sat forward as though to get up. "We picked up pierogis and farmer sausage on the way home."

"And I'll cook them." Dad pushed himself out of the chair. "You stay right there."

Her sigh sounded dredged from the bottom of the

river. "Yes, sir. I guess you can have my kitchen for a day or two. I am a little tired."

"I'll help. Haven't had pierogis for months." Trevor stood and followed his dad into the kitchen. He stopped in the doorway and leaned back toward his mom. "Can I get you anything?"

"A glass of water would be nice. Thanks, son."

Trevor filled a tall glass with water from the fridge and brought it to his mother. "Here you go."

She reached up and placed her palm against his cheek. Her gaze held his. "Don't let fear hold you back, dear boy. Follow your heart."

Trevor's throat constricted. He bent lower and brushed his lips against her forehead before escaping to the kitchen. Why did this decision have to be so hard? Could a restless heart be trusted? Maybe he should talk to someone impartial. But who? Work consumed his time and energy. He couldn't think of anyone he'd trust to advise him.

He slit open the package of frozen pierogis and lifted the lid of the enameled red Dutch oven. Steam swirled out of the boiling water, nearly scalding him. Trevor dropped the lid with a clang and stared at the pot. Through the hot mist, its color triggered a memory of another shade of red. Spiky…red… hair.

"You all right?"

Trevor dumped the pierogis into the boiling water and grinned at his dad. "Yes, I am. After supper, I've got a call to make."

~*~

Hayley leaned into Lydia's embrace. Warm hands stroked her hair as Lydia whispered, her lips close to

Hayley's ear. "Thank you for sharing with us. I know it wasn't easy, and we appreciate your trust. God loves you, dear child, and so do we."

Pastor Dave cleared his throat. "May I cut in?"

Hayley smiled, disentangled herself from Lydia's hug, and walked into the big man's open arms. "Of course."

He folded her close to his soft, cotton shirt, and Hayley relaxed into his pine-scented hug. She sniffled and blinked back tears. Why couldn't her parents respond like this?

After a few moments, Dave opened one arm to include Lydia in a love huddle.

Hayley inhaled the life-giving elixir of their acceptance and opened her mouth to thank them but found herself praying aloud for the first time. "Thank You, Lord Jesus, for Pastor Dave and Lydia. Thank you for loving me through them and Nila, and for forgiving me." She froze, stunned.

Dave and Lydia both squeezed her one more time and stepped back, questions in their eyes. Lydia spoke first. "What is it, sweetheart?"

Hayley gestured with both hands from her heart up into the air. "It's gone! The pressure is gone." Her mouth stretched into a wide grin. "I feel like dancing."

Dave grabbed her hand, and Lydia took the other. "Then by all means, let's dance." He began to skip around the living room, pulling the two women behind him. Giggles bubbled up inside Hayley and erupted in laughter. Twice around the room they pranced, and then Hayley plopped into the couch while Dave sank into his recliner and Lydia took the glider.

Hayley massaged a muscle spasm in her leg while

she caught her breath. "Whew! That was the most fun I've had in *ages.* You guys are the best. Thank you."

"Our pleasure, my dear." Pastor Dave beamed. "It's been a while since I've skipped, but forgiveness is worth celebrating."

"It sure is. Now it's not just here, where it didn't really help." Hayley touched her forehead and then moved her hand to her chest. "It's here too. I know in my heart I'm forgiven." She sighed and shook her head. "You can't imagine what a difference that makes."

"Actually, we can. While we haven't experienced the same trials you have, we do know what it's like to need to be forgiven." Dave's deep voice rumbled. "And only God can free us from guilt. You are free, my child, and that makes this a blessed day."

Hayley hugged her knees. "This has been the best day ever. I can't imagine anything better…"

Her cell phone chimed from deep in her pocket.

~*~

The following evening, street lights blinked on as Trevor drove toward the address Hayley had given him. Echoes of their phone conversation still resonated, especially the tone of her voice. At first he'd thought he'd gotten the wrong number. The cheerful voice that answered didn't sound like the withdrawn but intriguing woman he'd met on the plane. But she'd greeted him almost breathlessly, and he had to admit, that gave his ego a boost. So instead of asking her to meet him for coffee, as he'd planned, he'd offered dinner. He shook his head. What was it about this woman? One chance encounter and she'd wormed past his well-practiced defenses.

He slowed, checked the address, and pulled into the driveway of a well-kept, older, two-story house. As he stared at the door, Trevor inhaled deeply to calm his onset of nerves, but some kind of winged insects had taken up lodging in his throat. He grimaced and opened his door. It had simply been too long since he'd been on a date. So why were his legs as wobbly as a newborn calf's as he climbed the front steps? He pushed the thought away and rang the doorbell.

A large, gray-haired man opened the door, one eyebrow raised. "You must be Trevor Hiebert. I'm Dave Harris. Come on in and have a seat. Hayley will be up in a minute or two."

Oh, great. The old protective father bit. He cleared his throat and held out his hand. "Pleased to meet you, sir." He followed the man into the living room, lowered himself into a Mission-style rocker, and promptly stood again as a smiling Asian woman with gray-streaked black hair entered the room.

Dave's face lit up as he introduced them. "Sweetheart, this is Trevor. Trevor, my wife, Lydia."

Trevor took her extended hand in his. It was warm, her grip firm. "I'm pleased to meet you, ma'am."

Her smile widened. "And I'm happy to meet you. Please, have a seat and tell us about yourself. You met our Hayley on the flight from Toronto?"

He waited until the older couple sat on the couch before perching on the rocker. "Yes, we shared a row on the plane. I…" A door off the kitchen opened, and his words fled.

Hayley hesitated in the doorway, a vision in black slacks and a deep green sweater that echoed her brilliant green eyes. Eyes without shadows. And she looked relaxed, happy. Not like on the plane.

He stood. "Hello, Hayley. You look…really good."

"Hi, Trevor. Thanks. You too." She lowered her chin as she headed for the entry closet, but not before Trevor caught a glimpse of the blush blooming on her cheeks. *Nice.*

He pulled back his jacket sleeve and looked at his watch. "We'd better get going. Our reservation is for six." He turned to Dave and Lydia. "It was nice to meet you."

"You, too." Lydia's smile widened as Trevor helped Hayley with her black wool coat. "You kids have a good time."

He nodded to her and shook Dave's hand.

"Take good care of her." Dave patted Trevor on the back as he and Hayley headed out the door.

"I'll do my best." Although he'd spoken casually, the promise twisted his gut. What had he gotten himself into?

~*~

At the Italian restaurant, Trevor seated Hayley, and then sat down.

Hayley's eyebrows lifted, and her cheeks bloomed pink. She looked down at the menu. "It all looks good." She shrugged her delicate shoulders. "I can't decide what to order. Do you have any recommendations?"

"The lasagne's good. That's what I'm getting."

"Sounds perfect." She glanced down, shifted, and finally met his eyes again. "I'm really glad you phoned. I didn't expect it."

He smiled as he placed their menus on the edge of the table. "To tell you the truth, I have an ulterior motive."

Her eyes widened, and she leaned back, obviously wary. "Oh?"

"You know that job in Toronto I mentioned?"

Hayley nodded, her expression shuttered.

The waiter appeared at their table, and they both ordered lasagne with Caesar salad. "Very good. Anything else to drink? Coffee, or maybe some wine?"

"No, thanks. Water's fine."

"Just water for me too," Hayley said, her attention on her full glass.

Once the waiter walked away, Trevor fiddled with his water glass as his mind raced. Where to start? His words came out in one long breath. "Toronto. You're from there. What's it like to live there? And what do you know about Lowrider Cycles?"

Hayley flinched and shrank back. Not a good start.

"I'm sorry. That sounded like an interrogation—not my intention." He sighed. "It's just that I'm struggling to decide whether to stay here and try to expand my custom work, or give Toronto a try."

Hayley's expression relaxed, and she leaned forward, resting her elbows on the table. "That's a huge decision. So what's drawing you toward Toronto? The bigger city and customer base? Because Lowrider's a busy shop, from what I've heard."

Trevor nodded. "That's one part of it. They have the equipment and space I need to build custom bikes better than anything I've done here. Our shop is too small and money's too tight."

"Then what's the problem? Sounds like you've been offered the job of your dreams."

He looked toward the ceiling as though he could find answers there. "It is. I think. But I'm not sure."

"Why?"

His gaze turned to Hayley again, and he was momentarily distracted by the compassion in her bright green eyes, the soft glow on her face.

She fidgeted and lifted a hand as though to tuck her hair behind her ear. Then she blushed as she clasped her hands. "Old habit. I used to have long hair."

That sparked his interest, and he opened his mouth to ask her about it, but she held up a hand. "You were going to tell me what's holding you back."

Right. Images of his mother, her arm in a cast, his father looking old and stooped, and Carlos with his generous encouragement but irritating preaching ran like a quick-time slide show through his mind. He grabbed the first reason. "My mom. Well, both my parents. They'd like to move off the farm, and they want me to take it over."

"Do you want to?"

"I'd love to, eventually, with the right person." With the right person? Where had that come from? Trevor shook his head. "But the timing…"

Movement from the side caught his attention, and they both leaned back as the waiter refilled their water glasses.

"Your order will be out in a few more minutes." His attention lingered on Hayley's face until she blushed and turned toward the dark window.

"Thank you," Trevor said more curtly than he'd intended.

The waiter raised his eyebrows and left.

"Sorry about that. Sure hope his serving skills

make up for his lack of manners. He made you uncomfortable, didn't he?"

Color brightened her face as she met his gaze. "A little. But tell me more about the farm and your parents. Why do they want to leave it?"

His gut clenched. This was where it got tricky. How much did he want her to know? She was basically a stranger, but maybe it was a good thing. If this went sideways, there was no reason he'd have to see her again. Even though he already wanted to.

One arched eyebrow lifted as Hayley tilted her head. A tiny dimple appeared beside her mouth, then disappeared. Fascinating. Her lips curved upward. "I'm waiting."

Trevor closed his eyes as heat rushed up the back of his neck. He needed to concentrate. And not on her face. "Sorry." But he wasn't, not really. "Um…my folks are getting older, and now with Mom's injury…"

"What happened?" Her smile disappeared, and a line appeared across her forehead.

"She fell and broke her arm. I got the message at the airport—the emergency I mentioned on the way here."

"Oh. I'm so sorry. But is she all right other than that?"

Trevor sighed and focused on his water glass. "I don't know. She'd been having dizzy spells, and that's why she fell. The doctor says there's no tumor, but I know Dad is worried. She needs extra help now, of course, and he's already struggling with the upkeep around there. His age is catching up to him."

"How old is he?"

"Dad's seventy-two and Mom's seventy-three."

Hayley's brow furrowed. "They must have been

well into their forties when they had you."

Trevor's jaw clenched shut like a beaver trap. He should have known this would come up. Hayley Blankenship attracted him like no other woman he'd met, and he wanted to know her better. But how would she respond if he admitted the truth, that until the Hieberts took him in, he was nobody's child?

8

Emotions flitted across Trevor's face. Had she said something wrong? Maybe he was sensitive about how old his parents were when he was born, but she couldn't imagine why.

"Here we go, two lasagnes with Caesar salad and garlic toast." The waiter set the loaded, steaming plates onto the table. "Can I get you anything else?" He directed his question and attention to Hayley, along with a wink.

She averted her eyes and shook her head. "No, thanks." She didn't look up until she heard his footsteps fade into the general restaurant noise. Then she peeked at Trevor. Would he want to say a blessing first?

No, he'd already picked up his fork. "Hope you're hungry."

Hayley inhaled and smiled. "I am, and this smells wonderful."

The only conversation for the next few minutes was appreciative comments about their delicious dinner. Hayley glanced up several times, but Trevor seemed deep in thought as he ate, his attention fixed on his food. Or maybe she'd upset him. Maybe her questions offended him.

She chewed and swallowed a tangy bite of salad. "Nice," she murmured.

"Pardon?"

For a second, all rational thought fled as his stormy gray eyes locked on hers. "Um…the salad. It's really good—the perfect amount of dressing." She stifled a groan. Witty conversationalist, she wasn't. *How not to impress a date.*

"It is good, isn't it?" He grinned. "Best in town."

Maybe he hadn't noticed her awkwardness. He dug into what was left of his pasta and held up his loaded fork. "How do you like the lasagne?"

"Delicious." She dabbed her mouth with her napkin. "Thank you."

He lowered his fork back onto his plate and leaned forward. He seemed to study her for a moment, and she fidgeted with the napkin in her lap. Was she wearing a blob of tomato sauce? She quickly wiped her mouth again, just in case.

"May I ask you something personal?" His low voice rumbled, soothing and exciting her at the same time.

"Um…sure." How personal? The bite she'd swallowed rolled into a hard lump.

"When we met on the plane, you seemed…I don't know…almost remote. Not rude or anything, but you seemed to be…in a lot of pain, and not just physically."

Hayley gulped. *Don't ask why. Please don't.*

"But tonight you're different. More confident and carefree." His quick smile flashed deep dimples. "When we talked on the phone last night, I wasn't sure I'd reached the right woman."

Relief swept away Hayley's apprehension, and she relaxed. She could do this. "You're right. I'd been through a rough time that included a car accident, so any kind of travel brings back some of the trauma. And when we hit turbulence, the rod in my leg…"

Trevor sat back, his brow puckered. "No wonder. But you're feeling better now?"

Hayley took a deep, slow breath. How to explain? "I'm still recovering physically, but I'm *much* better emotionally. Spiritually." She sensed his withdrawal but plunged on before her courage failed. "The accident was my fault, and I've been carrying a huge load of guilt ever since. But my friends helped me realize Jesus paid for what I did. I have a lot to learn, but already I feel lighter." She tried to figure out the expressions flitting across Trevor's face. "That probably didn't make any sense."

Trevor closed his eyes, and when he looked at her again, their turbulence tugged at her sinking heart.

She'd offended him. She opened her mouth, not sure what she should say, but he held up a hand, his face unreadable.

"I'm glad you're feeling better. If faith helps, good. For you."

~*~

Was there some kind of faith epidemic going on? First Carlos, and now his first date in months. Both excited about Jesus. Trevor wanted to walk away, but his mother had taught him better manners than that. Besides, there had to be more to Hayley's story, and his curiosity was piqued. But he could wait. "So, about Toronto…Did you like living there?"

One side of Hayley's mouth quirked. Shadows crossed her features, and he wondered what those memories were that pulled her lips downward.

She sighed, looked out the dark window and back

at him. "It has its good points. Lots to do, always. I used to love the busyness, the noise, all the people. Maybe I used it to drown out my loneliness." She tilted her head and seemed to study him. "If a big city is what you want, I think you'll like Toronto."

I used it to drown out my loneliness. Those words resounded in his heart. He swallowed hard and grabbed at the next sane thought. "Do you know much about Lowrider Cycles?"

"Not really. I went there a couple times years ago with a guy I knew." Her mouth twisted, making him wonder. "It was big, the guys were loud, lots of colourful language, and the bikes looked amazing. That's really all I remember about it."

That fit with his visit there. He'd sensed an intense competitiveness too, that attracted and repelled him. His head began to ache as his decision twisted his mind. Why did it have to be so complicated? And what had he expected of this date? She'd draw him a picture of his future? Might as well make the best of the evening, get to know this fascinating woman. He pushed his plate aside and leaned his elbows on the table. "Let's forget Toronto for now. How long do you plan to be in Saskatoon?"

A smile appeared and disappeared from her face. "I'm not sure. I haven't planned very far ahead. Just taking one day at a time."

What had she said on the plane about her time at the University of Saskatchewan? Memory clicked. "You said you were studying accounting when you were here before. Is that your goal?"

Hayley shrugged as she traced the edge of her glass. "It was, but I don't know anymore." She shook her head. "I sound hopeless, don't I? But so much has happened, I'm not the same person I was a year ago."

Now that sounded interesting. Did he dare ask what had happened, or would it make her withdraw again? Was the accident she'd mentioned so life-changing? And what if she took his interest as a reason to preach about Jesus the way Carlos did?

Curiosity won. Trevor leaned forward. "You don't sound hopeless, just confused. Trust me, I understand. But I'd like to know what happened. What were you like before, and what changed you?"

She stared out the window again for several heartbeats. Unreadable expressions flitted across her reflected face. Then she closed her eyes, took a deep breath, and exhaled through pursed lips. When she turned back to him, Hayley's eyes seemed a deeper green than before, and lines had appeared between her eyebrows. "I won't bore you with the whole sorry tale, but I wasn't a nice person. Totally self-centered, out for a good time no matter who got hurt. And people did." A spasm etched lines between her eyebrows. "I have a lot of regrets."

Her obvious pain burned his heart. "Listen, you don't have to tell me…"

She shook her head. "No, you asked, and I want to explain. The main reason I came to Saskatoon was to spend time with Dave and Lydia. He was my pastor when I was here before, and he and his wife are the most caring people I've ever met. They don't care about your past. Their home and their arms are always open to anyone in need. And I need it."

Trevor squirmed. Hayley stretched her hand across the table and placed it on his. A tingle shot up his arm, and her eyes widened. Had she felt it too?

"I won't preach at you." She smiled. "At least not

tonight. All I'll say is that God's love, through Dave and Lydia, is changing me. I'm learning forgiveness is possible. And it makes all the difference." She pulled her hand away and leaned back.

Trevor missed its warmth and power to distract from her words. His gut churned. It must be some sort of conspiracy, all this talk about God and forgiveness wherever he turned. He grabbed his water glass and downed its contents as though to drown out the effect of her words. He set his glass down with a thump, and Hayley shrank back.

"Sorry." He pulled up his sleeve and glanced at his watch. "I've got work tomorrow…"

Hayley blushed. "I'm sorry. I didn't mean to…" She ducked her head and scooted her chair back.

Shame flooded Trevor and burned his face. She'd only answered what he'd asked. "Wait, Hayley. Would you like a cup of coffee or something? We don't need to go yet. I'd still like to hear what you think about the job in Toronto. I could use an impartial opinion."

Hayley sighed, and the wistfulness of the sound shamed him even more. But her expression cleared, and she scooted her chair toward the table again.

"All right." She leaned her elbows on the table and propped her chin on her palms as she studied his face. "You obviously care a lot about your parents, and you don't want to leave them when they need you."

Trevor nodded as the weight of his responsibility settled onto his shoulders.

"But you want to grow in your career, and that can only happen in Toronto. Right?"

Was she right? If he knew the answer to that question, he'd know what to do. He rubbed his chin, and part of his brain registered thankfulness he'd taken the time to shave before this date. "I do want to expand my custom motorcycle business, but I don't know if I have to be at Lowrider for that. There's my problem. My parents or my career—how do I choose?"

One side of Hayley's mouth lifted, but her eyes held only sympathy. "You've got a tough decision to make. I wish I had the solution for you." Her head tilted. "What do your parents say?"

Trevor gazed at the dining room's ceiling as recent conversations replayed. "They want me to follow my heart. And they're praying." A trace of bitterness had crept into his voice, and he struggled to restrain it. "If I could find someone to help Mom until she heals and a guy to assist Dad with chores, I could leave with a clear conscience."

Hayley's face brightened. "Dave and Lydia know lots of people. They might know the perfect ones to help your parents. Do you want me to ask?"

Church people. Trevor's jaw clenched as he considered. Not his first choice, but his folks would welcome like-minded people. And they'd certainly helped enough families through the years. Maybe it was time for the tide of giving to turn back. They might not want assistance, but it could be the answer. He'd be free to leave and follow his dream.

Hayley's fingers played a rhythm on the tablecloth, and the silent movement caught his attention. The pink bloom on her cheeks when she realized he'd noticed stirred a warm glow deep in his chest and made his fingers want to trace the curve of her rosy cheeks.

Concentrate. Don't think about her, think about her suggestion. It might be the solution he needed. Trevor cleared his throat. "That's a good idea." Hope for a good resolution swept over him, and he grinned. "I knew there was a reason I couldn't quit thinking about you." Heat rushed up his neck. "I mean…thank you."

Hayley ducked her head, but not before he saw a sparkle in her eyes. She made a show of looking at her watch, and when she faced him again, her lips twitched upward. "You're welcome. But it is getting late. We should go, and I'll talk to Dave and Lydia. I'll call you with their suggestions. Is that OK?"

"Absolutely." A little thrill shot through him. He knew a phone call wouldn't be enough. He wanted to see her again.

She gathered her coat. Trevor stood and held out his hand, a silent request. She smiled at him, handed him the heavy garment, and turned her back to him, waiting.

Trevor stared at her spiky red hair, the delicate curve of her neck, and her thin shoulders. His gaze travelled down to the swell of her narrow hips. She turned, questions in her eyes, and embarrassment turned his movements jerky as he held her coat open. She slipped her arms into the sleeves, and he pulled the silk-lined coat onto her shoulders. His hands didn't want to let go. He leaned a little closer and breathed in her scent. Something fresh and flowery. Reminded him of his mom's flower garden.

Hayley turned, and her eyes widened. She took a step back. "Thank you for this evening, Trevor." Her voice wavered.

Was that fear in her eyes, or something else?

9

Hayley opened one eye and squinted at the glowing red numbers of the bedside clock. Two-thirty. What had woken her? She strained to hear, but other than its usual creaking and the sound of the furnace blowing heat, the old house was quiet. She flopped back against her pillow and sighed.

Think about something pleasant, but what? Her date with Trevor Hiebert. Given the way he'd hurried out of the airport without a backward glance, she hadn't expected to hear from him. So when she heard his voice on the phone, a thrill zinged through her.

She smiled in the darkness of her basement room. She would never forget the extra-hard thump of her heart when she came up the stairs and saw him talking to Dave and Lydia. His dark brown hair curled over the collar of his leather jacket, his posture straight but relaxed, and his worn denim jeans hugged his muscular thighs. The eyes she remembered as stormy gray seemed to glow like mercury when he'd spotted her.

She'd tried to forget the strong pull she'd felt on the plane, but the instant their eyes met in Dave and Lydia's entrance hall, all her senses switched to high. She couldn't have backed away if she'd tried. A deep, contented sigh bubbled up. Hayley closed her eyes, willing herself to dream about Trevor.

But just as she drifted toward sleep, a chilly breeze tickled her ear. She jolted upward, and her whisper forced its way past fear-tightened vocal cords. "Who's there?" She held her breath and listened. Nothing. Must have been her imagination. Hayley settled back against the pillow, but her eyes refused to close.

Movement near the window caught her attention. What was that?

Hayley pulled her blankets up around her shaking shoulders. "Is s-someone there?"

Her leg began to ache as though a storm brewed, from a dull discomfort to deep, searing pain in seconds. She sat up and massaged the tormented limb, but it only made it worse. Groaning, she crawled out of bed without turning on the light, pulled open the bottom drawer of her desk, and rummaged under some papers. Where were they?

Another hot spasm shot up her leg, and she bit her lip to keep from crying out. Stretching her arm as far as she could, her fingers touched a small, plastic case. She drew it out and clenched it in her fist.

Pain overwhelmed all other thoughts, and Hayley opened the pill container. She picked out two capsules, but halfway to her mouth her hand stopped as though it had hit a wall. Shock rippled through her as realization hit. These pills were her escape route from life, the narcotics that would end her misery forever.

Take them. You need them. The raspy whisper swirled around her face.

Hayley threw the pills back into the drawer and slammed it shut. "No! Not now." She began to sob. "I want to *live.*" Still sobbing, Hayley crawled back into bed and curled into a fetal position. Breathe. In and out. *I am OK. I am strong. The past is gone, the future is*

God's. Over and over she repeated the words, until finally the throbbing pain ebbed, and she relaxed.

As she slid into a deep sleep, she heard another sound, and it tore at her soul. Faintly, as though through a dense fog, a baby's cry hung in the air.

~*~

Darkness still shrouded the city when Trevor emerged from a deep, restful sleep. He shut off his alarm radio before it could interrupt his peace and propped his hands behind his head. He could take a few minutes to enjoy the comfort of his own bed. Since he'd returned from Toronto, he'd stayed at the farm to help his dad with chores. Now it felt good to be back in his own place, even for one night.

His thoughts drifted to the farm with its problems and possibilities. He'd always dreamed of eventually taking it over when his parents retired and he'd found the woman who could share his dream, a real helpmate. This farm was the perfect place to do for some hurting kid what his parents had done for him. Give a child a secure home and help him find his way to a better life.

His lips twisted as memories took him where he didn't want to go. Anything would have been better than his last foster home. He shoved the haunting images away and picked up a brighter one.

Hayley. She'd surprised him. Several times. Her empathy towards the difficulty of his decision, her willingness to open up even a little, and especially the change in her demeanour. The timid, hurting beauty from the plane had morphed into a more confident, positive woman. She'd figured God had helped her.

Fine. At least she hadn't tried to preach at him.

And if she could find someone to help his mom, he'd be indebted to her. Pleasure radiated through his chest. Another reason to see her again, and he could go for that. Better give her a day or two to talk to those friends of hers, though.

Trevor glanced at the clock. If he wanted to get to the shop before the other guys claimed work space, he had to get going. Sometime during the night, his subconscious figured out the solution to the gas tank issue on his next creation. But would this be the last custom bike he'd build in Saskatoon? Pleasure twisted into unease.

He wrenched the covers off his restless body and hurried to shower.

~*~

The bedside clock read ten forty-five when Hayley sat up and rubbed gritty residue from her eyes. She hadn't slept well until she'd heard footsteps above her indicating Dave and Lydia's comforting presence. She padded across the hardwood floor and pulled her plush moss-green bathrobe out of the closet. Its warmth enveloped her as she wrapped it around her weary body. She smoothed the rose-embroidered silk lapel, tied the belt, and cringed as its long ends mocked her thinness.

A few minutes later, she grabbed the handrail as she took one stair at a time, her injured leg lagging behind like a reluctant puppy. She pushed open the door at the top of the stairs and blinked.

Bright sunshine streamed in through sheer curtains at the kitchen's bay window. Hayley shielded her eyes with her hand as she crossed to the cupboard for a mug. But after her rough night, tea didn't appeal. "Coffee. I need coffee."

The stainless thermos carafe felt heavy, and when Hayley poured out its dark liquid, fragrant steam wafted into her face. "Mm-mm." It smelled good for the first time since the accident.

She took a careful sip, swallowed, and smiled. It tasted good too. Wonder flitted through her mind, but pleasure overrode it. Hayley sat at the round oak table, sipped her coffee, and marveled at the stark beauty of Lydia's garden outside the bay window.

Nothing bloomed yet, of course, as temperatures still dropped well below freezing most nights. But the cedar gazebo and benches, metal fire pit, and bare but stately trees and shrubs created a still life picture which promised more loveliness to come.

Lost in contemplation, Hayley jumped when something touched her shoulder.

"I didn't mean to startle you." Lydia sat next to Hayley. "Did you have a good evening?" Concern textured her voice. She must have noticed the shadows under Hayley's eyes. Or maybe it was just the lateness of the hour.

Hayley felt her face warm. "Trevor was great, and so was the meal. I'm really glad he called." Memory of a promise clicked, and she turned to face Lydia head-on. "I have to ask you something, though."

Lydia patted Hayley's hand. "Anything, dear."

"Trevor's worried about his parents. They live out on a farm near….Langham, I think he said. Anyway, his mom broke her arm, and his dad is having trouble keeping up with the chores, and that's keeping Trevor from taking the job of his dreams in Toronto."

Lydia's head tilted. "His last name is Hiebert, right?" Hayley nodded, and Lydia continued. "I wonder if they might be Franklin and Laureen Hiebert. I met Laureen at a women's ministry luncheon a couple years ago. Lovely lady."

Hayley shrugged. "I don't think he mentioned their names. But I told him you might know someone who could help them, at least until his mom's arm heals. Oh, and she's been having dizzy spells, so his dad is afraid to leave her alone."

"Oh, dear. Let me think…better yet, let's pray." Without waiting for a response, Lydia bowed her head. "Father God, You know this situation inside and out. You know the cause of these dizzy spells, and You know Trevor's desire to take care of his parents. If he is to go to Toronto, please provide a helper for them. Thank You, in Jesus's name."

The calm assurance in Lydia's voice surprised and soothed Hayley. How did Lydia know God heard her? How could she expect He would care enough to act?

Before she could formulate a question, Lydia patted Hayley's hand and stood. "Have you eaten yet, dear?"

"No, but I'm not really hungry. I'll wait for lunch."

Lydia peered at her. "Are you sure?"

Hayley nodded as echoes of her bad dream settled like a lump in her stomach. "Thanks, anyway."

"Dave has a luncheon meeting, so it's just the two of us for lunch. Would you like something light? Maybe grilled cheese sandwiches and a tossed salad?"

Her distress melted away, and Hayley smiled her pleasure. "That sounds perfect. Do I have time to get dressed first?"

"Of course, but it's not necessary. Whenever

you're ready, we'll make lunch together. And afterward, while we wait for God's response to our prayer, how about some more cooking lessons? We can make some meals for the Hiebert family. The poor woman won't be able to do much with her arm in a cast." She pulled a tattered cookbook from the cupboard and began flipping pages.

Hayley propped her chin on her hand and stared at Lydia's back. "You're amazing, Lydia, always doing things for others. I wish I could be just like you."

Lydia stilled. "No, you don't." One side of her mouth lifted as she returned to the table. "I'm far from perfect, my dear. Don't aspire to be like me. You haven't been here long enough to know how imperfect I am, but trust me." Her eyes twinkled as she shook her head. "You are becoming the woman God designed you to be, and that's a very good thing. Much better than trying to be like anyone else."

Hayley nibbled her lower lip. "I don't understand." God had a design for her? How could He? Why…? She shook her head and pushed back her chair. Maybe a quick shower would clear her mind and untangle her thoughts. She headed for the basement stairs. "I'll get dressed and be right back—with some questions."

What if Lydia was right?

And if God had a plan for her, what could it possibly be?

~*~

Five hours later, three casseroles and two meat loaves shared space in Lydia's convection oven, while six dozen cookies and four dozen buns cooled on racks. Hayley grimaced at the misshapen blobs she'd formed. "Maybe we should keep these here, hmm?"

Lydia grinned. "You should have seen my first batch of buns. Good thing Dave loves my cooking, no matter what. Yours don't look bad. Let's give them a taste test." She picked up two sorry-looking specimens, handed one to Hayley, and sliced open the other. "Come on, help yourself to the butter."

Hayley waited until Lydia took a bite, chewed, and swallowed. At least she hadn't choked or gagged. "How was it?"

Lydia winked. "Try one." She took another bite.

Hayley took a tentative nibble. Not bad. She chewed and analyzed. It tasted yeasty, like buns should, soft inside with a slightly crisp crust. "It's good." Relief lifted her lips. "They look funny, but they're all right."

Lydia nodded as she packed cooled cookies into freezer containers. "Shaping them takes a little practice, but I'm impressed with how well you did. Maybe tomorrow we'll make some hot cross buns to freeze. A tasty Easter tradition."

Hayley sank onto a chair at the table and massaged her leg. "I can't wait. That was fun. I've always envied people who could turn ingredients into something tasty and nutritious. But I never imagined I could do it."

Lydia reached for another container. "Why not?"

"My parents didn't cook much, and when I tried....well, that was the disaster I told you about."

"Then I suggest we make up for lost time now that you're here. I love having such an eager student." Her smile felt like a benediction.

Warmth flooded Hayley until one word pricked

her conscience. Student. Her accounting books waited downstairs, and she hadn't even thought about them for two days. And now she dreaded facing them. She imagined herself at her father's accounting firm, wrestling with numbers and forms. Day after day. A shudder rippled through her.

"Are you cold?" Lydia's soft voice dispelled the vision.

Hayley forced a smile. "No, I'm fine. A little tired. But I'll help with supper."

"You already did." Lydia's eyes twinkled. "One of the meat loaves is for our supper. I'll pop some potatoes in the microwave, heat up some green beans, and there's salad left from lunch, so we're set. Why don't you relax, maybe put your leg up for a while? We'll eat in about forty-five minutes."

Hayley pushed to her feet. "I should probably work on my studies."

Lydia turned back to the baked goods. "All right, dear. Thanks for all your help. Have fun."

Hayley plodded toward her room. Fun? Not the word she'd choose for her studies. Destiny, maybe. Or obligation. Her father's note nudged her conscience. She'd made a promise to succeed. She straightened her shoulders. She would do it. She had to. Fun didn't enter the equation.

10

Trevor flicked a speck of dust off his prized 1938 Indian Chief, the project which had sparked his love of motorcycles so long ago. Was that a scratch on the tank? He pulled a soft cloth from his back pocket and polished the headdress logo. As the line disappeared, tension in his neck eased but didn't disappear. He glanced at the clock on the wall.

The reporter, Greg Lewis, said he'd arrive at ten, and it was two minutes after.

Trevor headed toward the coffee maker. Maybe a hot drink would help his nerves. He'd never been interviewed before, and while the guy promised it would be "a piece of cake," Trevor wasn't at all anxious to expose himself to strangers. He grimaced and one corner of his mouth twitched upward.

As he picked up the coffee carafe, the bell on the front door jangled, announcing his interviewer's arrival.

Lewis spotted him and strode over to the counter, hand extended. "Thanks for this. Are you ready?"

Good question. Was he? He could talk all day about bikes, but if the guy tried to get into his past… He set the carafe back on its warmer and shook the reporter's hand. "Sure." He gestured to his Chief. "This is the one we discussed yesterday. My first. Put it together from a box of parts." Pride straightened his spine. "What do you know about Indian Motorcycles?"

Lewis pulled out a camera and photographed the bike from several angles. "I did some research. Old ones like this one are pretty rare—and expensive. How did you find it?"

Trevor clenched his jaw. No way was this reporter getting his whole story.

~*~

An hour and a half later, Trevor dumped his cold coffee and started a fresh pot. While it brewed, he sank onto one of the vinyl-covered, chrome stools behind the counter. Nervous tension spiraled away, leaving him depleted. Had he given enough information? Had he said too much about his past? He replayed the interview.

Lewis asked good questions. He'd skirted close to the limits of Trevor's personal stuff, and the guy hadn't backed off easily. "Look," Lewis had said, "A big part of this series and contest is letting the public get to know you, not just your work."

So Trevor had admitted to his single status, tidbits from his life on the farm, and…what else? He slowed the mental replay and cringed. When Lewis asked him if he had any brothers or sisters, he'd hesitated—and the reporter had noticed. Hopefully, his "no" was emphatic enough.

The coffee maker gurgled its readiness, and Trevor refilled his cup. As he sipped the hot brew, he wondered which of his bikes would appear in the newspaper, the Honda CX500 café racer or his 1938 Indian Chief. The older bike's rarity made it special, even without its personal story.

"Hey, do I smell fresh joe?" Carlos made a beeline for the almost-full pot. "That reporter gone?"

Trevor nodded. "Yeah, he took plenty of photos of both bikes. And me. Wanted me to pose on the bikes like some kind of fashion model." He grunted. "That didn't happen. The guy seemed to know motorcycles, but said he might have more questions. Might want to talk to you too, since I gave the shop a plug."

Carlos traced a pattern on the counter. "Did you say anything about Toronto?"

"Nope. Didn't think that would be fair. Besides, I haven't decided yet."

"Thanks. You got what, two days to let Starr know?"

Pressure settled onto Trevor's shoulders. "Two. Short. Days."

The weight of Carlos's hand warmed Trevor's arm. "I'm praying for you, T. God's gonna work this out. You'll see."

"Yeah, sure."

As soon as Carlos disappeared into his office, Trevor pulled out his phone and found Hayley's number. He needed a distraction, and he couldn't imagine anyone more distracting than a certain green-eyed redhead. "Hello, Hayley. Any chance I could see you tonight? We could catch a movie, if you'd like. There's a new one in town I think you'd enjoy."

~*~

"Great movie. I can't remember when I laughed so hard." Hayley grinned as she slid into a booth at the popular coffee shop, careful not to spill her hot chocolate. "You surprised me with your choice. Never pictured you as a cartoon kind of guy." But as a romantic lead? Easy. Warmth rushed to her face.

"Well, I didn't figure you'd care for my usual high body-count movie. Besides, laughter's good for a soul, right?" He sipped his black coffee.

So was sitting across from such a good-looking and considerate man. "Yes, it must be. Other than a pain in my side from laughing so hard, I feel wonderful."

Trevor's perusal caressed her. "You look pretty wonderful too. Thanks for agreeing to come with me on such short notice."

Hayley shook her head. "My social life's not exactly hectic. And I like spending time with you." Where had that come from? She hardly knew this guy. But it was the truth. Something about him tugged on her heart. Made her want to smooth out the crease on his forehead.

"Likewise. You're easy to talk to." His smile didn't quite reach his eyes now.

"Have you reached a decision about the Toronto job?" Was that the reason for the stress lines?

Trevor sighed. "No. As much as I want to grab the opportunity, I can't leave my folks in the lurch. And the more I think about actually moving and starting over in Toronto, the less sure I am. I've never been so torn." He looked at the ceiling as though searching for answers. "Dad, Mom, and Carlos all say they're praying, but I gotta admit, that just drives me away."

Hayley propped her chin on her hands as a weight of disappointment settled into her heart. The frustrated look on Trevor's face pulled the question from her. "Why?"

"Do you really want to know?" His gaze

hardened, burned. "It's not pretty."

Back off. You're in over your head. The raspy, silent whisper sent shivers up and down her spine. What should she say? *God, help me*. "Yes, I want to know." She reached out, covered Trevor's hands with hers, and lowered her voice. "Tell me, Trevor."

His eyes looked wary, but he didn't look away. His sigh sounded as if it was drawn from a bottomless pit. "My parents tried to teach me to love God, but by the time I met them, I'd seen too much evil to believe in a good God."

"Wh-what? When you met your parents? I don't understand."

"I grew up in foster care, Hayley. Nobody's kid. Franklin and Laureen rescued me when I was twelve years old and on my way to jail for beating my last foster dad. Larry Kirby." His mouth twisted. "I wish I'd killed him."

Hayley tried but couldn't suppress a gasp. "What did he do? I mean, he must have been awful…"

"I caught him raping my foster sister. She was only ten." Tears filled his eyes, but he didn't seem to notice. "When I saw him on top of her, I lost it. Grabbed a baseball bat and hit him. Over and over."

The gleam of satisfaction in his eyes chilled Hayley, while the pain etched on his face echoed in her soul. "Then what happened?"

"His wife yanked me back and called the cops. By the time they got there, 'Mom and Dad' had a story figured out where I was the abuser and had wigged out when they'd caught me." Bitterness laced his words. "The cops believed them, because they were such good church people. And to top it off, several years later I heard from a buddy…my little sister killed herself." His voice lowered to a whisper. "Where was God in all of that?"

Tears ran down Hayley's face, but she kept her hands on Trevor's clenched fists. "I'm so sorry. I don't have the answer. I wish I did." Helplessness and sorrow squeezed her heart. At the same time, she knew Trevor had offered her a precious gift—the truth of his past. Now what should she do with it?

Trevor pulled his hands away from hers and rubbed his face. "I don't know why I told you. I don't expect you to have answers that don't exist. Sorry to dump on you." He shifted on the vinyl bench. "How's your cocoa?"

Hayley couldn't switch gears so quickly. "Pardon? Oh, it's fine." She sipped her now-cooled beverage as her brain raced to catch up. It stuck on one part of Trevor's story. Did she dare ask? "May I make one observation?"

"Sure. Go ahead." He leaned back, his arms crossed.

"You said your parents rescued you from jail—and a horrible foster home. They obviously loved you enough to adopt you. Seems to me God must have been at work there. Or would you call their entry into your life a coincidence?"

Pinned by Trevor's steely glare, Hayley couldn't move. Could barely breathe. Why had she said that? Who was she to talk about God?

~*~

Trevor stared into the wide, green eyes of the woman across from him. If not for the compassion radiating from her, he'd get up and walk away. No, wait. He'd brought her here; he couldn't desert her. So he considered her question. Franklin and Laureen often said God brought him into their lives, but he'd always brushed off the thought. God didn't care about him. Now Trevor tried to hang on to his outrage against their God, but felt it slipping through his mental fingers. "I don't know," he finally admitted. "I'll have to think about it, but not now. Can we change the subject?"

Hayley forced a smile and dabbed her face with a tissue. "Of course. Let's get back to your job in Toronto. Is anything besides your parents' health holding you back?"

Other than the fascinating beauty sitting across from him? He pulled his gaze away. Yeah, there was the farm, and his parents' hopes that he'd take it over. But the lure of the Toronto job pulled. More money, more freedom, a chance to prove he could succeed on his own merit. How could he turn that down? Trevor shook his head. "Not really. It's a big move, so a little nervousness is normal, I'm sure."

An offhand remark by Vince Starr during the job interview brushed the edges of Trevor's memory with a sense of uneasiness, but it refused to come into focus. No matter what happened in Toronto, he could deal with it. How else could he make a name for himself and show he was better than his past? He had to take the chance. "You know, I think I've made my decision. I'll give my two weeks' notice tomorrow. Assuming my folks can find someone to help them, I'm moving to Toronto. They say God will provide. I hope they're right, because you've helped me realize this is an opportunity I can't pass up."

Hayley's smile slid away from her face, and the

woeful look in her eyes nearly undid him. But then she sat up straight and smiled brightly "I'm happy for you, Trevor. I hope you'll be happy in your new job."

He reached across the table and wiped an unexpected tear from her face, his finger lingering on the curve of her cheek. He was giving up a lot for that job. Maybe too much?

~*~

"Did we get everything? Do you have the directions I scribbled?" Lydia started the car.

Hayley held up the carefully detailed instructions while she mentally reviewed the food nestled in the car's trunk. "Pretty sure we're set. How long do you think it will take to get to the Hiebert farm? From these directions, it sounds like quite a distance."

"Shouldn't take much more than half an hour." Lydia signaled and turned on to Circle Drive North. "Traffic's pretty light. That helps. I wish I could bring better news to Laureen. Dave and I have both put out feelers for someone to stay with her, but so far, nothing."

She sighed while braking for a red light. "It's too bad Tessa Peters—I mean, Tessa Cruz—and Orlando are still in Belize." Lydia glanced at Hayley. "Did you meet them when you were here before?"

"She's Will's mom's friend, right? Nila wrote me about Tessa and Orlando's wedding and how their honeymoon turned into a mission trip. Tessa's a nurse? Then she'd be perfect for Mrs. Hiebert. It's too bad…"

"She would, but I'm not sure the Hieberts could afford her, and I'm sure Tessa will need an income when they get home. But remember, we've given this to God, and He's more than capable to work everything out."

"I hope so. I told Trevor last night we were bringing some food to his parents today."

"How did he respond?"

"I think he was pleased, but not so much when I told him we haven't found anyone to stay with Laureen yet. Or to help his dad."

"But he's moving to Toronto anyway?" Lydia took the exit onto Highway 16 toward Langham. "That doesn't fit with the impression I got."

"He won't go until someone steps in to help his parents. But he really wants that job, and he has to give his decision by tomorrow." Hayley had hoped Trevor would decide to stay in Saskatoon. He was one of the few friends she'd made in the area, and she'd wondered if they could be more than friends. *God, why would You let him leave now? Can't You stop him? Was I wrong about him? About You?*

11

Hayley wrinkled her nose. "What's that smell?"

Lydia laughed. "We call it 'Eau de Farm.' Manure piles are thawing, so country air gets rather pungent this time of year."

Hayley gripped the armrest as Lydia swerved around a huge pothole. "Oh! This road is awful."

"Roads are thawing too, and potholes are pretty much a springtime ritual." Lydia glanced at Hayley before dodging another water-filled hole. "You haven't been out in the country much, have you?"

The odor increased the further they travelled down the muddy, rough road, and Hayley forced herself to take shallow breaths. "No, I haven't. City born and raised, I'm afraid." She covered her nose and mouth with her hand and spoke through her fingers. "Do people actually get used to this?" She couldn't imagine enduring such a stench day after day.

Lydia chuckled and slowed the car. "Yes, they do. You would too, if you spent enough time on a farm. We should be close now. What did Laureen say to look for?"

Hand still covering her face, Hayley checked the instructions. "A long row of spruce trees and then a red sign saying *Hieberts' Haven*. This row of trees could be theirs, and I think I see the sign."

"You're right." Lydia slowed and signalled to turn

right.

Who was Lydia signaling to? The road was empty, something Hayley had never experienced before. Country life seemed like a different world. Fascinating. She gazed around. On her right, three rows of shorter evergreens lined the wide driveway, echoed a short distance on her left. When they exited the dark green hallway of trees, Hayley's eyes widened. "Oh, it's so pretty."

"What beautiful stonework," Lydia said. "And I'll bet Laureen has already started plants for her flower beds. We enjoyed sharing gardening stories at the women's ministry luncheon."

The Hieberts' home stood tall and square with two stories of stonework topped with white dormers, a full-length, white-pillared front porch, and an empty brick flowerbed on both sides of the broad steps. At one end of the porch, someone had installed a ramp, newer than the house but well used.

The driveway continued on past the house, where Hayley could see a long Quonset near the back wall of evergreens opposite a large, metal building. Then she glimpsed some kind of airy white structure tucked behind the house. Could it be a Victorian-style gazebo? She craned her neck as Lydia pulled close to the porch and stopped.

"Here we are," Lydia said. "Isn't this beautiful? I can almost picture those lilac bushes in bloom. See? The buds are already showing. And that looks like a crab apple tree in front of the big window. I wonder if the flowers are white or pink?" She grinned at Hayley. "Look at me, getting distracted by this well-designed yard. Let's get these boxes into the house, shall we?"

Hayley opened her door and winced at the strong

manure smell. "People really get used to this?"

Lydia nodded, smiling, and popped the trunk open. "If you grab the smaller box, I can get the casseroles. I'll come back for the last box."

"Welcome!" A man's gravelly voice coupled with a cold, wet nudge on her leg startled Hayley as she leaned into the trunk, and she banged her head. "Ouch." She quickly touched the tender spot. No blood—good. She retrieved the carton and straightened.

"You must be Lydia Harris and Hayley Blankenship." A gray-haired man, medium height and slightly stooped, walked toward them. "Franklin Hiebert. Laureen told me you were coming." He pointed at the dog rubbing against Hayley's leg. "Roscoe, down."

The black and white animal sat immediately, and Hayley tentatively patted its head. "Nice dog. Sure obeys well."

"Roscoe's a Border Collie. Smart dogs, bred to herd." Mr. Hiebert smiled and clasped Lydia's extended hand between his palms. "Thank you for coming. My dear wife is struggling with this enforced inactivity, I'm afraid, but she brightened right up when you called." He smiled at Hayley. "She's looking forward to meeting you too, young lady. I believe you know our son." One bushy eyebrow lifted.

What had Trevor said about her?

Obviously a response wasn't necessary as Mr. Hiebert reached past her into the trunk. "Let me help you ladies." He hoisted two and peered into one. "Is this all for *us*?" He sounded like a little boy at Christmas.

Hayley couldn't hold back a grin as she adjusted

her grip on the box.

Lydia moved in to retrieve the last box and close the trunk. "Yes, it is. Everything can be stored in the freezer, and we enjoyed ourselves preparing them. Right, Hayley?"

Hayley tilted her head and nodded. "It was fun—and educational."

"Sounds like a story there," Mr. Hiebert said. "But let's get inside before Laureen comes looking for us."

Side by side, Hayley and Lydia followed him up the walkway to the steps where Hayley hesitated. Lydia noticed and tilted her head, but Hayley mouthed, "I'm OK." She shifted her box so she could grab the sturdy-looking wooden handrail.

"Feel free to use the ramp. It's handy when you're carrying a load."

The words melted over Hayley, rich, sweet, and soothing. Her hand paused midair as she looked for the owner of the voice. Leaning against the wide-open door stood a slender woman with a waterfall of white hair cascading to her shoulders, periwinkle eyes, and a cast on her right arm. Her lined face beamed a benediction on Hayley. So this was Trevor's mom.

"I'm fine, thanks." Had Trevor told his mom about Hayley's bad leg? She kept a hand on the rail and went up the four broad steps, careful to keep her left foot from dragging.

In the short time it took her to reach the porch, Franklin was back outside and reaching for the box in her arms. "Let me get that for you."

Before she had a chance to feel embarrassed about her weakness, Laureen took Hayley's hand.

"Welcome, my dear. Please, come make yourself at home." Laureen turned, still holding Hayley's hand,

and escorted her into the spacious living room. "Sit wherever you'd like, while I help Lydia take care of these gracious gifts."

Hayley gazed around the high-ceilinged room. Afghan-covered couches lined two walls and flanked a brick-backed, wood stove. A big, black recliner and a plump, floral armchair, end tables covered with photographs, and a book-laden oak coffee table completed the inviting space.

The overstuffed chair invited Hayley to sink into its comfort. With a sigh, she pulled a padded footstool closer and swung her stiff leg onto it. Cozy. For such a large room, it oozed warmth. She leaned back and closed her eyes.

What a contrast to her parents' starkly modern living room with its white walls and black furniture. Abstract art in broad strokes of clashing colors—Hayley had always hated them.

But here, Laureen and Franklin had created an oasis, mismatched and worn but comfortable. She could live here. Hayley's eyes popped open. Where had that thought come from?

"We made tea and coffee. Which do you prefer, Hayley?" Laureen re-entered the living room through the arched doorway leading to the kitchen.

Lydia followed, carrying a tray loaded with mugs, two carafes, dainty china cream and sugar containers, and a plate of cinnamon buns.

"Thank you, Lydia." Laureen moved aside some books on the coffee table. "You can set the tray here." She and Lydia sat on the couch facing the large picture window. "Those cinnamon buns looked too delicious to put away, and I'd love to share them with you." She picked up a cobalt mug decorated with a bright red heart and raised her eyebrows at Hayley. "Tea or coffee, dear?"

"Tea, thanks, and I take it black."

"Easy to please. I like that." Laureen nodded as she poured the tea. "Lydia?"

"Coffee for me, with just enough milk to change the color. Thank you."

Laureen adjusted the carafe's lid, poured the steaming brew into a lily-printed china mug, added a splash of milk, and handed it to Lydia, who watched with a gentle smile. Why hadn't Lydia offered to do the pouring? A twinge of disappointment pricked Hayley. Maybe Lydia wasn't the model of Christian perfection she'd thought.

"Hayley, would you like a cinnamon bun? Lydia told me you made them, and they look fantastic." Laureen's warm caramel voice roused Hayley from her musings.

"Um, no thanks. I'm not hungry."

Laureen tilted her head. "I hope you're not dieting."

Hayley turned away from the compassion in the older woman's eyes. "I'm not."

"Well, I'd love one." Lydia spoke up, but she waited until Laureen placed a sticky bun onto a small plate covered with pink blossoms and handed it to her. "Thank you."

Hayley opened her mouth, realized she didn't know what to say, and closed it again.

Laureen nibbled on a bun, set it back on her plate, and sipped her coffee. Then she leaned back and rested her cast on the arm of the couch. "I can't thank you ladies enough for this—coming all the way out here, bringing such treats, and letting me play hostess. I wondered if that particular joy would have to wait until my arm healed, but you've allowed me to serve you, and I appreciate your patience."

Lydia patted Laureen's knee. "It's our pleasure, my friend." She directed a smile across the coffee table. "Right, Hayley?"

Hayley's face warmed. "Of course." She sipped her tea to cover her embarrassment. "You have a lovely home, Mrs. Hiebert."

"Thank you, dear, but please call me Laureen. Lydia tells me this is your first time on a farm." Her inflection turned it into a question.

"Um, yes. Other than a few months at the University of Saskatchewan, I've always lived in Toronto." She inhaled and smiled when she realized the barnyard smell hadn't followed them indoors. "This is a new world for me. How long have you lived here?"

"More than forty years. We'd been saving up for a home of our own since our marriage, and when we saw this place, we knew it was the one for us. I can't imagine living anywhere else, but…" Laureen's voice trailed off, and Hayley noticed her swallow hard.

Hayley spoke softly, as though treading on eggs. "Trevor told me you want to move into the city."

Laureen lifted her chin, her smile thin. "Depends on the day and the mood. Realistically, it's time, but I dread the thought of the noise and busyness of Saskatoon. I'm spoiled, I know, but I love this farm."

Lydia set her coffee mug on the table. "I can certainly understand. It's so peaceful here. Although it probably hasn't always been this quiet." Her brown, almond-shaped eyes twinkled.

Laureen chuckled. "You got that right. For a while

we had six kids under the age of eight. Peace and quiet were a rarity then."

Six kids less than eight years old? How…and why? Hayley replayed Laureen's remark. *For a while.* Realization dawned. "Foster parents." So Trevor wasn't their first. She didn't realize she'd spoken aloud until Laureen nodded.

"Ever since we found out we wouldn't be contributing to the world's population, we opened our home to children in need. Not an easy venture, but oh, my, I wouldn't trade any of it for anything." Laureen's smile eased into a look of contentment that smoothed the wrinkles on her face.

"Was Trevor your last?" Curiosity pried the question from Hayley. "He told me a bit about what happened at his other foster home…" She tried to suppress a shudder as his anger-filled voice echoed. *"I caught him raping my little foster sister."*

Laureen's gasp startled Hayley. "He told you?" No psychiatrist had ever examined her as thoroughly as Trevor's mom did now.

Hayley shrank against the chair but couldn't look away from Laureen's slightly raised eyebrows and piercing blue eyes. Silence pulsed for several heartbeats. Heartbeats Hayley feared the other women could hear.

But then Laureen's smile returned, brighter than before, and she scooted forward as though to stand. "Would you ladies like a tour of the house?"

Pressure eased, and Hayley inhaled with relief. "Yes, please."

"Sounds lovely." Lydia stood and offered her hand to their hostess. "Shall I carry our dishes to the kitchen?"

"Sure. Thanks. Hayley hasn't seen our 'heart of the home' yet, so it's a good place to start." Laureen headed toward the arched doorway. "This is my favorite room of the whole house."

Hayley helped Lydia reload the floral-patterned tray before following their hostess. In the arch, Hayley paused and traced the marks in the doorway. *T.J., 3 ½, Raylene, 4, Jonas, 5, Cherie, 2…*Some were only listed once, while a few repeated three or four times, with dates after each one.

Hayley searched for one name and found it at her eye level: *Trevor, 12 ½,* with marks for four more years spaced a distance above. He'd been almost her height when he'd been twelve. She tried to picture him, tall, probably gangly at that age, and certainly angry after what he'd experienced. Hayley's heart ached for the boy—and the couple who'd taken him in. How had the Hieberts handled Trevor's anger? The ache lessened, and she sighed. Probably with a lot of prayer, if they were anything like Dave and Lydia.

"Coming, Hayley?" Lydia's voice drew her through the memory-filled passageway into a bright, open kitchen/dining area.

A large, rectangular oak trestle table with countless scratches and mismatched chairs centered the kitchen. Lydia patted the spot beside her, and Hayley sat.

While Laureen placed their dishes in the gleaming stainless dishwasher, she and Lydia chatted about their plans for the upcoming gardening season.

Hayley indulged her curiosity and gazed around the huge room. Upper cupboards were a mix of white and dark wood, some with glass fronts, and the lower cabinets, all dark, were a mixture of doors and deep drawers. Behind her, a large, double-door stainless refrigerator shone, surrounded by deep cabinets on all sides. An old-fashioned, white double sink sat under a wide window with a stained-glass transom. Beautiful. No wonder Laureen loved this space.

Hayley twisted around. The far wall held two antique-looking china cabinets, and their contents brought a smile to her face. She got up to look at them more closely. Several popsicle-stick structures shared space with antique dishes, delicate teacups and misshapen clay…somethings. One might be a cow, but she couldn't be sure.

"My treasures." Laureen joined her, opened one door, and pulled out a twig-framed drawing of a fantasy-type motorcycle. "Look at this." She handed it to Hayley.

"Trevor?" The penciled details were amazing, especially for a child.

Laureen nodded. "He was thirteen when he drew that. So when Franklin went to a farm auction not long after and found a rusty frame and box full of motorcycle parts, he bought it. My guys built the old Indian Chief together, and it's a thing of beauty now. Became a turning point for our boy." Her shoulders drooped. "And now we're facing another change." Laureen's hand shook as she put the picture back into the cabinet, her smile wobbly. "Are you ready to see the rest?"

By the time the three women had peeked into the main floor master bedroom, climbed the stairs to the four bedrooms on the second floor, and glanced into the mudroom while sharing bits of their lives the entire time, Hayley's leg threatened to drag.

Laureen was leaning against the walls outside the

bedrooms too.

Hayley hoped they hadn't overtired her. Guilt stung. She and Lydia should leave and let Laureen rest. Hayley pulled back her sleeve to expose her watch, and Lydia caught the hint and checked hers.

"Oh dear, I didn't realize how late it was. We need to get back to the city before Dave wonders where his supper is." A smile softened her words, and she laid a hand on Laureen's good arm. "Thank you, my friend, for a lovely afternoon."

The crinkles beside Laureen's eyes deepened as she smiled. "My pleasure. It's been wonderful to get reacquainted with you, Lydia." She turned to Hayley. "And I hope we can visit again soon. I can see why my son is taken with you."

Heat rushed up the back of Hayley's neck. Taken with her? Where did she get that idea? And if Trevor was taken with her, why was he so eager to move away?

12

A sharp tap on his shoulder alerted Trevor. He switched off the metal grinder and swiveled.

Carlos pointed at Trevor's left thigh. "A spark got you."

Trevor slapped the smouldering spot on his coveralls and poked his finger through the hole. At least it hadn't burned through his jeans. Then he realized Carlos wasn't alone. One step behind him stood a bald guy with a bushy gray beard, vivid tattoos on his neck and arms, and deep-set eyes that seemed to bore through him. Nobody he knew. He raised an eyebrow at his boss.

"T, this is Max, the guy who introduced me to Jesus." Carlos grinned, but then his lips thinned. "He's got a proposal for you. Come into my office."

Trevor glanced back at his project before following the two men. Just a few more minutes, and his gas tank would have been ready to sand and prep for paint. But Carlos was still his boss. This better not be another preaching session, though.

Trevor sat on the edge of the green vinyl chair, Carlos swiveled his leather throne, and Max leaned back as if he had all the time in the world. A prickle of annoyance irritated the back of Trevor's neck. He had work to do and no time to sit around playing nice. Two weeks—that's all he had to get the gas tank done. Not enough time to finish the project, but Carlos and the other guys would do it up right. He needed to make sure his logo got onto that tank, to mark this design as his. Even if he wouldn't be there to take credit.

"So, Trevor, Carlos told me about your situation." Max's voice rumbled like a well-tuned bike. "Your new job is in Toronto, but your folks need some assistance here. Correct?"

Trevor glared at Carlos, but his eyes were closed. Praying again?

Trevor grunted under his breath and turned to Carlos's friend. "Yeah. So what?" He hadn't meant to be rude. Pressure must be getting to him. "I mean, yes. You're right."

Max's lips lifted in a half-smile. "I'd like to meet your folks. See if we can work something out. That is, if you're determined to leave."

Heat rushed to Trevor's face. How dare he? This Max character didn't know him, except for whatever Carlos told him. What right did he have to question his decision? Trevor gritted his teeth and lifted his chin. "I'm going, and I've got two weeks to make sure someone reliable is on hand to help at the farm." The challenge rang in the small room.

"Then how about I meet you out there this evening? We can talk, and we'll see what happens."

Trevor's gut churned. Max didn't look like his parents' answer to prayer, but what did he know about prayer? Or the God his parents trusted.

~*~

Later that evening, Max, Trevor, and his parents sat at the kitchen table, a plate of chocolate chip cookies centered between them.

Trevor took one and bit into it. Hayley had made them, his mom said. Crisp outside, soft inside—perfect. He grabbed two more, only half-listening to his parents chatting with Max. Weather, memories, normal getting-to-know-you stuff. Until…

"You look awfully familiar, Max. Are you sure we haven't met before?" That was his mom.

Trevor stared at the stranger as he waited for the response.

Max sipped his coffee, set the mug down, and leaned back in his chair. "No, ma'am, not that I recall." His deep rumble sounded almost southern.

Trevor's back stiffened. There'd been no accent in Carlos's office. What was this guy trying to pull? "Where're you from?"

Those deep-set eyes turned on him, and Trevor felt pinned. "I've lived all over North America. Spent some time on a ranch in Texas. Most recently, I worked at King's Ranch in central Alberta. The foreman there will vouch for me."

"What brought you to this part of the country?" Franklin's quiet question echoed Trevor's thoughts.

Max shrugged. "God told me it was time to move on."

Trevor's throat spasmed, and he inhaled some coffee. Coughing and sputtering, he pushed away from the table and his mother's concerned face, and stumbled into the living room. He wanted to keep going, get in his vehicle and drive away from this farce. All the way to Toronto. But how could he leave when the only guy offering to help his folks was a religious nut? Then again, Carlos had vouched for him, and he trusted his boss. His current boss.

Trevor paced the living room several times, unable to ignore the voices in the kitchen. Sounded like his folks had already decided to welcome Max with open arms. A twinge of jealousy surprised him. This was good news. Wasn't it? He headed into the kitchen, grabbed another cookie, and plunked down on his chair.

"You all right?" Mom reached across the table and squeezed his hand.

"Yeah. Coffee went down the wrong way, that's all." That and his misgivings about Carlos's friend.

"Great news," Dad beamed. "Max here has agreed to work with me, and he's confident God will provide a helper for your mom before you leave. He rents a place in Langham, so he's just five minutes away. Praise God."

If Trevor's smile looked as fake as it felt…well, he couldn't help it. His throat convulsed. He'd made up his mind and given his notice. He'd been offered the job of his dreams. So why did it feel as though he was making the biggest mistake of his life?

~*~

The following afternoon, Hayley hit "Send" and closed her laptop. Another accounting lesson done in spite of her tendency to daydream. She stood and stretched her back, and then shifted her weight to her left leg. One hand on the desk steadied her as she tested her leg's strength and flexibility. Up on tiptoes, Hayley smiled. Much better. Not quite ready for a marathon, but definitely stronger. But strong enough? She needed to talk to Lydia.

Upstairs, Hayley found Lydia and Dave in quiet

conversation in the living room. Not wanting to disturb them, Hayley backed as quietly as possible toward the basement door. Her movement must have caught Dave's attention, because he beckoned her to join them.

"Come on in. You're not interrupting."

Hayley hesitated. "Are you sure?" They both nodded, so she crossed the room and settled into the mission-style rocker. "I need some guidance." Hayley hoped she wasn't making a fool of herself. Not that it would be the first time. She cleared her throat. "I keep thinking about Laureen Hiebert. I even dreamed about her last night."

Lydia's mouth curved upward, and her eyes shone, almost as if she knew what was coming. "She's a lovely woman. I'm glad you got to meet her."

"Me too." Hayley inhaled deeply. "But I keep wondering…do you think I might be able to be the helper she needs?"

Dave's bushy eyebrows shot up. "You realize you'd have to move out there?"

Hayley nodded slowly, her lips pursed. "I know." Would they think her ungrateful? After all, Dave and Lydia had opened their home—and their hearts—to her. She couldn't bear to hurt them. "I can't thank you enough for welcoming me into your home…"

"And we're happy to have you here for as long as you want." Dave sighed. "But we won't stand in the way of God's will for you."

Lydia leaned forward. "Have you prayed about this?"

Hayley squirmed. She assumed God spoke to her through the dreams, thoughts of Laureen, and the farm that kept popping into her mind. "Um, no, I guess I haven't."

Lydia tucked her hand into Dave's and bowed her head. "Then let's pray. Lord God, you know Hayley's heart and Laureen's need. We're asking you to make it clear if Hayley is to move to the farm until Laureen recovers her strength. Thank you for what you are doing."

"Please show me, Jesus," Hayley mumbled. "I don't want to make another mistake."

Pastor Dave cleared his throat. "Father, you have a plan for Hayley. You have chosen her, and while we aren't ready to say good-bye, we hold this young lady with open hands before you. Guide her. Use her. Protect her from evil, I pray in Jesus's name." His bass rumble soothed Hayley's anxiety.

Hayley couldn't imagine anything wicked at the Hiebert farm. Why had Dave prayed to protect her from evil? Fear prickled her spine.

13

Hayley glanced out the living room window for the fifth time as she watched for the Hieberts' arrival. Excitement merged with nervousness and created what felt like moths tumbling in her stomach.

Delicious smells emanated from Lydia's kitchen and hinted at the meal she'd helped prepare. Odors of sweet and sour pork, jasmine rice, and sautéed Oriental vegetables scented the air and made her stomach rumble. Hayley pressed her hand to her abdomen as she struggled to calm her nerves.

What if the Hieberts refused her help? Would they believe she was capable? Maybe she'd have to be content with a future of a cubicle, calculating taxes for strangers. A mental picture of the Hiebert farm and Laureen's warm smile swam into focus. They *had* to accept her offer. She hoped.

A maroon Dodge minivan pulled into the driveway.

"They're here." Hayley rushed to open the front door.

"Perfect timing." Lydia wiped her hands on her apron as she joined Hayley at the entry. "Everything is ready." Lydia smiled at her husband as he exited his office. "Except, perhaps, for you, my dear." Lydia reached up and smoothed Dave's rumpled gray hair. "Been working on next week's sermon already?"

Dave nodded. "And praying." He patted Hayley's shoulder.

Her insides settled down. Somewhat.

Outside, Franklin helped Laureen from the car and held her arm as they climbed the steps. Franklin's face looked drawn, but Laureen beamed.

Hayley hoped she would still be smiling after they'd discussed her proposition.

"Welcome to our home." Pastor Dave stepped aside with a flourish. "We're glad you could make it."

Lydia pulled Laureen into a hug. "Yes, we are." She stepped back as Dave and Franklin shook hands. "You haven't met my husband before, have you? Franklin, Laureen, this is Dave. And you know Hayley, of course."

Hayley smiled but hung back, certain her inadequacies must be written across her forehead.

"I've heard good things about you folks," Dave said. "May I hang up your coats?"

"Thank you." Laureen slipped off her bright red wool cape, while Franklin shrugged out of his brown suede jacket.

"Come on into the dining room," Lydia invited. "Supper is ready."

Laureen slid her arm around Hayley's waist as they all followed Lydia. "You can't imagine how excited I've been ever since you phoned." She lowered her voice. "I must admit I've been feeling quite housebound since my little episode." She inhaled, and her smile widened. "Something smells wonderful, ladies."

At the table, Dave pulled out a chair near Laureen. "Have a seat. Franklin, you can sit beside your lovely wife."

Lydia and Dave sat in their usual places while Hayley served the meal. Her hands shook a bit as she set the rice on the table. *Please don't let the Hieberts notice.* She needed to prove—to herself as well as their guests—that she was strong and capable.

Moments later, Hayley checked the various serving dishes: rice, sweet and sour pork, vegetables, salad, dressings, and rolls warm from the oven. All set, with nothing forgotten or spilled. So far, so good.

"Looks great, my dears." Dave's smile warmed Hayley as he held out his hands. "Let's pray."

Lydia's hand squeezed Hayley's as Dave prayed.

"Father God, thank You for allowing us to share this meal with Franklin and Laureen, Your servants. Bless the hands that prepared this bounty, and bless our time together, I pray in Jesus's name. Amen."

Hayley nibbled her lower lip. *Yes, please, Lord Jesus. I want this so much.*

Several minutes later, Laureen set down her fork and dabbed at her mouth with a napkin. "Delicious. Absolutely delicious. Do you share recipes, Lydia? I'd love to add this one to my collection."

"Of course. Hayley cooked most of the meal, though." Lydia winked at Hayley. "I think she's discovered an untapped talent."

"Well done, Miss Hayley."

The warmth in Franklin's gravelly voice brought heat to Hayley's face. "Thank you. Lydia's a great teacher."

Was this the right time? Nerves hit, and one of those pesky internal moths flew into her throat. Hayley grabbed her water and gulped the entire glass. Better, but now everyone was looking at her. She took a deep breath, let it out, and opened herself to rejection. "Mr.

and Mrs. Hiebert, would you consider me for your helper position?" At their raised eyebrows, she rushed on. "I'm no expert at housekeeping or cooking, but I'm eager to learn, and I'll work hard." She met Laureen's gaze. "I also know pain and some ways to deal with it."

Laureen and Franklin shared a long look, and Hayley squirmed. Those moths in her stomach were having a food fight. She pressed a fist to her abdomen while clenching and unclenching her jaw. *Please, say yes.*

Finally, Franklin cleared his throat. "You are an answer to prayer, young lady." He exchanged another glance with Laureen. "We rather hoped you'd turn out to be the one our Lord chose."

Hayley gasped. "Really?" They'd wanted her even before she'd asked? Wonder bubbled up, turned into tears, and trickled down her face. She grabbed her napkin to blot her cheeks, but Franklin spoke again.

"Two questions. How soon can you start, and do you have your own vehicle?"

Twisted metal, broken glass, and excruciating pain exploded in Hayley's mind. Her hands flew to her face.

~*~

Trevor's stomach rumbled, and he looked up at the Honda wall clock. Almost one. No wonder he was hungry, especially since he'd skipped breakfast. Burger and fries would hit the spot, but he didn't feel like eating alone.

A glance into the office warned him off inviting Carlos. The scowl and the way he pummeled the keyboard shouted "do not disturb." Happened every month about this time, when bookwork demanded attention. Better Carlos than him.

Trevor spied Ryan in the far corner polishing the chrome on a rebuild. "Hey, Ry, want to grab a bite?"

Ryan looked up, eyebrows raised. "Yeah, sure. Just let me tell the boss. Maybe we could bring something back for him."

Shame punched Trevor. Between the opportunity in Toronto and the mess with his folks, he'd pretty much shut out everyone else. His mind skimmed over his interactions with coworkers the last couple weeks. Rejecting invitations, growling when asked for his opinion, general surliness…he'd been a jerk.

He'd given his notice and he would miss these guys, especially Ryan. Trevor had enjoyed mentoring the younger man in repairing old bikes. Would he find someone to teach at Lowrider Cycle, or would he be the one occupying the bottom rung of the ladder? He shrugged off the unpleasant thought, grabbed his jacket, and held the door open for Ryan.

Thirty minutes later, his plate empty, Trevor relaxed against the hard plastic booth while Ryan finished his bacon cheeseburger. It felt good to be away from the shop for a few minutes. Away from the twinges of guilt attacking him, the solemn looks from Carlos, and the eagerness of a couple of the newer guys as if they couldn't wait to take over his work. A grunt escaped.

Ryan looked up. "What?"

"Just thinking."

"About the new job?"

"Yeah. Only nine more days." Emotions Trevor didn't want to name warred for dominance.

Ryan leaned back and crossed his arms. "So you're

really going." His mouth twisted. "Can't blame you. I know you've got big dreams, and I hope it all works out for you."

The doubt in Ryan's voice irked Trevor, and he glared at his friend. "You don't think it will?"

Ryan held up his arms as though to ward off a blow. "Whoa, I didn't say that. But I've heard some things. How well do you know the boss there?"

Trevor frowned "Not well. I had a couple of interviews with him. He knows his business. Good enough for me."

Ryan rubbed the back of his neck, looked away and back again. "OK, let's change the subject. Have you seen today's paper? The Harley chopper by the guy at Bridge City Choppers was featured today. Pretty fancy, but nothing compared to yours." He grinned. "Yours is up next. Bet the phone will ring off the hook tomorrow."

Trevor had forgotten about the interview and newspaper contest. So what if his bike won the People's Choice contest? He'd be gone before it'd do him any good. Might bring work to the shop, though. "Afraid I can't get too pumped about it now."

Ryan's grin disappeared. "No, I guess not." He slid out of the booth. "I'll pick up Carlos's lunch, and we can get back to work. Some of us appreciate what we've got here." Ryan stalked to the order counter.

Trevor's lunch settled in his gut like an entire socket set. The kid must be jealous. He obviously resented that Trevor had gained a job at one of the biggest motorcycle shops in Canada. Then something Ryan said earlier prodded his memory.

What had Ryan heard about Vince Starr?

14

As Saskatoon disappeared behind them, Hayley breathed out to ease the excitement and anxiety. Her fingers danced on her thighs. "I hope I got everything."

Lydia smiled but kept her attention on the highway. "Even if you didn't, we can deliver anything you missed. It's not far. Or you can come for a visit."

"Yes, of course." She clasped her hands. "I still can hardly believe I'm moving to the Hieberts' farm. It happened so fast. I'm not dreaming, am I?"

Lydia chuckled and patted Hayley's jiggling leg. "God works that way sometimes. I can certainly see His hand in this."

"Me too." Hayley ducked her head. "But I can't believe you weren't going to tell me about Lily's phone call. With her husband out of town and the kids home for spring break, I'm not surprised your daughter begged you to come to Winnipeg."

"Well, Dave couldn't leave the church at all this month, and we have to be careful about appearances, so we decided I'd have to turn down her invitation."

"But now you're free to go. I'd feel horrible if I'd kept you from your daughter when she needed you."

"That's why we didn't plan to mention it. Sacrifices are part of life." Lydia braked as they neared their exit. "And now we're both able to fulfill a joyful duty. Almost there."

Butterflies tumbled in Hayley's stomach. She'd

flown to Saskatoon to find a purpose, a reason to keep taking one shaky step after another. Laureen needed help, and Hayley would do anything to help Trevor's mother. Was this part of God's design, the one Lydia mentioned?

As the tall spruce trees came into view, the barnyard odor she'd forgotten assaulted Hayley's nostrils. Hopefully she wouldn't have to work outdoors. She couldn't hold her breath that long. She pinched her nose. How could anyone get used to such a stench?

~*~

As soon as the car stopped, Franklin Hiebert hurried down the front steps. Laureen followed more slowly and gripped the railing as she descended one careful step at a time. Both faces shone like sunbeams of welcome, warming Hayley's soul. Her mouth lifted in an answering smile as she exited the car.

Franklin placed his gnarled hands on her shoulders. Not a hug, but close enough. "Welcome, my dear. You may never know how much this means to us." He squeezed once, let go, and moved to the back of the car. "I'll bring your things in. You ladies go on in and make yourselves at home."

"No, there's too much. I can carry my own stuff." Hayley lifted the trunk lid and cringed at just how much "stuff" she'd brought. She lifted her laptop and case of toiletries, arranged their straps on her arm, and hefted a bag full of books. Too heavy. The books could wait. "On second thought, I appreciate your help."

Franklin chuckled and grabbed the books and large suitcase. As he met his wife at the bottom of the steps, he kissed her cheek and whispered in her ear. She nodded and patted his back as he passed.

Laureen leaned against the railing, and when Hayley reached her, the lines on the older woman's face looked like a relief map of pain. Until she smiled. Then the warmth in her eyes melted those deep grooves into folds of maternal softness. "Welcome, Hayley. I hope you'll be happy here. You certainly are an answer to prayer."

Hayley wanted to lean into her warmth. "I hope I don't disappoint you. Thank you for giving me this chance."

Laureen pulled her closer and kissed Hayley's cheek.

Hayley blinked several times, and swallowed hard. Such a simple gesture, so much tenderness. She didn't deserve it. She stepped away, eyes on the stairs. "Where should I put my things?"

Franklin called over his shoulder, "Follow me," as he and Lydia carried their loads up the steps. "We prepared the bedroom overlooking the front yard for you."

Hayley froze. "B-but that's the special room, the one you keep for visiting missionaries. I can't take that one."

Laureen's smooth, alto voice came from behind her. "And why not? God sent you to us, just as He sends missionaries to those who need His message. You are God's message to us."

Wonder rose inside her. Hayley swallowed hard. Forgiven or not, she would always be damaged goods. She'd do her best, but God's messenger? Not likely. Although it would be amazing if He could use her.

She straightened her shoulders and followed

Franklin and Lydia up the stairs to the large, sunny bedroom. A sleigh bed draped with a scrap quilt in shades of blue and green, an oak desk and chair, and a large armoire filled the room. She'd admired it when Laureen showed it to her and Lydia, and now it seemed even lovelier as she took in more details. Lace curtains framed the bay window, and a built-in seat below looked like the perfect spot for quiet reading. This was a sanctuary. And it was hers. A sigh escaped as Hayley placed her laptop and bag on the window seat and turned toward the door.

Franklin had set her large suitcase on the bed and her box of books on the desk. Hayley peeked out the window. He and Lydia had reloaded their arms with her stuff and were on their way up again. Heat rushed to her cheeks. She'd been daydreaming while these sweet older people carried her heavy belongings. What must they think?

~*~

After supper, Hayley headed upstairs to work on her accounting lesson, but halfway up, loud barking outside stopped her. Sounded like Roscoe, but not his normal, cheerful *woof*. Franklin jumped up from his easy chair. Laureen leaned forward as though to rise, but Franklin shook his head while heading to the mud room.

"That yearling heifer must be in trouble. I expected as much. I'll go see. Maybe give Max a call."

Laureen pushed to her feet. "But Max said he'd be out of town until tomorrow, remember?"

Roscoe's frantic barking intensified when Franklin opened the back door.

Hayley hurried down the stairs. "Can I help?" Then the barnyard odor hit, and she took a step back.

Franklin stopped just long enough to glance at her while Roscoe whined. "I'll let you know." The door slammed behind the farmer and his dog.

"Hayley, come here." Laureen sank onto the couch and patted the spot beside her.

Hayley sat obediently and wondered what she'd gotten herself into.

Laureen's smile didn't quite reach her eyes. "Well, my little city girl, you may be in for an education tonight. I don't suppose you've helped birth a calf before?"

"No." It sounded like a squeak.

"How brave are you?"

She was shaking; not a positive sign. "Um, not very, I guess." She looked at her clasped hands. "Do I need to be?"

Laureen patted her leg. "Always, my dear. But tonight we may need your help. If that heifer's baby is breech, someone has to turn it. Franklin's hands are too big with his arthritis, and I'm out of commission. And if the mama is in trouble, Trevor wouldn't make it in time, even if he could come right away."

Hayley struggled to control the wobble in her voice. "So that leaves me. To…turn…a calf." Her gaze sought Laureen's. "What exactly does that mean?"

Laureen described the procedure, and Hayley's mind whirled. So did her supper. She pressed a fist to her abdomen and forced herself to breathe slowly. "I'd have to reach *inside* the cow?"

"We don't know yet if it'll be necessary, but I thought I should prepare you."

The back door slammed open, and Franklin

stumbled into the room. His face was mottled red, and he bent over, breathing heavily. "It's a breech. Can't turn it. Cow is weakening."

Laureen stood, steadied herself, and then walked into the mudroom. "Hayley, if you're ready, come get my coveralls and boots." She stopped by her husband's side and put her hand on his bowed back. "Franklin, sit down, please." Her voice lowered to a whisper. "You know what the doctor said."

Franklin sank onto the wooden bench beside the back door, grabbed his wife's hand, and held it to his cheek, his eyes closed.

Hayley hesitated, but just for a moment. These sweet people needed her. *God, help me.* She shrugged into the baggy coveralls and pulled on Laureen's felt-lined rubber boots. She didn't want to think about what caked the soles.

Moments later, she trudged beside Franklin to the barn, grateful for his halogen flashlight illuminating the path. Franklin still breathed hard, but his face had lost some of its redness. The closer they got to the large, faded structure, the stronger the odor became. Hayley tried to breathe shallowly, but Franklin's hurried pace and the muddy ground forced her to gasp for breath. She wiped her mouth on her sleeve. She could *taste* the smell.

Inside the barn, the laboring heifer struggled. Hayley stared, the stink forgotten. The animal moaned as a contraction rippled her heaving sides. Hayley held her breath until two tiny hooves appeared, upside down. She turned to Franklin. "She's doing it, right? She'll be OK?"

Franklin reached for a box on the wall and pulled out an arm-length glove. "No. Those are the back feet.

It's in a breech position. The calf needs to be turned so the front legs come out, followed by the head." He handed Hayley the strange apparel. "Put this on and come here, right behind her."

Her stomach knotted into a ball, but Hayley did as Franklin directed. With lubricant on the glove, Hayley followed Franklin's instructions, gently pushing the calf's feet back inside and following them with her hand. She blanked out her squeamishness and concentrated on Franklin's calm voice and the feel of the calf and walls of the womb. A few times she wanted to give up. Her arm throbbed, her whole body ached, and an inner voice kept screaming, *You can't do this!* But the cow would strain with another contraction, each one weaker, and Hayley knew she couldn't quit. Gently, ever so gently, she righted the calf until the front hooves thrust through the opening.

"You did it, girl!" Franklin clapped her on the back.

Hayley stumbled away from the cow. "I did?" A black muzzle followed the tiny hooves. "I did." Warmth flooded her in the cold barn.

On the next contraction, Franklin grabbed the calf's front legs and pulled.

The cow bellowed, and a sloppy calf flopped onto the straw. It didn't move. Didn't breathe.

Hayley's whole body slumped. She sank to the straw-covered barn floor. She'd fought for this life. Were all her efforts for nothing?

Franklin took a piece of straw and wiggled it around inside the calf's nostril. The little one jerked, snorted, and expelled mucus from its nose. "That's better." He rubbed its sides and checked it over. "It's a heifer." He grinned at Hayley. "Good job. You've earned the right to name her. What'll it be?"

Hayley studied the wobbly creature as it struggled to its knees and then stood to suckle its mama, who turned and nuzzled it. Sure was determined, first to live, and now to thrive. Her gaze lingered on the tiny animal's finely shaped head and big, brown eyes. So beautiful. Hayley grinned up at Franklin as he leaned against the barn wall. "Isn't she perfect? All I can think of is Bellavita, beautiful life." Just like her own desire, her own dream.

Franklin rubbed his chin.

The gesture reminded Hayley of Trevor. What would he think if he saw her now?

"I think that's a fine name. Mind you, we'll probably just call her Bella." He pushed himself off the wall. "You look beat. You did good work, Hayley. Glad you're here. I'll just get some fresh water and hay for the cow while you head inside."

"I can help." Hayley stood, wobbled, and leaned against the rough boards. "In a minute."

Franklin gently pushed her toward the open door. "Go on in. You'll have other chances to help with chores, if you want. But you'd best get inside before your legs refuse to carry you."

Despite her exhaustion, she studied Franklin. Near-normal color, but he looked as wiped out as she felt. "We only have one flashlight, so it makes sense to go back together. I'll get the water." She reached for the bucket.

The little heifer she'd helped birth stood, it's tail flicking.

Her fingers ached to caress the small but sturdy body. *Beautiful life.* Yes, it was. She breathed deeply. After wrestling for this tiny creature's survival, the smell didn't even bother her. She looked down at herself, covered with gory evidence of her hard work. Tired? Yes. Dirty? Most definitely. Time to clean up and get some rest. With the pail in her hand and her eyes on the uneven, straw-strewn floor, she forced her legs to move toward the barn door. That was when she bumped into a solid chest. Startled, she looked up into stormy gray eyes.

"What are *you* doing here?" Trevor stared back at her.

15

Trevor had groaned, pushed back his desk chair, and checked the clock. Eight-thirty. His stomach rumbled, reminding him he'd forgotten to eat supper. On the way to his compact kitchen, the blinking message light on the landline caught his attention. He pushed the button.

"Hey, Trevor, it's Mom. Just wondering if you're OK, since we haven't been able to get hold of you. Working late?"

Yeah, he sure was. Not his choice. Then his mother's smooth voice continued. "We're fine here, except a yearling heifer's in trouble..."

His gut clenched. Where was that Max guy? Why wasn't he there?

Trevor grabbed his coat and car keys and ran to his Jeep. Visions of his dad collapsed in the barn shoved aside the motorcycle design he'd been working on. He shouldn't have turned off the ringer on his phone. He slapped the steering wheel. No police cars in sight, Trevor pressed the accelerator as he left the city. No time to phone his mom back. He had to hurry. Less than half an hour later, he drove past the house to the outbuildings, stomped on the brake, and jumped out. He ran into the barn, expecting the worst, and ran into...*Hayley*?

"What are *you* doing here?" The words burst from

his lips before he could think.

She blanched and stumbled back, dropping the water bucket. She was a mess. A filthy, bloody, glowing wreck.

Trevor couldn't move. His mind refused to function. This was the city girl who'd sabotaged his concentration all week.

He tore his gaze from Hayley and noticed the heifer he'd taken to the barn earlier in the day, and her obviously newborn calf. He shook his head. He hadn't been needed after all.

His dad peered over the edge of the hayloft, and a thread of steel laced his voice. "Hayley, take the flashlight and go clean up. Relax. Trevor will help me finish here."

She looked up, eyes wide, and nodded. She handed the bucket to Trevor, grabbed the flashlight, and walked out. The barn seemed dimmer, and the flashlight hadn't even been on.

Franklin pitched some hay into the stall and climbed down the ladder, breathing hard. He stalked up to Trevor and pinned him with a glare. "What was that about? Didn't you get our message?"

Trevor hadn't heard that tone from his father for many years. It made him want to shuffle his feet and look away. Instead, he lifted his chin. "Mom said you needed help. That's all I heard before I rushed out here."

Franklin thrust the bucket at him. "Go get some water for the new mama. Then we'll talk." He turned his back and began to spread fresh straw in the stall.

Trevor stomped to the faucet, opened the valve, and watched water gush into the pail. Its churning echoed the sensation in Trevor's chest. Where was

Max? He said he'd help with chores. And why was Hayley even at the farm?

Yeah, he'd barked at her, but only because she'd caught him off guard. Water splashed onto his jeans and spilled on the ground. Trevor shut the valve with more force than was necessary and retraced his steps to the stall and his father.

"You were rude." Franklin leaned on the pitchfork, and his shoulders heaved.

Trevor stopped and more water sloshed onto his shoes. He mentally rewound the scene and what he'd said. No wonder she'd stepped back as if he'd slapped her. He hadn't meant…

"Didn't you get our text? We phoned, but you didn't answer either call. So we left a text message to let you know Hayley agreed to help your mom. And when I needed help with this breech, she stepped right up. Did a fine job too. Pretty impressive for a city girl."

Trevor emptied the bucket into the trough. "I'd muted my cell and turned the ringer off the landline. Sorry." He straightened and took in his father's sagging shoulders, the exhaustion etched on his face. "What happened with Max? Shouldn't he be here?"

Franklin hung up the pitchfork, pushed back his cap and wiped an arm across his forehead. "Not until tomorrow. He needed to go out of town for a few days. As agreed, remember?"

"I missed that part." He looked at the cow as she nuzzled her newborn. He tried to picture Hayley working to turn the calf. The vision did not compute. "Seems like I've missed a lot. I really am sorry I snapped at Hayley."

"Apology accepted, from me. But she needs to hear it." He clapped Trevor on the back. "Let's go in.

Your mom's probably wondering what's keeping us."

A couple of minutes later, they left their footwear in the warm mudroom and shrugged out of their coats.

"Franklin?" Laureen called from the kitchen. "I'm making hot cocoa. It'll help you warm up."

Trevor followed the sound of her voice. "Hey, Mom, got enough for me too?"

Laureen swiveled, wobbled, and grabbed the edge of the stove. "Trevor! When did you get here?"

His throat tightened at his mom's weakness. What if something happened when he was away? No. He couldn't think that. He straightened. "Just a few minutes ago. I got your message—at least part of it. I ran out of the house when I heard Dad needed help. Apparently he didn't. He's washing up, by the way."

Laureen pulled out a chair. "Of course. Have a seat. You should have listened to the whole message. And what about the text we left this morning?"

"Sorry. It's been crazy at the shop, especially today. I shut off the sound on my phones so I could get stuff done."

"Why? What happened?"

Trevor tilted his chair back, caught the look from his mother, and plopped it down again. "Remember the newspaper contest I told you about, where readers vote on their favorite custom bike? Well, today's paper featured my interview. And pictures of both the Indian and the Honda. Phone rang all day, and between congratulations and answering questions, I didn't get anything else done. Then I got an email from Vince Starr in Toronto." He leaned back and crossed his arms. "He wants me to have two new designs ready to build when I get there next weekend."

"Next weekend?" His mom's face paled.

"Already?" She took a deep breath and picked up the whisk. "Right. I guess I'd imagined time would slow down. I really hoped you'd be here for Easter. We're going to a special Good Friday service in the city. We thought you might come with us." Her smile wavered, and then disappeared.

Trevor uncrossed his arms, trying not to appear defensive. "Sorry. Can't. Time seems to have sped up since I gave my notice. And new designs? I don't know how I'm gonna manage. Plus, I've been hearing some stuff about Lowrider." A deep sigh escaped, and his voice dropped to a whisper. "Mom, what if I made the wrong choice?"

~*~

Hayley shut off the shower in the second floor bathroom and heard Trevor's voice drift up through the heat ducts. She automatically checked the lock on the door. Good. He'd never deliberately barge in, she was sure. His mother had raised him right. But mistakes could happen.

She grabbed a towel from the rack, rubbed herself dry, and pulled on clean jeans and a green turtleneck sweater. She had to face Trevor—and his challenge—so she needed to look as capable as possible. Hayley wiped off the mirror and crinkled her nose at her reflection. With no makeup and her red hair at attention all over her head, she could scare small children. A giggle escaped. At least her cheeks were rosier than they'd been in ages. Must have been the hard work. Not because of Trevor.

A few minutes later, she descended the stairs, hair tamed and a touch of mascara emphasizing her green eyes. Ready or not, it was time to face him. But as she neared the kitchen, Trevor's voice muffled and faded to silence.

There was a catch in Laureen's voice. "Oh, honey."

Not a good time. Hayley turned to sneak back upstairs.

Franklin shuffled out of the master bedroom. "There's my farm girl."

The approval on his face and in his voice warmed her all the way down to her toes. Hayley halted and grinned. "That was amazing." She rubbed her arm, rubbery from its workout. "I still can hardly believe it."

Franklin patted her shoulder. "*You* were amazing. I know you grew up in a big city, but I'd say you're a natural farmer."

She hadn't enjoyed champagne since before the accident, but now the same kind of bubbly pleasure zinged through her. Without thinking, she pulled the older man into a quick hug. Just as quickly, she stepped back. Her face burned, and she stuttered. "I-I…"

Laureen appeared in the doorway. "There you are. Cocoa's ready."

Franklin's eyes lit up. "Sounds good. Come on, Miss Hayley, let's celebrate."

But Trevor waited in there. The guy who'd made her feel special, and then, when she'd finally done something really good, barked as though she'd trespassed. How could she face him now?

Franklin turned, looked at her with one eyebrow raised, and motioned with his head.

Hayley inhaled, squared her shoulders, and followed Trevor's father into the kitchen. Or was it the lion's den?

16

The scent of hot cocoa caressed Hayley's nose as she entered the kitchen.

Laureen held out a full mug, its fragrant steam drifting toward her, enticing Hayley closer. "Here you go, sweetheart. How's your arm?"

"Thanks. It'll be fine." Hayley accepted the mug with both hands, careful to avoid looking at Trevor. His presence seemed to fill the room, but that didn't mean she had to face him. Not yet, anyway. She took a tentative sip of the cocoa and nearly purred as its heat soaked into her still-chilled bones.

Franklin pulled out the chair next to him. "Here, have a seat. You must be beat."

Now she'd have no choice but to deal with Trevor. But she didn't want to see condemnation on his face. Hayley lowered onto the chair, mindful of her hot drink.

"Hey." Trevor sounded embarrassed, uncertain.

She met his gaze and saw regret. His gray eyes captivated her; their flecks of steel blue sparkled under the dining room light. She couldn't look away.

Trevor cleared his throat and fidgeted on his chair. "Listen, I'm sorry I snapped at you out there. I didn't get Mom's message about you moving here, and…I guess the shock made me act stupid." He looked away, breaking the spell.

Hayley tried to picture herself as he'd seen her,

covered with birthing gore among other things, probably red-faced, and wearing coveralls several sizes too big. How *not* to make a good impression. A giggle bubbled up and escaped. "Apology accepted. I *was* rather out of my element."

Their gazes locked again, and Trevor reached across the table, palm up. "Friends?"

Hayley placed her hand in his. A shockwave zinged up her arm. She jumped but couldn't break contact. His pupils widened, and a fine line appeared between his eyebrows. But he didn't pull back. Hayley swallowed hard and willed her voice not to squeak. "Friends."

Trevor smiled, squeezed her hand, and let go. He glanced around, and his brow furrowed. "When did Mom and Dad leave?"

Heat warmed Hayley's cheeks. She hadn't noticed anything other than him. Was this how Laureen felt when a dizzy spell hit? Perhaps the hot cocoa would restore some of her equilibrium. She took a sip.

"My folks must have figured we needed some privacy. Not sure why, but I'm OK with it." Trevor stood. "I need more cocoa. Want yours topped up?"

She shook her head, her throat tight. Maybe she hadn't thought this through enough. Trevor would be moving away soon and he'd probably come out to see his parents as often as possible.

"Hey, are you all right?"

"I'm fine." She shifted on her chair, and her leg muscles protested. "A bit sore from helping that cow."

Trevor grinned and his eyebrows lifted. "No doubt. Dad's really proud of you, the way you jumped right in. First time, I assume?"

"First time in a barn, even." Hayley felt the grin

forming. "But helping bring a tiny calf into the world? That was incredible."

Something gleamed in Trevor's eyes, but then he turned toward the pot of hot chocolate without saying a word.

~*~

Trevor refilled his mug. When they'd first met, he would've called Hayley frail, but already she looked healthier. And the green sweater reflected her gorgeous eyes. Nice. "Ow!" Hot cocoa splashed onto his hand, and he jerked, spilling it onto the counter and floor. Irritation flared. He clenched his jaw against an ugly exclamation.

Hayley jumped up and grabbed some paper towels. She wiped the mess off the counter and crouched to clean the floor.

Trevor tapped her arm. "Not your problem. I made the mess. I'll clean it."

"Sorry." As Hayley handed him the towel, he saw a flash of something shimmer in her eyes. Tears?

I'm such a heel. He'd snapped at her in the barn, and now he'd done it again. He'd made a mess, and not just with the cocoa. He finished the clean-up, tossed the towel in the garbage, and returned to the table. Time to make amends.

Hayley's attention seemed focused on the center of the table. Was her lower lip trembling?

"Ah, man, I'm sorry."

Hayley glanced up, her mouth grimaced, and she went back to studying the table. He tried again. "I didn't mean to bark at you." A thought hit, and he cringed. She'd worked hard on the heifer and probably had some aches and pains to show for it. "Did I hurt your arm?"

"No. I didn't mean to get in your way. I just wanted to help."

Shame punched him in the solar plexus. "I really am sorry. I don't know what's wrong with me. I don't usually blow up. I didn't mean to—especially at you." Warmth rushed up the back of his neck. That last bit had slipped out without thought. Now she'd want to know what he meant. He couldn't even explain to himself why this particular redhead had gotten under his skin.

Her eyes widened, and pink bloomed on her pale cheeks. "Are you upset because I'm here? I-I'm not chasing you, if that's what you think."

"Yeah. No. I mean…" Trevor stared at a spot near her left shoulder. "I'm glad you're helping Mom. She told me you two hit it off. I was just surprised, that's all." Although an admission of attraction wouldn't have hurt his feelings. Friends. That's what they'd agreed to be. That would have to do. "I assume you're OK with me showing up here as much as possible until I leave?"

Hayley cleared her throat and tilted her head, drawing his attention back to her lustrous eyes. "Of course I don't mind. This is your home, your family. Besides, we're friends. Right?"

For a city girl, she sure could lasso a guy. With his own words, even. Trevor grinned and reached across the table. "Right."

She placed her small hand in his, and a jolt shot up his arm. She didn't pull away, though, and Trevor enjoyed the rosiness in her cheeks with a flush of warmth creeping up his own neck. Time to be honest.

"I'm glad you're here, Hayley. I wish I had more than a week and a half before my Toronto gig starts. I want to know you better."

Hayley's mouth lifted in a smile that tugged at his midsection. "Me, too."

Trevor squeezed her hand before releasing it. "Good." He looked past her to the kitchen doorway. "Shall we let my folks know we're OK now? Nice of them to give us some privacy."

"They're pretty amazing. You're a lucky man, Trevor, to have such great parents."

Her voice trailed off on the last sentence, and he wondered why. She took both their mugs to the dishwasher. She seemed to favor her leg. Not surprising, after the strenuous work of pulling that calf.

Trevor got up, closed the dishwasher, and gently took her arm. "You must be exhausted. Let's relax in the living room. That's probably where Mom and Dad are."

They were, snuggled together on the loveseat with their Bible spanning their laps. Laureen smiled a welcome. Franklin closed the Bible. "Got everything sorted out?"

"I think so." Trevor avoided looking at the Bible as he sat beside Hayley and pulled a footstool close for her weak leg.

"Yes." Hayley confirmed. Her eyes were shining as she murmured, "Thank you."

Her appreciative expression imprinted on his heart. Another image to haunt his dreams. Trevor glanced at his watch and regret surged through him. "It's ten o'clock. I'd better get home. Didn't realize it was so late. You all need your rest, and I've got another hectic day starting in just a few hours."

Laureen opened her arms in invitation. He crossed the room and hugged his mother. She patted his back as he clasped his father's hand. "Will we see you tomorrow?"

Trevor looked at Hayley and mentally ran through his long to-do list. He'd have to start early and work through lunch again, but how could he refuse the invitation in those jade eyes? He caught the look that passed between his parents. He'd think about it later. "I'll try to be here for supper."

A few minutes later, Trevor cranked up the heater in his Jeep. After the warmth of his parents' home—and the fire that burned every time he got near Hayley Blankenship—the frosty night air chilled his bones.

He had his life planned. He wanted to make his name famous in the custom bike world. Then he'd save up and eventually buy the farm from his folks. Even with the deal they'd offered, he'd have to earn more than he could with Carlos. And someday, when the time was right, he would find someone who could share his dream of living in the country and helping kids who needed security, discipline, and lots of love. Kids like him. Hayley's enchanting face appeared in his thoughts. And now, he'd met someone who might be everything he'd ever wanted.

But in a week and a half, he was moving two provinces away. To a different world, a different life. Not what he wanted to do forever, but the job in Toronto would be a stepping stone to the fulfillment of his dreams.

He'd given his word to Vince Starr, and his dad had taught him the importance of his word. But what if he could fast-track this part of his plan? How long would it take to gain the recognition he craved, to prove his value? And why did he think he had to be famous to prove his worth? He swatted the thought away like a pesky fly. His plan would succeed, no matter what he had to sacrifice.

A whisper seemed to hang in the dimness of the car's interior. *Even Hayley?*

17

As soon as the door closed behind Trevor, Franklin pushed to his feet, stretched, and held out his hand to Laureen. "I'm gonna check on our new mama and baby one more time. Feel up to joining me?"

A smile lit Laureen's face as she clasped her husband's hand to stand.

Hayley's cheeks warmed at the love that flowed between them.

Laureen looked at Hayley. "Want to come?"

"No thanks. If you don't mind, I think I'll head to bed."

Franklin pulled his wife close. "Of course we don't mind. And feel free to sleep in tomorrow morning. You earned it."

"But…" Hayley's exhausted brain couldn't form a coherent protest.

They helped one another into work coats and boots, and then Laureen leaned into Franklin's side as they exited.

The sigh that had threatened earlier escaped from her, as Hayley pulled her weary frame up the stairs. Her head hit the plump pillow and sleep claimed her. Sometime later, images sped by like a slide show on steroids. Hayley wrapped her arms tight around Trevor as they roared down an empty road on his motorcycle. Its powerful engine rumbled beneath her, and she opened her mouth wide and laughed into the wind. Trevor leaned into a curve, and she followed his lead. No, too far! The bike slid, and the scene changed.

She sat in the driver's seat of a sports car—she didn't know what kind—and pressed the accelerator to the floor. Fence posts flew by so fast they barely registered. Suddenly, a cow stood in the middle of the road. Hayley swerved—too late. A sickening crunch, and then the scene switched to a barn. The cow lay bleeding in the straw, its calf lifeless behind it. Sobs bubbled up from deep inside as Hayley reached for the stillborn calf, and it morphed into a human baby. Her baby.

Hayley bolted upright, gasping for breath. Her head pounded in time with her racing heartbeat. She rubbed her face to force herself awake. It was just a horrible dream, but the blackness seemed impenetrable as she peered between her fingers. Where was she? A whisper of movement touched her face. "Wh-who's there?" She couldn't hear anything above her hammering heartbeat. Heaviness pressed down, and she curled into a fetal position. Her whisper seemed to echo in the dark room. "Don't hurt me, please." Who could help her? "Jesus, where are you?"

The oppressive weight lifted, and Hayley sat up again. Moonlight filtered in around the window shades, and she recognized the room. The farm—she'd moved to Franklin and Laureen's home. Her pulse and breathing slowed to a normal rhythm as memory returned.

Then a vision of her cache of pills swung pendulum-like before her eyes, a caricature of a smile. She gasped against their lure. "Not now!"

Laureen needed Hayley's help. She had a purpose;

she could be useful.

Hayley lay back against her pillow and closed her eyes. Maybe she should get rid of those pills, remove the temptation. But what if she failed again? Or if it turned out that God wasn't true, and life wasn't worth living after all? No, she'd hang on to them. For a while.

Several hours later, noise from below and the scent of coffee jarred Hayley from a restless sleep. She rubbed the dried salt of tears from her eyes and peered at the alarm clock. Seven-thirty? Her first day as Laureen's personal assistant, and she'd slept in. She pulled on her jeans and a long-sleeved cotton shirt, ran a comb through her hair, and hurried down the stairs. Her big chance to prove her value to Laureen waited in the kitchen, judging from the soft rumble of voices. Maybe Trevor… Her heart beat a little faster. Hayley pasted on a smile as she entered the kitchen. And stopped short.

Where Trevor sat last night, a muscular, tattooed, bald and bearded stranger relaxed with his elbows propped on the table. His gaze seemed to bore deep into her soul as though, somehow, he knew her.

Heart fluttering, Hayley stepped back.

"Good morning, dear. Did you sleep well?" Laureen's cheerful voice halted her retreat.

"I-I didn't mean to sleep in. I set the alarm…I'm really sorry."

"No apology needed, Hayley. I turned off the alarm. Figured you needed extra sleep after yesterday's adventure." She patted the chair beside her. "Come, have some coffee and meet Max."

Max? Franklin had mentioned the man they'd hired to help with farm chores, but she certainly hadn't pictured someone who looked as if he'd be more at home in a smoky bar or gang hangout.

Hayley preferred to keep her distance. The way he looked at her…she shivered and sat at the opposite end of the table.

"You cold?" Franklin got up, filled a cobalt mug with coffee, and set it in front of her. "Cream and sugar are right there."

"Th-thank you." Hayley cradled the mug in her shaky hands and stared into its depths. She needed to prove—to herself as well as the Hieberts—that she was capable. Hayley lifted the mug, took a sip, and let the hot brew slide down her tight throat. Better.

"Glad to meetcha, Miss Hayley."

Coffee splashed onto her fingers. "Ow." She plunked the cup onto the table and wiped her fingers on her jeans, carefully avoiding Max's gaze. At least she hadn't dropped Laureen's beautiful blue mug.

"Didn't mean to startle you." His deep rumble carried a hint of a chuckle. "Don't worry, I'm not as mean as I look."

Hayley stared at the vivid tattoo on his left arm. A majestic lion, mouth wide to roar, stared back at her. She'd reserve judgement.

Max must have noticed her reaction. "Ever read *The Chronicles of Narnia*?"

Hayley nodded as warmth filled her. Grandmother Blankenship had given her the complete set of books for her eighth Christmas, and Hayley had fallen in love with the characters, especially the lion.

"That's one of my favorite series of all time." Laureen leaned forward. "Wonderful stories, especially for kids who need a strong hero."

Hayley dared another glance at Max. So did he imagine himself to be a hero or did the tattoo confess his need for one?

"Want to help me make breakfast?" Laureen broke into Hayley's musings.

Hayley pushed her chair back. "Of course. What are we making?" Butterflies fluttered in her stomach. Her first test—she didn't dare mess up.

"Bacon, scrambled eggs, and toast. How's that sound?"

Hayley's stomach growled, and heat rushed to her face as the others grinned. "Really good, apparently."

Half an hour later, Hayley gathered the dirty dishes from the table. The men headed outside to do chores and Laureen filled the sink with hot, soapy water. Hayley took a deep breath. The delicious scent of bacon permeated the kitchen. She grinned. She'd eaten much more than usual and would have to work it off.

"Do you mind scrubbing the pans?" Laureen grimaced at the cast on her arm.

"Sure. I'd love to."

"I love your attitude. Most people don't exactly jump at the chance to wash pots and pans. While you do that, let's work out a menu and shopping list for the next few days. I have an appointment tomorrow afternoon. I thought maybe you could drive me to the doctor's office, and then we could do some grocery shopping afterwards."

Hayley's shoulders slumped. She'd hoped she could convince the Hieberts of her value before they learned she didn't drive. "I-I haven't driven for a long time. That accident I mentioned at Dave and Lydia's? I haven't gotten behind a wheel since then." The dishwater churned as Hayley's hands began to shake. She stared at the murky water as it echoed her inner turmoil. So much for proving her competence.

A warm hand settled on her shoulder. "Oh, honey." Laureen rubbed Hayley's bowed back. "That crash damaged more than just your car, didn't it?"

~*~

A chime from his pocket alerted Trevor to a new email. He considered ignoring it. Every message from Vince Starr brought more demands. The man seemed to think Trevor had nothing to do until he got to Toronto. Trevor set down the socket wrench, pulled out his phone, and read the message from a Nate Smith.

"Heard you haven't found a place here yet. I've got a room and space for a couple bikes. Half hour commute to work. $750/month, shared utilities. Let me know."

Trevor searched his memory, but he couldn't remember meeting anyone named Nate at Lowrider. Then again, only a few of the guys had bothered to introduce themselves. A frisson of unease rippled through Trevor. Why did it matter? He'd be busy building his own creations. He wasn't moving there to make friends. Trevor glanced around the small shop.

Ryan looked up, nodded, and resumed reassembling a Suzuki racer. Yeah, friends made a difference. Someone to talk to and relax with at the end of a long day.

A certain redhead came to mind. Hayley had promised friendship, but he wanted more. Her face, those wide jade eyes framed with dark lashes, narrow straight nose, high cheekbones, and full, tempting lips. Her mouth… He swallowed hard and pushed her image away. No time for daydreaming. Too much to do in the next nine days. But his heart twisted as her image faded.

With effort he turned back to Nate's email. His offer sounded a lot better than anything Trevor had found online. He punched Nate Smith into the search engine. With a name like Smith, there were several. He scanned the most promising, but none mentioned Lowrider Cycles. He read the email again. Nate's offer sounded good. Maybe too good.

18

Franklin latched his seatbelt and turned toward Hayley. "Ready?"

Hayley gripped the steering wheel until her knuckles whitened. The minivan felt huge, maybe too big for her to handle. "I think so. But I'm still scared."

"The road's usually empty, and if it's too much for you, we can just drive around the yard. Go ahead, start 'er up." Franklin's calm encouragement helped settle her nerves.

Hayley turned the key in the ignition. The engine roared to life, and Hayley jerked her foot off the gas. "Sorry."

"No problem." Franklin chuckled as he patted the dash. "This old car's handled all kinds of drivers. Now back up a bit, and you can either go past the Quonset and around the machine shed or out to the road."

Hayley stepped on the brake and grabbed the gear shift with a trembling hand. "Maybe I'll stay on the yard for now."

"Whatever you want. We prayed about this, remember? You're not alone. And I'm not just talking about me."

"You're right. It's been so long, though…"

"That's why we're doing this. Don't let fear imprison you, young lady. You got bucked off real good, but it's time to remount this horse."

That brought a smile. Hayley put the car into

reverse, checked all her mirrors, and crept backward to the broad, gravel driveway.

The first time around the farm buildings seemed to take forever, as she flinched with every turn, but on the second and third circuits, Hayley's shoulders relaxed and her grip eased. When they arrived back beside the garage, she turned to speak to Franklin. His gray head rested against the headrest and his eyes were closed. Until she put the van into park.

Franklin's eyes opened, and he winked at her. Hayley's cheeks warmed. "I thought you were asleep."

He sat up straighter and shook his head. "Nope. Just resting and enjoying the ride. Noticed you got some confidence as you went around. Smoother, less hesitation."

"This car is easy to drive. And your calm attitude…well, it helped me relax and concentrate on driving."

"Good." His eyes twinkled. "Want to try the road?"

The driveway was safe, but it didn't get her anywhere. In the city, buses and taxis were available. But out in the country, it was drive or stay home. She gripped the steering wheel again. "I do."

"Good, young lady. God's got you, and you've got this. Let's go." Franklin grinned.

Where the driveway met the road, Hayley stopped the car and leaned forward. The nice thing about flat country was that one could see a long way. No vehicles appeared, so she eased out onto the gravel road and increased her speed. Ever so slightly.

After a couple minutes, Franklin began to wring his hands.

Hayley eased off the gas. "Am I going too fast?"

She checked the speedometer. "Um, too slow?"

"You're doing fine. No traffic to hold up, anyway. How's it feel?"

"I could probably speed up a bit, but the potholes are tricky."

"Don't go any faster than you're comfortable with. Why'd you think I was upset?"

Hayley dodged another depression in the roadway. "Your hands."

"Oh, that's just my way of tryin' to rub the ache outta them."

"Oh." Trevor had massaged her hand on the plane; it was soothing. *Thunk.* A shallow pothole caught a tire, and Hayley jerked her attention back to the road. "Sorry."

Franklin pointed. "See that cloud of dust? Looks like we're gonna meet another vehicle soon."

Tension gripped Hayley as she clutched the steering wheel. "What should I do?" Her voice sounded shrill, but she couldn't help it.

"Take it easy." Franklin's calm voice soothed her frazzled nerves. "You're already going nice and slow, so let's wait and see what it is. If it's a car or truck, just stay on your side of the road, and you'll be fine. If it's a big piece of machinery, you'll want to pull onto an approach."

"O-OK." Hayley maneuvered close to the edge of the road, which was tricky because it sloped toward the ditch. Her knuckles whitened.

A massive form appeared under the cloud.

Hayley glanced from side to side, looking for a place to pull off.

Franklin touched her arm. "Look, it's just a farm truck. No problem."

The *just-a-farm-truck* seemed to take up most of the roadway. Hayley tensed and held her breath as the vehicle rumbled past them.

"There you go. Piece of cake." Franklin's smile disappeared. "Hey, young lady, you're awfully pale. Had enough for today?"

"Um-hm. I think so. Maybe I'll turn around at the next driveway." A few minutes later, Hayley inched into the garage, set the gear into Park, and turned off the engine. She closed her eyes and sighed.

"Well done, Miss Hayley." Franklin undid his seatbelt and opened his door. "A few more times on our little road, and you'll be ready to hit the highway. Then there'll be no stopping you." He stepped out of the van and stroked Roscoe's head before sauntering to the house.

But visions of vehicles zipping past as though on a race track stalled Hayley as she reached for her seatbelt. This country road was scary enough. How could she ever venture onto a highway? And if she couldn't, would the Hieberts look for someone to replace her?

~*~

Trevor sat in his truck in Easy Rider's parking lot. Mom and Hayley would have supper on the table in less than an hour, but this phone call couldn't wait. And he couldn't call from the shop. He rechecked the latest email from Nate Smith and entered the phone number. Smith's emails answered some questions, but Trevor needed to hear the man's voice.

"Hello, Nate Smith here."

The well-modulated voice carried a faint accent,

but Trevor couldn't place it. Sounded pleasant enough. "Hello, Nate. This is Trevor. Just got a few more questions for you."

"Shoot."

"How long have you worked for Lowrider, and what do you do there?"

"Fourteen months as a delivery driver. It's a decent job."

Must pay well, to afford the house pictured in his emails. Or he'd held a better job before. A now-familiar unease tickled Trevor's spine. "Look, Nate, I'm not used to moving in with someone I don't know, so I'll be blunt. Why are you doing this—offering part of your home to a complete stranger?"

A low chuckle came over the line. "That's where you're wrong, Hiebert. I looked you up, and I talked to your boss. Pretty easy to find a story about your bikes, and Carlos sang your praises. I'm not worried."

That made one of them. His phone beeped a reminder to get on the road. Didn't want to be late for supper—and time with his mother's stunning helper. "Listen, Nate, I've got to go. I'll call you again tomorrow with more questions, if you don't mind."

"No problem. Around the same time will be good. Should be home from work."

That raised another question. Were personal calls forbidden at Lowrider? Or was something else going on?

Trevor said goodbye, disconnected, and shoved his phone into his jacket. If only his apprehension could be thrust away as easily. He grunted, started his Jeep, and pulled out onto the road. He'd see Hayley soon. She could erase his anxiety with just a smile. He merged onto Highway 16, and his pulse escalated as he pressed the gas pedal.

~*~

"Great supper, Mom. I'm sure going to miss your cooking." Trevor speared a chunk of potato and used it to wipe up the last bit of gravy. "Mm-mm. You spoil me." He pushed his chair back, got up, and kissed his mother's cheek. "And I love you for it."

Laureen patted his hand. "Gotta feed you while I have the chance." Her hand trembled, and she tucked it under the table. "Can I ask a favor?"

"Anything, Mom."

"Would you join us for the Good Friday service at Dave Harris's church? They're doing something different—a play."

Trevor shook his head, unable to meet her eyes. "Sorry, I can't. Starting the new job Monday means I have to leave Friday morning at the latest." He dared a glance and bit his lip at the dampness on his mother's lashes.

"Oh. I didn't realize." Her smile trembled, and then evened out. "I understand."

Franklin patted her hand and cleared his throat with a little cough. "Hayley made rhubarb crisp for dessert. Do you want it now, or later?"

"Later sounds good." Trevor rubbed his full belly. "If I'd known, I wouldn't have taken thirds."

Hayley had begun clearing the table, but Franklin's touch on her arm stopped her. "I'll clear the table. Why don't you and Trev check on the cows tonight? If you don't mind..."

Trevor's attention swiveled from Hayley to his dad. Was his face redder than usual? "You all right,

Dad?"

Franklin rubbed his chin. "I'm fine. But why should an old guy like me have to trudge outside in the dark, when there's young folk here who could do it?"

Trevor peered at his father for another heartbeat and was rewarded with a slow wink. Oh, so that was his game. The sly, old matchmaker. Well, it suited him fine. He'd hoped for a few minutes alone with a certain redhead. He glanced at Hayley. Pink glowed on her cheeks, but she didn't look away. A good sign. "You up for a walk to the barnyard? Shouldn't be much to do, and I'll do the chores if you'll keep me company."

"No." Hayley's face relaxed into a smile. "Not good enough."

Was she ticked off at him? But she was smiling...

"You have to let me help." Her grin widened.

His breath whooshed out in a chuckle. "Good one, Red."

Her eyebrows shot up. Oops. Maybe she didn't like nicknames.

"Red, eh?" Hayley scowled, hands on her hips, but her eyes sparkled. "Now I have to come up with a good one for you. Let. Me. See." She steepled her fingers as though deep in thought. After a moment, she opened her hands, palms up, and sighed. "Can't think of one. Not yet."

He'd hoped she'd come up with a name revealing her impression of him. Not that "Red" covered his feelings for her. A few minutes later, dressed in work jackets and lined rubber boots, Trevor opened the back door with a flourish. "After you, milady."

She giggled and attempted an awkward curtsy in Laureen's bulky coat and boots. "Thank you, kind sir."

Roscoe dashed between them and trotted toward

the barn as if he owned the place. At least he knew where he belonged. A slight grimace twisted Trevor's lips. Pathetic. He was jealous of a mutt. Halfway to the gate, the dog stopped and looked back at them, as though wondering why they were so slow. But Trevor didn't want to hurry. Not tonight.

A gust of wind hit them from the direction of the barn, and Hayley's nose scrunched up. "Whew. How long does it take to get used to that smell?"

"Depends on how sensitive you are." He made a show of inhaling. "I don't smell anything. Just good, fresh farm air." He grinned at her unladylike snort.

"Maybe you should bottle some of this and take it to Toronto with you, so you'll feel at home."

Trevor's throat tightened. Yeah, he'd miss this place. And the people here. He swallowed hard and reached for Hayley's hand. "Come on, let's go see that baby of yours."

Hayley gasped and stumbled.

19

Hayley's heart slammed against her ribs as her breath caught. She flinched when Trevor grasped her arm.

"You OK?" His voice rumbled in her ear.

She turned, sure her face exposed her shock, and stared into his eyes. So close, she could feel his breath on her face. He didn't know about her baby. He'd meant Bella, of course. Embarrassment slid into something else, something warm and wonderful and…Roscoe barked, and Hayley pulled back with a twinge of regret.

Trevor straightened and scowled at the dog.

Then his hand moved to the small of her back, and its heat penetrated the bulky work coat. Hayley leaned into his strength for a moment, until the barn scent reminded her of chores that waited. She shifted, putting some space between them. "The cows…" Hayley glanced up as his eyes refocused on her.

"Yeah…right." He exhaled. "Don't want you to fall, though. The path can be tricky in the dark, even with the yard light." He drew her close to his side, his arm around her waist.

It wasn't that dark yet, but Hayley basked in his warmth. The chill of the night disappeared as Hayley matched her steps to Trevor's. Or rather, he matched his to hers. A true gentleman. If her friends from her former life could see her now, they would be shocked.

They'd never understand her eagerness to muck out barn stalls and check cows and calves. Well, maybe they would…if they met Trevor. On second thought, she was glad they weren't here. The shameless flirts. Trevor was hers. Hayley stumbled again. Where had that thought come from? Her cheeks flamed as Trevor tugged her closer. Good thing he couldn't read her mind.

"Careful. We're almost to the barn, and I'll switch on the lights. Guess you're not used to dark pathways. But after we finish chores, I want to show you something. In the dark."

Hayley couldn't read his expression. His eyes seemed to glow, or was it a reflection from the yard light? What could he be planning? She shivered, whether from trepidation or anticipation, she wasn't sure. Maybe a little of both. As soon as they reached the barnyard, Hayley searched the dimly lit area for Bella, "her" calf. There she was, close to her mama, Molly. Bella seemed bigger already, and warmth filled Hayley's chest. She grinned. She was in love—with a tiny heifer calf.

Trevor's breath tickled her ear. "New life is amazing, isn't it?" His voice dropped even lower. "I still can't believe you turned a calf, but there she is, healthy and growing. Thanks to you."

Hayley wanted to turn toward him, but they stood so close, he might think she was inviting him to kiss her. She stifled a sigh. A kiss would be…frustrating. Because Trevor would be leaving for Toronto in less than a week. She shrugged off the longing and stepped away from the tall temptation beside her. "I'm getting cold. Let's get this done, OK?"

"Right."

A short time later, the cows and their offspring were checked and the other chores accomplished.

Hayley hung the pitchfork on the wall and grinned at Trevor. "That didn't take long."

"We work well together. You're becoming quite the farm hand." He took a step toward her, and his smile faded into something softer.

Hayley's heart rate increased.

But he stopped more than an arm's reach away, his expression hooded. "Will you come with me, or are you too cold?"

He'd said he had something to show her. In the dark. A shiver worked its way up her spine.

Trevor held out his hand, and Hayley grasped it. Without another word, he led her out of the barn and further from the house. He held the flashlight in front of them and pulled her close to his side.

"I won't let you fall."

Too late. She was already falling—for him. Even though it was hopeless. "I know. You're a good man, Trevor Hiebert." Timing was everything, and hers was way off. He turned toward her, but she couldn't read his expression in the dark.

He led the way to a barbed wire fence far from the house, where the barn blocked the yard light's glow. Trevor stepped on the lower wire and pulled the middle one upwards. "Careful. Bend low, and try not to get caught on the barbs. I'll follow you."

She bent over, lifted one leg to put it through the opening, and lost her balance. Trevor grabbed her arm, and she could hear a smile in his voice.

"Not quite a farm girl yet." He stood firm as she ducked through the fence like an ungraceful dancer.

Carefully, not quite sure she'd cleared the barbs,

she stood. Unscathed. "I did it!" She barely restrained a fist pump. Hayley's face warmed, and she breathed a prayer of thanks for the darkness.

"Good job. Now hold the light while I come through."

A moment later, Trevor stood by her side and reached for the flashlight. "Stay close, and watch out for cow pies. We're almost there."

"Um, do you have bulls here?"

Trevor swung the flashlight in a small arc, sidestepping now and then. "Nope. Used to, but now it's easier to rent one. Why?"

"I just don't want to run into one. I've heard they can be dangerous."

"That's one reason we don't have any." He stopped, turned in a circle, and tugged on her hand. "This will do. Come here, lean on me so you don't lose your balance, and look up."

Hayley snuggled against his ribs, and caught her breath when his arms wrapped around her.

His warm baritone sounded above her head. "I've got you. Tilt your head back." He switched off the light.

Hayley closed her eyes to quicken their adjustment. She'd seen stars before, but she'd look at them with this guy. Any time. Even though he was determined to leave, she'd cherish this moment. And pray he'd return. To her and to God. Hayley lifted her chin, and let her head rest against Trevor's chest. Nice. Solid. Tantalizing.

"Now look."

How had he known her eyes were closed? She opened her eyes. And gasped. Dancing curtains of green, orange and white undulated across the blackness. "Northern lights. Amazing." She whispered as though in a cathedral, enraptured by the heaven's display. "I've never seen them like this, so bright and colorful against a dark sky." She reached heavenward. "They look close enough to touch."

"They do, don't they?" Trevor's arms tightened. "I understand the scientific explanation, but to me, they're magical."

Trevor's woodsy scent enveloped her. His muscular arms enfolded her, as the heavenly light cast their spell. She wanted to dance with him, up there in the magical night sky. "They are. Like an amazing gift from the Creator."

Trevor froze.

~*~

Why'd she have to bring God into it? He glanced at the woman in his arms and then stared at the sky. He felt a different kind of longing, to share her faith and the peace she'd found.

The colorful light show swirled above them in spectacular choreography until two lines of green intersected—like a cross.

"Trevor, look! Is it a sign from God? For us?"

His mouth opened in wonder. He knew God existed; that just made sense. But what if he'd been wrong about Him? Could God care about him? Enough to send a sign? What did it mean?

Hayley squirmed, and he loosened his grip. But instead of moving away, she turned to face him. Her bare hands reached up to cradle his face, their touch sending frissons up and down his backbone. Her jade eyes widened, hypnotizing him, and her mouth trembled. "Thank you, Trevor." She pulled his face down and touched her lips to his. Warmth. Sweetness. Enchantment. Desire.

Trevor clasped Hayley tighter, one hand moving up to the back of her head as he deepened the kiss. She tasted like cinnamon. Smelled like peaches. Her slender body molded to his as her arms slid around his neck. Time and gravity suspended.

His heart threatened to pound out of his chest when Hayley pulled back with a gasp. Trevor loosened his grip with reluctance. He thudded back to earth. And wanted to fly again.

"Oh…" Her voice sounded as shaky as he felt. "I can't even think straight."

Trevor touched his forehead to hers. "I've wanted to do that ever since our first date. Maybe since we met." His voice trembled, too. He took a deep breath and stepped back without releasing Hayley. "Are you all right?"

"Yeah. More than." She traced his face with one finger, leaving flames in its wake. "I wish…"

"What?"

"I don't know." She sighed, a mournful sound that echoed in his heart. "I…I wish you knew Jesus, and I wish you'd stay."

He crushed her to him and whispered against her hair. "I do too. But I can't."

20

The next afternoon, Laureen spoke over the top of Franklin's head as he fastened her red wool cape. "We'll be home before suppertime, Hayley. Since pork chops are in the slow cooker, we'll just need some baked potatoes and a salad."

Hayley handed Laureen her black leather purse and soft, knit scarf. "No problem. Will Max be here?"

"I think so. He's doing all the chores, but you may want to check with him about his supper plans."

"I will." She sighed. Too bad Trevor couldn't join them, but he'd warned her the next week would be hectic. He'd promised to come tomorrow. Would they get a chance to walk in the fields again? Her lips tingled as she relived his kiss. Heat rushed to her face, and she ducked her head.

Franklin opened the door, his attention on his wife. "Let's get on the road, my dear. We need to hurry to the doctor's office so we can spend lots of quality time in his waiting room." He winked at Hayley before offering his arm to Laureen. "Enjoy your quiet time, young lady."

Hayley moved to the window to watch them leave. Franklin treated Laureen like a precious treasure as he fastened her seatbelt and tucked her cloak around her. Yearning threatened to swamp Hayley, and her eyes filled. *That's what I want, Lord. A forever love like theirs.* The tenderness between Franklin and Laureen had forced Hayley to rethink her definition of love. The bickering and carelessness her parents displayed had sent her searching for love from anyone who offered it. *And look how that turned out.* She clenched her jaw. Never again.

Hayley climbed the stairs. Was she making the same mistake with Trevor? They hadn't known each other long. And Trevor would leave for Toronto, the place of her darkest moments, in less than a week. With a sigh, she sat at her desk and opened her computer. Enough daydreams. They couldn't support her, and she couldn't expect to stay at the farm once Laureen healed. Time to catch up on her accounting course. And her dull, cubicled future.

A couple hours later, Hayley rolled her shoulders as she hit *Send*. Almost caught up. She'd grab a drink, start the potatoes baking, and then tackle another lesson before the Hieberts returned.

A door slammed, and Hayley glanced at her watch. That was fast. She hurried down the stairs and into the kitchen. Hunched over the sink stood Max. Big, scary Max.

Hayley turned to leave but remembered she had to ask him about supper. She cleared her throat just as the water shut off.

Max swiveled. "Miss Hayley. Didn't hear you when I came in."

"I-I was upstairs. Studying." She straightened her spine. "Will you be here for supper? There's plenty. Laureen wants to know."

He tilted his head. "But you don't, right?"

Hayley wished she could disappear. "That's not what I meant."

Max grinned, and it lit his whole face. Crinkles

framed his bright, deep-set eyes, and the tops of his ears turned pink. "I shouldn't tease. I apologize, Miss Hayley. I appreciate your kind invitation for supper. Any time I can get a home-cooked meal, it just makes my day."

"Guess your day's been made, then."

Laughter burst from the big man. "Well done! Glad to see you've got some backbone." He lowered his bulk onto an oak press-backed chair that looked too delicate for his large frame. "Franklin tells me you're studying to be an accountant."

Hayley nodded.

"You good at it?"

"I will be."

"Great answer. So what's your ambition? Big city office? Small town? Maybe do books for small businesses and farmers?"

Hayley stared at him. Why hadn't she thought of that? She'd assumed she would join her father's firm—a thought less appealing by the day. She *didn't* want to follow in his footsteps, steps leading away from his family to cater to the rich and powerful. But helping small businesses or farmers? Yes, that appealed, especially if it meant she wouldn't have to move back to Toronto. She sank into the chair opposite Max. "Small businesses. Farmers. I…could…do that." Her smile stretched wide. "Thank you."

"Glad to help." Max leaned forward, his big hands clasped. "Got a message for you. You are a special young lady, Miss Hayley, and God saved you for a purpose. Do you understand?"

"I-I…don't know. I mean, I know Jesus died so I could be forgiven. But a purpose? For me?" She shook her head. "No, I don't understand."

"Got a Bible?"

Hayley nodded.

"Good. Read it. Ephesians." Max stood and walked out.

~*~

Trevor snapped the computerized till shut and grinned as his customer headed for the door. Sold! His latest custom bike, still unfinished, had brought a higher price than anything else he'd built. Pride swelled his chest until reality hit. This would be the last T. Hiebert creation built at Easy Rider. He spun away from the counter and nearly stepped on his boss's toes. "Carlos. Didn't hear you come up."

"No problem. You did good, T-man. I watched you open up to that guy. Made him want it. Great sales technique. And I noticed you've been grinning and humming all day." Carlos's dark gaze speared Trevor, and his voice softened. "You that happy to leave?"

"No, man."

Carlos stroked his goatee. "Then what? Care to share?"

Last night's sky illuminated with glorious northern lights, Hayley's delicate hand in his, her warm lips pressed against his mouth. "Um…No, I don't think so." His face burned.

Carlos stared at him for a full minute, his eyebrows forming a V.

Trevor stood tall, but had to press his lips together, or his tell-tale grin would reappear.

Several heartbeats later, Carlos chortled and slapped Trevor on the back. "You got yourself a woman! Way to go, T." Carlos started to walk away but paused and looked back. His smile disappeared. "Not the best timing, though, eh?"

"We're still getting to know each other, and there are issues." Not-so-small problems like her faith and his lack of it. For some reason, that seemed more significant than the distance between Saskatoon and Toronto. Last night, he'd shivered, whether from cold or the thrill of Hayley in his arms, he didn't know. The caress of her breath as she'd whispered, *I wish you knew Jesus, and I wish you'd stay.* It haunted him. She haunted him.

Carlos cleared his throat. "If you change your mind about talking, I'll be in my office."

"Thanks for the offer, but no."

What good would talking do? Carlos's stormy divorce a couple years back had affected the whole shop. But that was the old Carlos. Before he'd "met Jesus." Both Carlos and Hayley had changed, and they'd both said Jesus made the difference. Maybe hashing things out with his boss wasn't such a bad idea. He looked around.

Ryan was helping the only customer in the shop, so Trevor caught his attention and pointed from himself to the office. Ryan nodded and turned back to the middle-aged lady trying on helmets.

Trevor wasn't sure what he'd say, but something pushed him toward Carlos's office.

The office door stood open. Carlos faced the wall behind his desk, his voice low as he spoke into his phone.

Trevor hesitated, leaned against the doorway. Maybe he should come back later.

Carlos swiveled his chair and held one finger up. *One minute.* A moment later, Carlos ended the call.

"What can I do for you, T?" He had an oddly excited look on his face.

Trevor had never seen his boss this…sparkly. "Um…I thought I'd take you up on your offer. You know, to talk."

"Take a load off." He indicated a chair.

May as well get comfortable. Trevor blurted the first thing that came to mind. "Her name's Hayley, she's incredible, and she's like you."

Carlos's eyebrows shot up. "How so? She got a stylin' beard?"

Trevor snorted. "Of course not. She's gorgeous. Fiery hair, hypnotic green eyes, and a killer body. But I mean, she believes in Jesus and everything."

"And she still likes you? Well, praise the Lord." Then his smirk morphed into a grimace. "I'll bet it's got you tied up in knots."

Yeah, that pretty much summed up the condition of his gut. "How can I know if it's true?" The words burst out. "That God is good, I mean. After what I've seen…and done…I just can't wrap my head around it."

Carlos clasped his hands, tilted back, and closed his eyes.

Trevor wanted to discuss God, not get pulled into His presence. Maybe this was a mistake. But when he tried to rise, an unseen pressure pushed him back.

When Carlos reopened his eyes, his glowing face mesmerized Trevor. "Listen, T, Jesus is the key. The Way, the Truth, and the Life. He is Emmanuel, God with us. You gotta get to know Jesus."

The words hit their mark—straight to Trevor's heart. And melded with Hayley's whisper. *I wish you knew Jesus, and I wish you'd stay.* But he couldn't stay. It was settled. And Jesus? Maybe. Someday. A dark haze filled his vision, and a silent voice whirled around his head. *Get out while you can. Don't give in. God never helped you. You know that.* Trevor struggled to his feet and fought the urge to drop to his knees. "I'll think about it." *But not now.* "Thanks, boss. Appreciate your opinion."

Disappointment flitted across Carlos's face before he nodded. "Not my opinion. It's the truth."

Keep going. No regrets.

Trevor stopped in the doorway. Looked back.

Carlos sat with his head bowed.

21

Hayley shut her accounting books and logged out of her computer. She'd stared at the same paragraph for…she looked at her watch…almost half an hour.

Max's words ran in a loop and pushed everything else into the background. *God saved you for a purpose. Read Ephesians.*

Curiosity drew her to the nightstand. She picked up her Bible, settled onto the bed, and opened it. Hayley had to flip through many pages before she found Ephesians. She skimmed the first couple of verses until her eyes locked on words that seemed to jump from the page.

In love he predestined us to be adopted as his sons through Jesus Christ, in accordance with his pleasure and will…

She'd been adopted by God? Hayley leaned back against the pillows. How could it be?

Read it. Max's words again.

She continued to read. Happiness began to bubble as she drank in the message God sent her.

For it is by grace you have been saved, through faith—and this not of yourselves, it is the gift of God—not by works, so that no one can boast. For we are God's workmanship, created in Christ Jesus to do good works, which God prepared in advance for us to do.

Max was right. God had had something for her to do. But what? She skimmed paragraphs that puzzled and thrilled her, until she reached chapter four. Then she inhaled sharply as the words leapt off the page.

Get rid of all bitterness, rage and anger, brawling and slander, along with every form of malice. Be kind and compassionate to one another, forgiving each other, just as in Christ God forgave you.

That couldn't be right. An image of Blake Horner, the father of her baby, with his arms around the wife he'd betrayed and concealed, filled her mind. Blake had used and discarded her. His deceit had nearly destroyed her—and had led to her baby's death. Forgive Blake? Her gaze fell to the printed words once more.

...just as in Christ God forgave you.

A vehicle drove into the yard.

Hayley put the Bible back on the nightstand and hurried downstairs. Apprehension and hope battled, and Hayley wiped sweaty palms on her jeans as she slowed her pace.

A door slammed outside and footsteps sounded on the porch. She took a deep breath, anxious to see Franklin and Laureen's faces.

The doorbell rang, and Hayley froze. Why would they ring their own doorbell? She swung the front door open. Blake Horner leaned against the doorway, a smirk on his handsome face.

Hayley shrank back as bile rose in her throat. "Wh-what are you doing here?"

He stepped inside and pulled her close, his mouth at her ear. "That's the welcome I get? I've missed you." He nuzzled her neck. "Why'd you run off? Took me forever to track you down."

"Let. Me. Go." She struggled, but his grip tightened, triggering panic. She twisted and shoved hard. "Get off me! What are you doing here? What do you want?"

Blake stumbled backward and banged into the still-open door. "Ow." His eyes glittered as he came toward her again. "So, you want to play rough? Fine by me."

Fear mutated to anger, and Hayley lifted her chin. "I don't want to play at all. Go away, Blake. I have nothing to say to you."

Forgive.

"Just leave."

"You don't know what you're saying. When people said you'd had a nervous breakdown, I stood up for you." His lips twisted into a sneer. "Maybe I was wrong. You're not the girl I knew."

"No, I'm not. Thank God."

Blake advanced again, and Hayley took a step back. "I don't know how you found me, Blake, or why you're here, but I have nothing to say to you."

"You don't mean that. Remember the good times we had? Or do you need a little reminder?"

The back door hinges squawked, and Roscoe ran into the room. He slid to a stop beside Hayley and stared at her nemesis, growling deep in his throat, his teeth bared.

Blake's pupils widened, and he raised both hands in front of him, palms out. "Nice doggy. Sit, boy."

Roscoe leaned forward and half crouched, ready to pounce.

"Call him off, will you?" Blake's voice squeaked like a teenager's.

Max appeared on the other side of Hayley. "Problem?" How did such a big man move so silently?

"No, Blake was just leaving." Hayley's relief

wobbled her smile.

Blake shoved his hands in his pockets. "But I do need to talk to you, Hayley. And I'm not giving up." He skulked out the door and ran toward his low-slung car. A moment later, tires spun on gravel as the car accelerated.

Hayley pushed the door shut, turned, and leaned against it. "Thank you, Max."

Roscoe sidled up to her and nudged her leg with his nose. Hayley grinned and ruffled his ears. "You too, boy. Good dog." Tears filled her eyes. "Thank you both. My guardian angels."

Something glinted in Max's expression, but it disappeared just as quickly.

Gravel crunched under car tires.

Hayley tensed.

Max moved to the window. "Franklin and Laureen."

"Good." Hayley let out a long breath and rubbed her face. But then her heart clutched again. "I wonder what the doctor said."

"Who's in charge, Miss Hayley?" Max moved to open the door.

She inhaled deeply, and her fear dissipated. "God."

"'Nuff said." The big man turned, stared outside for a long moment, and then ran down the steps.

~*~

Trevor set down his wrench and glanced up. Should be quitting time, but not today. His unfinished custom bike was sold, so now he had to get it done. If he could get the mock-up done to ensure all the parts fit together, tomorrow he could send everything to be painted or chromed. Sweat beaded on his brow. If anything went wrong at this stage, he'd never finish in time.

"Closin' time, T." Carlos leaned against the workbench holding Trevor's bike frame. "Working late again?"

"Yeah. Gotta get this thing done."

Carlos shrugged. "It's not mandatory, you know. Ryan or I could finish it up. The design is yours, no matter who puts the parts together."

Trevor picked up the wrench again. "I know." He stared at the wrench. "Maybe it's pride, but I want to be the one to finish it. Since it's my last project here."

Carlos nodded, but the lines beside his mouth deepened. "I guess it will be."

Trevor's shoulders sagged and guilt ate at his gut. He rubbed it with his arm.

Carlos slapped him on the back. "Well, you still need to eat. How's Italian sound? My treat."

Maybe that hollow sensation wasn't guilt. He nodded. "Great. I could go for some lasagna."

"All right. Let me lock the front, and we can take my truck."

Trevor frowned. "That's not necessary. Then you'd have to bring me back here. I can drive."

"No problem. Gives us more time to talk."

Trevor's stomach clenched. A few minutes later, Trevor leaned back against the heated leather seat in Carlos's GMC half ton. The warmth worked its magic, and within a couple minutes Trevor's knotted muscles began to relax. "Man, this is nice. My next vehicle's got to have heated seats."

Carlos grinned as he turned onto Idylwyld Drive.

"You get used to it real quick." His grin faded. "Some things are easier to get used to than others."

A small car swung into their lane without signaling, and Carlos stomped on the brake.

The seatbelt dug into Trevor's chest, but the lack of cursing from Carlos impacted him harder. Trevor stared at his mentor. "You really have changed. A few months ago the air in here would be dark blue."

Carlos snorted. "Thank God."

Trevor's mind wrestled with questions. And frustration. "You said you wanted to talk. What about?"

Carlos slowed and flicked on the turn signal. "Almost there now. It'll wait until we've ordered."

Fine. Carlos was still boss, so Trevor would play it his way. He didn't speak again until after Carlos led the way to a booth near the back of the family-run Italian restaurant.

A perky blonde grinned a thousand-watt smile as she placed menus in front of them. "What can I get for you gentlemen this evening? Water, coffee, tea, beer? Or something else?"

"Lasagna and coffee for me, thanks."

"Same here."

The girl took the menus. "OK, then. I'll be right back with your coffees. Cream?"

"Just black, please."

"Cream for me, thanks," Carlos said. As the waitress flounced away, Carlos smirked. "And another heart gets broken by the T-Man."

Trevor grimaced. "Give me a break. She wants a big tip is all. Probably works for her most of the time."

Carlos grinned even wider. "Worked with you, until recently. Something to do with a certain redhead?"

Trevor was not going there. "So what did you want to talk about?" he asked, his tone wary.

"You. And I've got some news too. Your choice. Which subject first?"

Curiosity won. "What's your news?"

Carlos didn't answer right away. He stroked his goatee, looked out the window, and released a well-deep sigh.

Trevor lifted one eyebrow. "Well?"

Carlos didn't meet Trevor's gaze. "You remember Eva."

How could anyone at Easy Rider forget Carlos's ex-wife? The last time he'd seen her, she'd been screaming at Carlos, hands gesturing wildly as invectives had filled the shop. Not a pleasant reminder.

Carlos seemed to be waiting for an answer, so Trevor nodded and wondered what she'd done now.

The lines on Carlos's face softened, and his mouth curved upward. "We're gonna try again."

"You're kidding."

"Truth. Turns out, I'm not the only one God's been working on. Eva phoned last week, and we've been talking. Lots of apologies, some hints of hope."

"When I came to your office. That was Eva on the phone?"

"Sure was. We're meeting Good Friday at her church for a drama they're putting on. I can hardly believe it."

Surprise didn't even come close to the whirl in Trevor's brain. Stunned. That summed it up. "Sounds good, man. I'm happy for you."

"God is doing some amazing stuff, T."

That smile on Carlos's face made Trevor squirm as

he braced for another sermon.

"Now I've got some questions for you."

"Shoot."

"Have you talked much to Nate Smith?"

Trevor jerked in shock. "Some. He offered me room and board. Nice house, great deal, not too far from Lowrider. Why?"

"He called me, and we talked quite a while. About you. About Lowrider and Vince Starr."

"And?" Trevor frowned. Maybe those rumbles of unease meant something after all.

"Seemed a little odd. I mean, Smith sounded like an up-front kind of guy, and I got a good vibe from him. But he asked more about you than Starr had. Questions about your integrity, your beliefs. Starr only wanted to know how well you obeyed orders and if you caused problems." Carlos fiddled with his knife and fork, and when he looked up, concern shone from his face. "I don't know what's going on at Lowrider, but I sure got the impression something's not right. So tell me, T, are you totally sure this is the right move for you?"

Images flashed. His parents, the farm, Hayley, the unease he'd felt after the interview with Vince Starr. Carlos and his friendship. Then once more, his mom and dad. How selfish was he? He rubbed his chin and sighed. "No, I'm not sure. But I gave my word."

22

Hayley followed Max out the front door and stopped short.

Franklin sat in the van, slumped over the steering wheel. Laureen was rubbing his back, and even from a distance, her eyes radiated distress.

Max opened the door, said something to the older couple, and half-lifted Franklin out of the car.

Hayley hurried to Laureen's side, fear staggering her steps. "What happened?"

Laureen pushed her door open, slid out, and leaned against Hayley for several breaths. "A car…almost hit us." Then she rallied and pulled Hayley around the front of the minivan to Franklin's side. "Are you OK, honey?"

Franklin raised his head and nodded. "Will be." He tried to stand on his own but wobbled. "Guess I do need some help. Shook me up some. Thanks, Max."

The four slowly ascended the front steps and entered the living room where Franklin and Laureen sank onto the couch. In spite of the warm spring day, the elderly couple shivered.

Hayley pulled a quilt off the back of the couch and tucked it around them. "I'll make some coffee." Hayley fled to the kitchen. When she tried to fill the coffee maker, water splashed onto the countertop, and she sagged against the counter, tears plopping into the puddle.

Blake. It had to have been his car that nearly hit the Hieberts. If she hadn't come here, this wouldn't have happened.

Pastor Dave's prayer, the night before she moved to the farm, echoed. *Protect her from evil, dear Lord.*

At the time, it hadn't made sense. The Hieberts were godly people, the farm a safe place. But now, evil had come. Because of her.

"It's not your fault, missy." Max's deep rumble came from right behind her.

Hayley spun around and lost her balance.

"Whoa." Max took her arm, his touch gentle, and pulled out a kitchen chair. "Sit. I'll finish here."

Moments later, the brew's fragrance broke through Hayley's fog of misery. She needed to apologize. Plead for forgiveness. She shoved her chair back and pushed upright.

Max raised one eyebrow as he turned, holding a mug out to her in silent invitation.

"I'm OK now. I need to check on Laureen and Franklin."

He nodded, set the mug on the counter and turned back to his preparations.

In the living room, Franklin's arm encircled his wife, and her head rested on his shoulder.

Their quiet conversation faded when Hayley entered, but she heard the word "angina" as Franklin rubbed his chest. Hayley's chest tightened. She couldn't move. What had she done?

Laureen raised her head and gestured. "Come in, dear. We didn't mean to worry you."

Moisture sprang to Hayley's eyes, but she blinked it away. "Are you all right? Really? I didn't mean…"

Laureen patted the cushion beside her. "Come, sit.

We're fine. That close call shook us up some, but no one was injured."

Franklin released a guttural sigh. "Prayed for the young man, though. Didn't seem to know how to drive on a gravel road."

Hayley's throat tightened. "He'd been here. I'm so sorry."

Laureen's eyes widened.

Max's entrance interrupted. "Coffee's ready." He set the tray on the table in front of the couch and handed out full mugs. "Cream and sugar?"

"Maybe both," Laureen said. "A little extra boost. How about you, Hayley?"

"No, thanks. Black is good." The dark brew matched her mood.

Max helped himself to a barrel-shaped mug and sat in the easy chair. He leaned forward, propped his elbows on his knees, and bowed his head for a moment. When he straightened, his bald head caught a beam of light, creating a halo effect.

"Glad you prayed. Young fellow needs it. But I take responsibility for his haste." His mouth quivered, one side sneaking upward in spite of his efforts. "I did encourage his departure."

Laureen's mouth formed an O.

"Who was that guy? And what did he want?" Franklin scowled.

Hayley sighed and set her cup down. Time for some honesty. "Blake was my boyfriend in Toronto. I didn't know he was married. When I found out, I was so upset, I drove too fast and got into an accident. It changed my life, and I came to Saskatchewan." Would it satisfy their curiosity? *Please, God.*

Before the Hieberts had a chance to respond, Max

redirected. "What did the doctor say? Any answers?"

Hayley flashed a grateful smile at him and turned to the older couple. "Yes, please tell us."

Franklin's scowl smoothed out. "Encouraging news, we think. This specialist seemed to know what he was doing."

"Nice young man," Laureen said. "He set up a hearing test for me right away, and as I suspected, my right ear is much worse than my left. I'd assumed old age was to blame, but maybe not this time."

Hayley's brow crinkled. "How's that good?"

Laureen chuckled. "I know, it doesn't sound positive, but it is. He said—and we hope he's right—my spells may be caused by Meniere's disease. It's the best of many scenarios, a disorder of the inner ear. Chronic but usually manageable."

"What's next?" Max beat Hayley to the question.

"A videonyst..." Laureen looked to Franklin for help.

"A dizzy test. That's what they call it, 'cause that's what it does. Brings on dizziness."

"I'm not looking forward to it." Laureen grimaced. "But if it's positive, then Meniere's is the likely culprit. If not..."

Hayley hunched forward and clasped her hands between her knees. "Then what?"

Franklin sighed. "Then we wait for an MRI."

~*~

Trevor cleaned up his tools, scrubbed his hands, and re-checked the front door before grabbing his coat off the rack. At the back door, he stopped and surveyed the work area. The closer his departure loomed, the less he wanted to leave.

But his parents had taught him his name was only as good as his word. *God, what am I supposed to do?* Was that a prayer? Trevor groaned. He must be desperate if he expected God to hear him. His mood as black as the night sky, Trevor turned off the shop lights, stomped outside, and locked the door. Much as he wished he could believe God cared, he knew otherwise.

Halfway to his SUV, Trevor shivered as though cold water trickled down his spine, accelerating his steps. Once inside the Jeep, he started its engine and checked the outside temp reading. Twelve degrees Celsius—no reason to shiver. He must be overtired.

Other than a few semis, Saskatoon's streets were quiet at one in the morning. Good for thinking.

After dropping the bombshell about Eva, Carlos had invited Trevor to meet them at the Good Friday service. Something Carlos mentioned tugged Trevor's memory, but he couldn't nail it down. He'd declined, of course, but he'd felt a pull, as though something inside him wanted to accept. Only six days until he had to leave. Maybe he could get out to the farm early in the afternoon. He needed to see Hayley, to be with her. And his folks, of course, but the thought of Hayley drew him like fuel to a spark plug.

A few minutes later, he tossed his keys on the table, scrubbed the day's grime off, and flopped onto his bed. His muscles ached from his feet to the back of his neck. He tried to find a comfortable position as he willed sleep to come, but the glowing red numbers on the bedside clock mocked him. Two o'clock. Two-thirty. Trevor moaned and pounded his pillow. He had to be out the door in another four hours—sooner if he wanted to get to the farm early afternoon.

Trevor finally drifted toward sleep. But then a dark force surrounded him, pressing down so hard, he gasped for breath. Shapes swirled, figures appeared. His mother and father reached for him but faded from sight. Carlos, running ahead on a narrow trail, turned and gestured at Trevor to hurry. But Carlos disappeared, too. More swirls and strange images, until Trevor found himself facing Larry Kirby, his last foster dad. Black hatred enveloped him as Kirby sneered and held up the limp body of Trevor's favorite foster sister.

Please, God, help her!

But God hadn't. Tears wet Trevor's face, but he couldn't rouse enough to wipe them. He shuddered and sank into the darkness.

~*~

A loud caw, so ear-splitting the crow must be perched right outside his window, pulled Trevor from his restless sleep. His eyes popped open. Sunlight peeked around the blinds. He'd overslept! Trevor tumbled out of bed, pulled on some clothes, and rushed out the door. He'd have to grab breakfast at a drive-through.

He'd wanted to have the bike at the paint shop by now. The break he'd promised himself—time with his folks, hours with sweet Hayley—his whole day, ruined. Trevor smacked his fist on the steering wheel as he braked for a red light.

The light turned green, and the truck ahead of Trevor belched black exhaust as the driver accelerated. Trevor stared, motionless, as the billowing darkness of his nightmare replayed, until the driver behind him leaned on his horn. Trevor jumped and turned right. Nasty dream, that one, but he couldn't let it slow him down.

From the moment the shop opened, customers filled the showroom, and several wanted to talk to Trevor. Saturdays were often busy, but this bordered on the absurd.

By midafternoon, he wished he'd never agreed to the interview with Lewis from the *Star Phoenix*. And he should have taken his Honda, declared the winner of the newspaper's contest, back home. It drew potential customers like bees to a honeycomb, until the room buzzed with conversations and questions.

"When can you build me one like that?"

He'd taken contact info from people with vague promises, hoping Carlos, Ryan, or one of the other guys could step up and satisfy the clients. But the guilt of his deception ate at him.

His head throbbed and his knees threatened to buckle as he murmured assurances to a forty-something guy that his dream bike could be built at Easy Rider. The man walked away with a smile on his face, so he must not have noticed Trevor's omission that he wouldn't be the builder.

"How're you holdin' up?" Carlos asked.

"Um, OK, I guess." He rubbed his cheeks, as though it would revive him.

Carlos peered at him, dark eyebrows nearly touching. "Did you get any lunch?"

"It's been so busy…Guess I forgot."

Carlos clapped him on the back. "Get out of here. Take your bike to the paint shop before they close, and don't come back until you've eaten." He glanced at his watch. "In fact, don't come back until Monday. It's been a long day for you."

Gratitude and exhaustion twisted Trevor's mouth into a half-smile. "Thanks, man."

Another potential customer headed toward Trevor, but he ducked into the back room, grabbed his jacket and keys, and headed out the door. The paint shop, then the farm. At least he'd be there in time for supper.

Pleasure warmed him as he pictured Hayley's face, her eyes glowing. Maybe she'd go for a walk in the fields. Maybe she'd let him kiss her again. He closed his eyes in anticipation, until his Jeep beeped a warning. His door was still open. Trevor slapped his face. *Focus!*

Before he could head to the farm and all its attractions, he had to get his disassembled custom job to the paint shop before they closed. He'd just stuck the key into the ignition when his phone buzzed. He pulled it out of his pocket and stared at the message from Nate Smith.

Call me. Urgent.

23

Hayley punched the bread dough more enthusiastically than necessary, but it relieved some of her pent-up anxiety. No wonder some people enjoyed making bread. Stress release and delicious results—what could be better? Except perhaps some time with someone who had kissed her senseless, left, and hadn't shown up since. Or even phoned. She thumped the dough again.

"That's it, press all the bubbles out." Laureen didn't look up from the bread pans she was greasing. "He's awfully busy, you know. Less than a week…"

Hayley swallowed hard. Exactly. In just a few days, the man who'd captured her heart would drive out of her life. And she'd miss him. She missed him now.

The cell phone she'd placed on the counter pierced the quiet.

Hayley grabbed it with doughy hands and pushed Talk. Her pulse sped up. *It's about time, Trevor Hiebert.* She smiled into the phone. "Hi. I've been waiting for you to call." Oops. She hadn't meant to say that. She peeked at Laureen in time to see the older woman bite back a grin.

"So you did miss me, eh? Glad to hear it." Blake.

Hayley's hand flew to her chest. She couldn't breathe, couldn't think.

"We need to talk. Meet me at Grainfield's on Circle

Drive at seven-thirty. It's good news, sweets, but I'm not coming out there again. At least not until you call off the watchdogs."

Hayley sputtered. So like Blake, to assume she'd do whatever he demanded. But then, she used to. "No, I won't meet you. I have nothing to say to you, and I never want to see you again. You're out of my life, and I want to keep it that way. Go. Away." Hayley pressed *End* and slumped against the counter. Her eyes stung with unshed tears.

"May I assume that wasn't my son?" Laureen's quiet voice conveyed concern, not the condemnation Hayley feared.

"No…no, I wish it had been, though."

Laureen's eyebrow quirked.

Hayley scrunched her face, knowing her expression probably showed her distaste. "That didn't come out right. Blake was on the phone. I would never talk to Trevor that way."

Laureen pulled out a chair and motioned with her hand.

Hayley plopped down and buried her face in her hands.

Laureen's hand traced circles on Hayley's back. "Sounds as if you and this Blake have some unfinished business."

Hayley lifted her head, her jaw clenched. "No, it's finished. Totally."

"Really? Then why the bitter response, my dear? I understand he wronged you—terribly. But trust me in this, his control over your emotions won't end until you forgive him."

Forgive? After everything he'd done? All the lies, deceit, and betrayal? Her baby was dead because of him. Outrage boiled over. "Never!"

Laureen bowed her head for several heartbeats.

Hayley cringed. This lovely woman didn't deserve such a hostile response.

Laureen sat up straight, her blue eyes bright. "Hayley, have you been forgiven?"

Hayley nodded.

"Did you deserve it?"

Hayley ducked her head, remembering how imprisoned she'd been by self-loathing. Nila, Pastor Dave, and Lydia had shown her the way to freedom, through forgiveness paid for by Jesus Christ. She had no right to deny Blake the same release. "But how do I…?"

Laureen covered Hayley's clasped hands with her own. "Give him to God. That doesn't mean what Blake did was right, but you need to release him and his actions to God. It's the only way to free yourself from the past."

And open the door to the future. Laureen didn't add that, but Hayley heard it loud and clear. She took a deep, steadying breath. "What do you think I should do? He said he wants to talk, but I'm afraid. I can't trust him."

Laureen blew out a long, slow breath. "It doesn't look as if Trevor's coming tonight. Maybe you could invite Blake to come here, where you can have privacy and protection at the same time." A sly smile lifted her lips and made her eyes twinkle. "Perhaps you'd like to keep Roscoe with you while you and Blake visit."

Hayley grinned. "Great idea. If his news is urgent, he'll come. I'll phone him right now and tell him this is his only chance. If he shows up here, fine. If not, even better."

~*~

Trevor pulled his key from the ignition, leaned back, and closed his eyes. Only six days until Good Friday, his moving day. Away from his folks. And Hayley. Too soon.

Did he really need to call Nate Smith tonight? Maybe it could wait. But what if Nate had changed his mind about sharing his house with Trevor? Trevor pressed the button, and Nate answered on the first ring. "Nate, it's Trevor Hiebert. What's up?"

"Trevor. Listen, I don't know how to say this, and I really shouldn't say anything." Nate's voice sounded agitated. "You'll have to trust me on this. No questions. Just stay away from Lowrider. Make whatever excuse you need to, but don't show up. It's for your own good."

Suspicions took flight in Trevor's mind, memories of those twinges of unease striking him like a gale-force wind. "You've got to give me more than that, man. I can't go back on my word for no good reason."

"I may have said too much already. Whatever you do, don't talk to Vince Starr or any of his guys. I'm depending on you to keep quiet—and far from here."

"But..."

"You'll understand soon enough. Just stay away."

The line went dead.

Trevor stared at his cell phone for several moments. What just happened? How could Smith demand he go back on his word, give up his dream, just on the word of a guy he'd never even met? Was this a sign, or a hoax?

~*~

At the farm, Blake Horner grinned as he pushed past Franklin into the kitchen where Hayley waited. His cocky grin disappeared at the sight of the Border Collie at Hayley's feet.

Roscoe lifted his lips in a silent snarl.

Blake's hands shot up, palms out. "Whoa. Easy, boy." He whirled and glared at Franklin. "Get your dog out of here."

Franklin looked past Blake to Hayley. "Your company's arrived. Got everything you need?"

"We're set." Hayley smiled, even though her lips trembled. She nodded toward the chair and addressed Blake. "Have a seat, and we can have a talk." She patted the dog's head. "Roscoe's staying."

Blake's eyebrows formed a deep V, and his mouth turned downward, but he sat. "Fine. I'd hoped for a more pleasant atmosphere…" His disdain should have scorched the kitchen as he gazed around. "But if this is what you want, I'll make do."

How could Hayley have ever thought this jerk was a gentleman? She saw the expression on Franklin's face and mouthed, "Sorry."

Franklin shook his head gently before addressing both of them. "We got some good reading material in our room, and leftovers are on the menu for supper. So take all the time you need."

As soon as Franklin backed out of the room, Blake leaned forward and grabbed Hayley's hand. Roscoe growled, showing his sharp teeth, and Blake let go and sat back, sullen.

"Can't you get rid of that mutt?"

Hayley ruffled the dog's ears. "Roscoe stays. He knows the rules, and you'd better pay attention. Do.

Not. Touch. Me. That's the big one. Don't raise your voice, and stay in the chair." She allowed a tiny smirk to twist her lips. "You'll be fine, as long as you behave."

Blake jumped to his feet. "You've got to be kidding! No one tells me…"

Roscoe lunged around the table without a sound, and Blake plopped back down onto the oak chair hard. Vulgar expletives burst from his mouth.

"That's another thing." Hayley leaned back and crossed her arms. "No swearing."

Blake stretched forward, his eyes wide open. A look Hayley remembered from the courtroom videos she'd watched with him. Typical lawyer drama. She braced herself.

"What have you gotten yourself into? Is this some kind of cult?"

Hayley shook her head. She knew him too well to respond. He'd twist whatever she said, anyway.

He started to push his chair back, and Roscoe crouched as though waiting for Blake to make a move. Blake glared at the dog and scooted his chair forward. Was that an admission of defeat?

"So, what did you come all the way from Toronto to tell me?"

Blake started to reach for her again but pulled back at a growled warning. "I've missed you. One day everything between us was great, and the next you were gone. And no one would tell me what happened." He could have out-puppy-dogged Roscoe, the way his blue eyes pleaded. "I had to find you, bring you back home."

"No, you didn't. You had no right. You lied to me and betrayed my trust."

Blake ran hands through his short blond hair, and it stuck up at odd angles. He would never do that in a courtroom. Maybe she was getting through to what was left of his conscience.

He shifted on his chair and glanced at the dog. "About my wife…That's why I came. Celine left me, and I really am single now." He did that puppy-dog look again. "I need you, Hayley."

For the first time, Hayley breathed a prayer of thanks for her terrible accident. In the past, she would have melted under his gaze and done whatever Blake asked. Now, all she felt was pity for the pathetic man on the other side of the table. *Thank You, Jesus.* But her pulse still fluttered like a trapped butterfly at what she had to say. "You need Jesus, not me."

Blake slapped the table. "I knew it! You've been taken in by a bunch of religious nuts. Well, I'm here to save you."

Hayley wished she could smack the smugness off his face. She bowed her head. *Sorry, Lord.* Peace filled her, and she smiled at the man she'd once thought of as her true love, her golden destiny. "My friends are not religious nuts, and I've already been saved. By Jesus Christ, who died so I could be forgiven. I needed it, desperately, and you do, too."

Blake turned his head toward the window and the darkness outside, his expression as smooth as a mannequin's.

Hayley knew that look. He was preparing a stinging comeback.

Roscoe sat up straight and stared at the doorway. Franklin or Laureen must have gone into the living room. But they'd honor their promise of privacy. Not like her former lover. He hadn't even honored his vows to his wife. Hayley reached across the table and touched his hand. "Listen to me, Blake. Because I've been forgiven, I can forgive you."

He swiveled to face her, his eyebrows high. "Forgive me? For what? You mean Celine?" His lips twisted in a smirk. "You should have known I was married. I didn't try *that* hard to hide it. You just didn't want to know. I don't need your forgiveness." He nearly spat the word.

Hayley bit her lip to hold back an angry retort. She breathed deeply, each breath a prayer for strength. She clasped her hands in her lap to hide their trembling. "I did *not* know you were married. The day I saw you with your wife, I'd come to tell you…I was pregnant. With your baby."

Blake sucked in a loud breath. His gasp echoed from the doorway.

Roscoe barked and ran out of the room.

Hayley pivoted toward the sound, but no one was there.

The front door slammed, an engine roared, and gravel clattered as tires spun.

Hayley ran to the window just in time to see the back of Trevor's Jeep as it raced down the driveway.

24

Hayley hugged herself, her forehead against the cold, dark window. Tears flowed. How much had Trevor heard?

She jumped when Blake's voice hissed in her ear. "Someone special? Didn't take you long to move on. So, what did you do with the kid?"

Pain knifed through Hayley, and she sagged against the window. "My baby is dead." Silence. For several slow heartbeats, Hayley waited for Blake's response. She shifted so she could see him.

His jaw clenched, and then he shrugged. "Just as well. I've already got two, and that's plenty." His face twisted into an expression of distaste. "You would have been a lousy mother, anyway."

Hayley shoved her fist against her mouth, but it couldn't stop the keening cry that ripped from her soul. She stumbled toward the doorway.

Franklin and Laureen stood there, anxious looks on their faces, and Roscoe stood at attention beside them, growling at Blake.

Laureen reached for Hayley, "Are you all right, honey?"

Hayley shook her head, and Laureen pulled her into the shelter of her arms.

Franklin glowered at Blake. "Thought I heard you leave."

"Not me, but I'm going now. Coming here was a

waste of time." His handsome features twisted as he sneered at Hayley. "You were a waste of my time."

Roscoe showed his teeth, crouched low, and advanced toward Blake.

Blake's eyebrows shot up. "Keep your mutt away from me!"

Franklin pointed down. "Stay, Roscoe. Let the miserable cuss take off. He's not worth it."

When Laureen placed a restraining hand on her husband's shoulder, Hayley pulled away and hurried toward the safety of her room.

But as she trudged up the stairs, she heard Franklin's choked voice. "Hayley Blankenship is worth two dozen of you. Get out, and don't come back."

~*~

Trevor paced his small living room blindly, not sure how he even got home. He rubbed a hand over his face. Must have been instinct, like a horse to its barn. Barn…farm…*Hayley*. His legs hit the couch and he half-fell onto it. He sprawled there, arm over his eyes, but he couldn't block out the images screening in a continuous loop. Hayley reaching toward the creep. Saying she forgave him. Making up with him. Trevor's heart clenched.

Then, confessing she'd been pregnant.

Trevor's breath whooshed out, and he bent forward, chest nearly touching his knees. Pain crashed over him like a tsunami. What had happened to the baby? Had she given it away, like his birth mother had done? Throwing it at Social Services to ignore and abuse? Or, even worse, had she ended the pregnancy, so she could pretend it never happened?

Nausea hit hard. Trevor stumbled to the bathroom and dropped to his knees in front of the toilet. A few minutes later, he rinsed his mouth and stared at his reflection in the scratched mirror above the sink. He didn't recognize the man staring back. How could he—after all he'd been through—have fallen for someone who cared so little for her own child?

Are you sure?

Trevor swung around, lost his balance, and grabbed the vanity. "Who's there?" He peered into the corners of the small room, but no one appeared. He shook his head, but carefully, because a hammer drill had begun to pummel his skull. Must be too much stress. That could cause hallucinations, couldn't it?

He'd certainly had enough stress lately. The job offer from Vince Starr at Lowrider. Worry about his mother's health. The thrill of getting to know Hayley and the pain of knowing he had to leave soon. Then today's warning from Nate Smith. So much uncertainty.

But the worst was the realization that the woman he'd fallen in love with had done the vilest thing he could imagine, the one act he could never forgive. She had gotten rid of her child.

The image in the mirror blurred as his heart cracked and splintered.

~*~*

Trevor pulled his pillow over his head, but the pounding got louder. Sounded like…the front door. Who was pounding on his door? He lurched out of bed, stumbled through the living room, and peered through the peephole.

Max. The last person he wanted to see.

Trevor raised his voice as much as he could without making his head burst. "Go away, Max. I don't want to talk to you. Why are you here instead of the farm?"

"I was. Already did the chores. We need to talk. Your mother sent me."

Right in the Achilles heel. Trevor groaned as he unlocked and opened the door. "Guess you'd better come in, then." Less than gracious, but it was the best he cared to do.

Max strode past Trevor, glanced around the living room, and sat on the worn couch. "We need to talk."

"So you said."

Trevor shut the door, barely restraining himself from slamming it. He stared at Max, and then sat in the beige recliner. "What about?"

Max leaned forward. His deep-set eyes smouldered like embers. "You heard part of a private conversation this evening." He held up a broad hand when Trevor opened his mouth. "Hear me out."

Trevor folded his arms across his chest. "Fine."

"Miss Hayley has a history. So do you. You're both sinners who need forgiveness. Hayley found it and was extending it to a man who'd hurt her. Now you're on that list too."

Trevor's jaw unclenched, and he stared at Max with shock. "What are you talking about? I didn't do anything to her. Besides, she's the one who threw away her child."

Max's eyebrows lifted. "You sure?"

Trevor jutted out his chin. "I heard her. She said she *had* been pregnant. Do you see a kid? Either she killed it, or she gave it away like so much trash. I can't deal with it." He shut his eyes. He would not allow the tears to win. For a minute or two, the only sound Trevor heard was his heartbeat thudding in his ears. How could he have been so wrong about Hayley Blankenship? Did Max expect him to forgive her? Not likely. Only if she could undo what she'd done.

Max's sonorous rumble sounded like it came from a deep well. "Your past is blinding you to the truth. Your birth mother did the best she could. She gave you life."

Trevor jumped up. "How could you possibly know anything about that woman? She gave me up. She didn't want me, and she didn't care what happened to me. I *hate* her for it." He needed to hit something. Or someone. But Max stood, too, and his bulk warned Trevor to control the urge.

Max shook his head, his eyes sad. "You know so little."

"And you know so much? Tell me, then, what you know about the woman who discarded me."

Max inhaled, like the pause before a wind gust. "She was fourteen. Her boyfriend said, 'Get rid of it.' Her parents kicked her out. But she vowed to give you life. She believed you would be adopted by good people. And eventually, you were."

Trevor buckled from the gut-punch, sank into the chair, and stared up at the older man. "You can't know that."

"Do you know it's not true?"

Trevor assumed, or someone had told him back in the mists of his childhood, he'd been thrown away. What if Max was right? What if he'd been wrong all those years? Something inside his chest stirred.

Max settled back onto the couch.

How many times had Trevor been told something horrible and assumed it to be true? Like tonight. With Hayley. One of the shards of his heart shifted and pierced his cynicism. Trevor murmured into his hands. "Oh God, what have I done? What am I supposed to do now?"

Max's voice flowed over him like a warm rain shower. "That's why I'm here."

~*~

Hayley had just reached for another tissue when she heard Laureen yell, "Hayley, come quick! I need you!"

She dashed back downstairs and saw Franklin slumped against the wall, his face ashen. Laureen was trying, with one good arm, to pull him to his feet.

"What happened?" Without waiting for an answer, Hayley ran to Franklin's other side and pulled his limp arm around her neck.

"Help me get him to the couch." Laureen spoke through gritted teeth.

As they struggled, Franklin came to and shook his head. "Unh. What are you doing?" He pushed himself upright and rubbed a hand over his face as its pallor warmed to a pale pink.

"Your nitro…where is it?" Laureen patted his pockets, sounding close to tears.

Franklin moved away from the wall, wobbled, and leaned against it again. "Guess I do need help from you ladies."

All three were breathing hard by the time Franklin sprawled on the couch. He popped a pill under his tongue and closed his eyes.

Laureen perched beside him, and the lines on her face deepened. She picked up his hand and held it to her face. "That was a bad one. I think I'd better call the doctor."

Franklin waved his hand. "Don't bother. I'm OK now. Shouldn't let my temper get the better of me." He moved his head so he could connect with Hayley. "Sorry, young lady. About all of that."

Hayley wiped her eyes on her sleeve. "Are you really all right?" She knelt beside the couch. "This is my fault. I shouldn't have asked Blake to come." She hung her head. "*I* shouldn't have come here. I've brought nothing but grief."

"You brought *life* to this home." Franklin's voice rang with conviction and he had a twinkle in his eyes.

"Mind you, grief is part of life."

Laureen swatted his arm. "You're obviously fine. Guess I don't have to bother the doctor tonight after all." Then she cupped Hayley's cheek. "My husband is right, you know, on both counts. We are blessed to have you here. You have brought much joy to this old house—and to our hearts. If grief comes, it's a normal part of life. Not a reason for doubt."

"But Trevor..." She gulped air. "I-I'd hoped he would see God's forgiveness in me and accept it for himself. But now..." Tears pushed past her closed eyelids and ran down her face. "He hates me."

Coolness settled on Hayley's face and in her heart, until she glanced up and saw Laureen and Franklin's clasped hands and bowed heads. She should have known that would be their response. The tight band around her chest loosened a bit. Hayley bowed her head. *Please, God, make this right. Somehow. Even if Trevor can never love me, help him love You.*

25

The following morning, Hayley rinsed the breakfast dishes in the sink. Outside the kitchen window, the gloom brightened until the rising sun peeked through the poplar trees, and its blaze of orange and red backlit the stark limbs and tight, pale green buds. Hayley stood transfixed and tried to absorb some of the sunrise's beautiful serenity.

"Reminds you of Easter, doesn't it?" Laureen leaned against the counter as she refilled her coffee cup. "I love spring sunrises and the promise of sweet life after winter's harshness."

"A renewal of hope." But Hayley felt stuck in winter. She could sure use some renewal. After last night, even Franklin and Laureen's love couldn't put a flame to her dream's smoking embers. A ray of sunshine hit Hayley's face, and she ducked her head. Too bright on a day when she wanted to hide in the shadows.

Trevor's parents had opened their arms when she'd confessed her story, but what about Trevor? Would she see him before he moved to Toronto? Her presence might keep him from spending time with his mom and dad.

The phone rang, and Hayley turned to her employers, sipping their cups of coffee at the table. "Should I get it?"

They both nodded, and Laureen spoke. "Please."

Hayley looked at them more closely as she walked to the phone. They both seemed older this morning. She sighed. They'd forgiven her, but could she forgive herself for causing so much stress? "Hello?"

Silence. Hayley listened to her heartbeat. Ten beats.

"Hayley."

Trevor. Hayley stifled a gasp by inhaling slowly. "Did you want to talk to your mom and dad?"

He cleared his throat. "I'll talk to them when I come out. I need to talk to them, but to you, too…may I?"

Hayley moved back to the kitchen window and lifted her face to the sun. "Yes, I'd like that."

"Are you guys going to church this morning?"

"No. Your folks don't feel up to it, so we plan to have our own little worship time here."

"Oh. Maybe I'll wait until later, then. I could come after lunch."

Hayley took a deep breath. Couldn't hurt to suggest it. "Or you could join us."

A short, potent silence.

"You're right, I could." Trevor's voice sounded even huskier than usual. "I'll see you soon."

~*~

Hayley told Trevor's parents what he'd said.

"We need to pray." Franklin's voice was soft.

For the next hour, the kitchen table became an altar as Franklin, Laureen, and Hayley held hands and prayed for Trevor. For his salvation and healing. And for protection. Hayley's home city of Toronto never seemed so huge and far away. So much could go wrong, as she knew all too well. *Please, God…*

Franklin took a deep, shaky breath. "Father God, You know our hearts, and You know Trevor's. Grant him the healing he needs, we pray. And grant us grace and wisdom this morning to share Your love with him. Open his ears to hear Your voice, in Jesus' name."

Gravel crunched, and Laureen squeezed Hayley's hand before letting go. "That must be our boy." She pushed herself upright, wobbled, and grabbed the table. "Hayley, could you help me into the living room?"

Franklin stood and leaned against the wall behind him.

Hayley glanced at him sharply. "Are you all right?"

He waved her off. "I'm fine. You two go ahead. I'll be right behind you."

The elderly couple had barely settled onto the couch, when footsteps pounded up the steps and the front door opened.

Trevor stood in the open doorway. How could a face look so ravaged and hopeful at the same time?

Laureen scooted closer to Franklin and patted the space beside her. "Come here, son. Have a seat."

Trevor ducked his head and crossed the room.

Hayley's heart sank, and her throat constricted. He hadn't even looked at her.

He clasped his hands between his knees. "I'm not sure where to start. So much has happened." Finally, Trevor looked at Hayley for a moment before he bowed forward and closed his eyes. Almost as if he was praying.

A tiny sprig of anticipation germinated in Hayley's chest.

Laureen rubbed her son's broad back and prayed aloud. "Dear Lord, help our son, for Jesus' sake."

Trevor faced his parents. "You've been praying for me for a long time, haven't you?"

"Of course." Franklin's voice quavered just a bit. "We love you, Trev."

Trevor glanced at Hayley again, and the corners of his mouth lifted. "I love you, too."

Shock tingled through Hayley. Did he mean her?

Trevor looked back at his folks, his gaze lingering on his father's face and then his mother's. "So I guess God's been listening to you, because He opened my eyes last night."

"Thank You, Jesus." Laureen beamed and clasped her hands. "What happened?"

Trevor's gaze shifted to Hayley once more, and she cringed at the pain etched in his face. She wanted to smooth away the lines around his mouth, beside his beautiful eyes. But uncertainty glued her to her chair.

He cleared his throat. "When I left here last night, I was a mess. I'd come seeking answers, but what I saw and heard..."

That tiny sprig of hope died. Hayley released a quiet moan, but he must have heard.

"Hayley, I'm sorry. I made assumptions I had no right to make." He turned to his mother, and his voice lowered. "You sent Max. Thank you. God used him to make me see what a jerk I've been and showed me how to give my doubts, my past to Him." Trevor slid off the couch, knelt in front of his parents, and clasped their hands in his. "Mom, Dad, I got down on my knees last night, just like this, and asked God to make me the man I should be."

"Thank You, Lord! Praise God from Whom all

blessings flow…" Laureen sang, hands raised, and Franklin joined in. Their voices cracked, but their smiles radiated.

The whole room seemed to glow from the joy on Laureen and Franklin's faces. Hayley pressed her fingers to her eyes, but tears broke free and ran down her face as her prayer from the previous night echoed. *Even if Trevor can't love me, help him love You.*

God had heard. And answered. *Thank You.*

But part of her heart ached. If only Trevor could care for her, too.

Lost in her musing, she started when Trevor touched her hand. She hadn't even noticed him stand. "Wh-what?"

"Will you come with me later? Maybe out to the gazebo?"

She looked into his dark-lashed gray eyes and nodded, unable to speak.

Trevor blew out a breath. "Thanks." He sat back on the couch. His jaw clenched and unclenched. "I've still got some unfinished business, but Max says I've got to learn to trust God. In everything."

Franklin nodded. "That's an ongoing lesson, son. But we're thrilled to know that wherever you go, God will be leading you."

Hayley bit her lip. She couldn't bear to think about Trevor moving to Toronto now.

Trevor's gaze moved from his parents to Hayley and back again. "I have more news." He paused for several heartbeats. "I'm not going to Toronto after all. I plan to phone Vince Starr first thing tomorrow morning."

Franklin whooped, Laureen clapped her hands, and Trevor grinned.

"And one more thing. Think I could move back here? I've already sub-let my place to my buddy Ryan, and it wouldn't be right to back out of our deal."

While Trevor's parents laughed and hugged him, Hayley's mind whirled. Her body felt numb. It was too much to absorb.

Trevor, living at the farm?

Oh, sweet torture.

~*~

His parents took turns praying, their hands on his head. The living room looked the same, but he could swear heaven had joined them in the familiar space. Afterward, his mom wiped her eyes and rested her head on his dad's shoulder. Trevor drew in a shaky breath. These two were the best thing that had ever happened to him. His breath caught, and he breathed it out in a prayer. *Thanks, God, for their love.* He gazed at the one who'd triggered his desperate surrender to God. She'd kept quiet while his parents prayed. Her head remained bowed, her eyes closed.

Could Hayley forgive him? Could she give their relationship—the attraction quickly escalating into something much more—a chance? Time to find out. He patted his mom's shoulder, stood, and crossed the room. Trevor held out his hand. "Hayley, will you come with me?"

She looked up, jade eyes wide, and nodded. She placed her cool, small hand in his, and a tremor ripped through him. So delicate, so easily crushed. Like her feelings. *Oh, God…*

Laureen nodded toward the coat closet. "You'll need your coat, dear. It's pretty chilly this morning."

"Yeah, it is." He pulled Hayley to her feet but didn't let go of her hand. He'd keep this gorgeous redhead warm, no matter how cold it was outside. Trevor held Hayley's black wool coat as she slipped her arms into its sleeves, then pulled it up over her shoulders. Instead of releasing her, he slid his arms around her waist and brought her close to his body. He breathed in the peachy scent of her hair and rested his cheek on it. "Nice," he murmured. "I like your hair this way." Soft, auburn waves caressed his face.

Hayley leaned against his chest and drew in a shaky breath. "Thanks. It's too long to spike now, and I'm glad. That phase of my life is over."

She sounded defensive, unsure. And he was the cause. He swallowed regret. "The gazebo or my car? Your choice."

Hayley tilted her head. "I love the gazebo. If it's not too cold outside."

Trevor tightened his arms around her and then loosened his grip, turning her to face him. "It's cool, but not freezing."

Her decision suited him just fine. If she did get chilled, he could offer some warmth. Even the idea triggered heat zinging from his toes to his face. He could almost taste her lips on his. *Get a grip, man.* Trevor opened the back door and followed Hayley.

"I love the way the deck wraps around the gazebo. The deck's traditional lines contrast perfectly with the Victorian gazebo. So pretty. Like a fairy tale setting."

Was that nerves talking? Probably. Oh well, he could chitchat if it made her feel better.

"Dad and I built the deck about ten years ago, but the gazebo was his gift to Mom for their fiftieth anniversary. She'd always wanted one for some reason." He shrugged. "A deck was doable for Dad and me, but not such a fancy structure. We used a kit, and it turned out pretty nice. Mom loves it."

Hayley traced the carved hearts on either side of the entrance, a soft smile on her face. Then she turned, the smile gone. Lines appeared beside her mouth and between her eyebrows. "Let's get this over with."

He wanted to smooth away those lines with his lips. Apologize for doubting her. He could kick himself for hurting her. Trevor sat on the cold wooden bench and pulled Hayley down beside him. Would she mind if he tugged her closer? "Come'ere. I'll keep you warm." Hayley scooted as close as possible without sitting on his lap, and Trevor wrapped his arm around her shoulders. "Better?"

She nodded. "It's colder out here than I thought." A deep sigh. "Want to go first, or should I?"

"Go ahead."

"It's not a pretty story."

He touched his lips to her temple. "You don't have to tell me anything you don't want to. And whatever you've done, you're already forgiven."

"You mean by God? I know that, but I need to know if you can deal with it." Her gaze sharpened.

"Give me a chance. Please."

As Hayley confessed her relationship with Blake Horner, her voice dropped to a monotone. Trevor struggled with discomfort that turned to anger and then rage at Horner's betrayal. He curled his hands into fists and wrestled the urge to lash out.

"I'm sorry." Hayley fell silent.

Trevor thumped the back of his head against the structure's post. "I'd like to strangle the jerk, but I'm not angry with you. Please continue, Red."

Hayley snuggled back against him, but folded her arms and ducked her head. "That's not the worst part."

Trevor steeled himself. The baby. *God, help me.* "Talk. I need to know."

The explanation of the accident, the death of her baby, and the terrible, wrenching despair that nearly killed her tumbled out as she spoke. Soft sobs accompanied her words.

Trevor felt tears chill on his cheeks. He lifted her unresisting form onto his lap. "Hayley, I'm so sorry."

She turned her face to his jacket and wrapped her arms around his neck. He held her and stroked her hair, her back, and her arms. If only he could absorb her pain the way his denim jacket soaked up her tears. "Forgive me." He choked on the words but forced them out. "I jumped to conclusions when I heard you talking to that guy. But even if what I'd assumed was true, I had no right to judge you." He lifted her chin and wiped her tears with the pad of his thumb. "Can you forgive me?"

Hayley touched his cheek with a gloved hand. "Yes, of course I forgive you. But I need you to do something for me."

Trevor swallowed hard. "Anything." The haunter of his dreams tightened her arms around his neck, pulled his head lower, and tickled his lips with hers.

"Kiss me, please."

26

Thrills shot through Hayley as Trevor touched his lips to hers. He smelled like her cedar-lined closet and tasted like honey. Then his hand cupped the back of her head, and he pressed his firm mouth against hers.

Hayley shivered, but not from cold. Heat radiated and spread like liquid fire through her entire body. Rational thought fled. Hayley trembled and pressed against Trevor. He moaned against her mouth. Her hands fisted in his hair, and her toes curled. Hayley melted against Trevor's chest as her bones liquefied.

"Hayley. Wait." Trevor's agonized whisper broke through her haze. He lifted his head a fraction of an inch, breaking her hold, and inhaled a deep, shaky breath.

Cold air blew away passion's heat. Hayley flushed, embarrassed. What just happened? Should she apologize? Maybe, if she could catch her breath. "I…I…didn't mean to get carried away." She ducked her head and rested her cheek against his broad chest. Even through his thick jacket, she could hear the rapid thump, thump of his racing heart.

"Give me a minute." Trevor groaned and leaned his head against the gazebo's frame.

Hayley scooted away, pulled her knees up, and wrapped her arms around them. She couldn't look at him.

"Hey." Trevor's finger traced the curve of her

cheek and tucked a short wave behind her ear. "That was…great."

Hayley glanced sideways at him.

His beautiful mouth curved upward, his head tilted. "You OK?"

"Still shaky. And kind of embarrassed. I didn't mean to lose control."

Trevor slid his arm behind her and hugged her to his side. "I hope you're not sorry we kissed. It was incredible. *You're* incredible." His lips grazed her temple, creating more shivers. "Are you cold?"

"Not yet."

"In that case…" Trevor stood and held out his hand. "Want to go for a walk? I'm having second thoughts."

Hayley's heart clenched. About them? Maybe there'd never really been a "them." Her mouth tingled, and her pulse increased again. No, that couldn't be it. She stood and took his outstretched hand.

They walked hand in hand past the barn and out into a hayfield. Tiny green shoots poked through last season's rubble, as fragile as Hayley's dreams.

Trevor must have noticed her trying to avoid stepping on the new growth, because he chuckled and shook his head. "We're not doing it any damage. Alfalfa's tougher than it looks."

"I'm tougher than I look too. So tell me, what are you having second thoughts about?"

Trevor pulled her close, his hand firm on her back, and rested his forehead on hers. His breath tickled her nose, and she inhaled his woodsy scent.

"Hayley, I'm sorry."

~*~

Hayley closed her eyes and stiffened in his arms.

Trevor touched her cheek and felt tears. Confusion stalled his thoughts. Why was she crying again? He moistened his still-tingling lips. He had to make her understand. "I don't think I should move back to the farm after all. You're just too much of a temptation, and I don't want to hurt you. Us."

"*That's* what you changed your mind about? I thought…" Hayley twisted in Trevor's embrace.

The move threw him off balance. He stepped back to regain stability, his arms still gripping Hayley, and they both tumbled to the ground.

"*Umph*!" Trevor gasped for air as he hit the dirt.

Hayley scrambled to get off him, but he couldn't move. Couldn't breathe. Her elbow had punched him in the solar plexus. He'd been hit there before. It would take a moment or two, but breath would return. He willed himself to relax. Wait for air.

Hayley's eyes grew wider as she stood over him. "Trevor, get up! What's wrong? Did I hurt you?"

Finally, blessed air whooshed into his lungs. He sat up and reached a hand to Hayley.

Once he stood upright again, Trevor shook his head and chuckled. "You knocked the wind out of me, Red. Not for the first time today." He winked, and rosy pink bloomed on her face. He drew her close, tucked his finger under her chin. "What? Did you think I had second thoughts about us?"

Hayley turned her head.

Trevor took it as affirmation. "Not us, Hayley. Not a chance." He rested his cheek on the top of her head. "You know, God's been chasing me for a long, long time. But He used you to lasso me in. He went to a lot of trouble to bring us together, and I have a hunch He's got more in store for us. Together. The way I see it, we'd better not fight Him on this."

Hayley gazed up at him. Her eyes shone, and her hand covered her open mouth. "Oh, Trevor."

He laughed softly, crushed her against him, and whispered in her ear. "One more thing, Red. The next time you kiss me like that, we'd better be married."

Hayley reared back, her eyebrows nearly to her hairline. "Is that a proposal, Trevor Hiebert?"

Trevor gulped, coughed. His heart raced. He'd spoken without thinking. But since he'd said it, he realized he meant it. "Not yet, sweetheart. It's a good idea, but this is not the time or place." He grinned. "Trust me, you'll know when I propose to you."

Her eyes twinkled, and she pulled his head down. Trevor braced himself to keep control. But Hayley just pecked him on the cheek and let go.

"Safe enough, sir?"

Her giggle was infectious, and they laughed together until Trevor's stomach rumbled noisily.

He rubbed his belly and grinned. "Guess you're not all I need, after all."

Hayley pushed up her coat sleeve and exposed her dainty, silver watch. She looked up at him, eyebrows raised. "It's almost one o'clock. Your parents must be wondering what happened to us."

Trevor took her hand in his. "Maybe, maybe not. Those two have always known me better than I know myself, so I doubt we'll surprise them."

As they walked hand in hand toward the farmhouse, Hayley reminded him they'd gotten distracted. "So where will you live, if not here? Maybe I should move back to Dave and Lydia's."

Trevor rubbed his chin. "Mom still needs your help for a while. And your being here gives Dad peace of mind. I don't want you to leave. Hopefully Ryan and I can work something out. It should only be for a few months, anyway. If I get my way."

He squeezed Hayley's hand, and her answering laughter rang out like chimes.

When they reached the back door, Trevor stopped with his hand on the doorknob. "I just realized I need to talk to Carlos. As of today, I don't have a job."

27

Monday morning, Trevor drove toward Easy Rider an hour earlier than usual. He'd burned the bridge to Toronto. Vince Starr's scorching curses still rang in his ears, and Carlos had every right to give Trevor's job to someone else. Trevor's belly cramped. Maybe re-heated, day-old coffee on an empty stomach wasn't such a good idea.

Trevor pulled into the lot behind the shop and parked beside Carlos's almost-antique, green half ton. No trade-ins for Carlos, even when he'd bought a new truck. The man loved that old truck, promised he'd keep it going forever. Knowing Carlos, he probably would.

That was one of many things Trevor admired about the new-and-improved Carlos. He didn't quit, didn't give up on anything. Or anyone. Trevor stood tall, took a deep breath, and pushed the door open.

Carlos looked up from the motorcycle parts on his worktable. "T-man. What are you doing here? Thought you'd be packing for Toronto." His eyebrows drew together as he regarded Trevor. "What's wrong?"

"Got a minute? Maybe in your office?"

Carlos peered at Trevor as though he could read his thoughts. The scrutiny made Trevor want to squirm, but he stared right back. Finally, Carlos nodded, wiped his hands on a rag, and headed into his office. "So what's up?"

Trevor rubbed his chin as he discarded several openings. Might as well blurt it out. "I'm not going to Toronto. Phoned Vince Starr before I came." He grimaced. "That didn't go well, but Starr's reaction convinced me my decision was the right one."

"Hallelujah!" Carlos leaned back, propped his feet on his desk, and clasped his hands behind his head. One side of his mouth quirked upward. "So what happened to change your mind? Gotta be quite the story."

"Something just didn't feel right about Lowrider. I couldn't put my finger on it, but a couple days ago, the guy I was going to room with phoned. Nate Smith. He warned me to stay away. I don't know what's going on there, but when I talked to Max…"

"You and Max?" Carlos lunged forward, his feet hitting the floor with a thump.

"Yeah, we talked. A lot. Pretty smart guy."

Carlos's face lit up, especially his eyes. They seemed to bore into his very soul, just as Max's had.

"Now I know what you meant, boss—him telling you stuff you didn't know about yourself. He did that to me. Made me see how wrong I was. About pretty much everything. Like quitting everything here for pride's sake." He blew out a breath. "And judging people and God based on my own perceptions."

"You mean…"

Trevor nodded. "Yeah, all about Jesus. I think I get it now." He blew out a breath. "Well, I'm starting to."

Carlos raised his arms and lifted his face toward the ceiling. "Thank You, Jesus!" Then he leaned over the desk, his hand thrust out for a handshake. "Welcome to the family, bro."

Family? That sounded pretty good. Trevor got up

and grasped Carlos's hand. "Thanks." Then he sank back into the armchair. "So…is there any chance this family member could get his job back?" Before Carlos could respond, Trevor held up a hand, palm out. "I know I don't deserve it. I was ready to leave without a backward glance after all you've done for me. I regret that. I regret a lot of things."

"Regret's not a bad thing, if it leads you to repentance. But once you repent, hanging onto guilt won't do you—or anyone else—a bit of good. *Comprende*?" Carlos stroked his goatee. "So now you want your job back."

The knot in Trevor's gut tightened. "Have you already filled the position?" Panic began to swirl his thoughts. *Please, God.*

A grin broke through Carlos's stern look. "Naw, your job's open. I been prayin' you'd come to your senses before it was too late." He chortled. "You should see your face."

"Thanks, man. I'll make this up to you somehow." With all the emotions warring for dominance—gratitude for getting his job at Easy Rider back, frustration at Carlos's teasing, shame for his actions, and eagerness to get back to work—his face probably did look ridiculous. He grinned. He didn't even care.

"Yeah, you will. You can start by getting to work. The interview you did for the paper is bringing in lots of interest, several orders. As you know." He opened a drawer and pulled out a sheaf of papers. "Here. Take your pick and get to work."

"You're too good to me, boss."

Carlos grinned. "Don't you forget it. Welcome home, T." He cleared his throat.

"What?"

"I just had an idea. Since your bikes—and your handsome mug—are so popular, let's spotlight your Indian in the window. Build a raised stand so it shows up better from outside."

Trevor mulled it over for a minute. "Sure, as long as it's secure. Don't want anything to happen to my Chief."

A cold breeze came out of nowhere. Trevor shivered as an icy tingle raced up and down his back.

~*~

Hayley paced her bedroom, the receiver pressed to her ear, as though it would calm her nerves. "Hi, Daddy."

"I got your text. What do you mean, you're not coming back? After all we've done for you? I suppose you quit your course too, after I paid for it." Her father's cultured voice rose with every word.

What had she expected? Her parents would rejoice with her that she'd found her way, a reason to live?

"No, I haven't quit. In fact, I'm nearly finished, and you should be proud of my grades. I've booked my exams at the University of Saskatchewan for the end of June, and I expect to graduate with honors. But I'm staying here. This is my home now."

Home. A fleeting image of Trevor and her working side by side on the farm and someday adopting hurting kids, spread warmth outward from her heart, all the way to her cold fingers clutching the phone. God had brought her here, and He would work out His plan. His very good plan.

"Are you pregnant again?"

Her father's harsh words slapped her romantic

dream into far-flung bits, and Hayley gasped at the pain. Tears flooded her eyes, and as she reached blindly for a tissue, she fumbled the phone. It dropped to the floor. She wiped her eyes on her sleeve and knelt to pick up the phone. "Daddy?"

No response. Had the fall disconnected them, or had he?

Hayley sank onto her bed, lay on her side, and pulled her knees up to her chest. Why couldn't her parents support her? Oh, they'd always supplied her physical needs and often her impulsive wants. But not what she yearned for, their love.

Jesus, what am I supposed to do? How can I make them understand?

Pray for them.

The answer resonated in her heart. Hayley slid off the bed and onto her knees.

~*~

After supper, while Trevor placed the dirty dishes into the dishwasher, Hayley put away leftovers, barely enough to keep. She'd tried something new, chicken fettuccini, and the Hiebert family had declared it a grand success. Laureen and Franklin had lavishly praised her expanding repertoire, while Trevor nodded in agreement and helped himself to thirds.

After the conversation with her father, she needed a boost to her confidence. But Hayley had hardly tasted it. In spite of her open-heart prayers, her father's harsh accusations reverberated and stole her appetite. *Dear Jesus, if they cannot love me, at least help them accept my decision. Please.*

Strong, warm arms encircled her from behind, and

Trevor's whiskery chin nuzzled her neck. "That was delicious, Red. And so are you. Mm-mm."

"Just a second." Hayley placed the covered dish into the refrigerator, closed its door, and turned into Trevor's embrace. She leaned her cheek against his broad chest. The steady beat of his heart calmed her. Here, she mattered. She was safe. This home, this man—everything she'd dreamed of was right here. *Thank You, Jesus.*

Trevor stroked her cheek and tucked a short strand behind her ear. "You're pretty quiet tonight. Want to talk about it?"

Did she? She hated to burden Trevor with the ugliness of her relationship with her parents, but if the dream she dared to cherish came true, he'd be related to them. "Yeah, I guess so. Just let me make sure your parents don't need us, and maybe we could go for a drive. Would that be all right?"

"Of course." He hesitated. "My car's not very clean."

Hayley reached up and pecked his cheek. "Silly man, it's you I want, not your car." Heat rushed to her face as she realized what she'd said. "I mean..."

"I like the way you think." Trevor chuckled, lifted her chin, and kissed her. Hard.

Hayley broke contact, gasping, and ducked her head to lean on his chest again. Trevor's heartbeat raced, and she smiled. His rapid breath tousled her hair as he rested his cheek on the top of her head.

"This...." He whispered, sounding winded. "Is why...I can't...live in...the same house...as you. Yet."

Hayley closed her eyes and waited for her pulse to slow. "You're right." She hugged him tightly. "But at least you'll be close. Not in Toronto." Her least favorite place. "I'm so thankful."

Trevor's large palm caressed her back, creating tingles from the curve of her hip to her shoulder before his hand slid down her arms to clasp hers. "Me too. Now let's go tell Mom and Dad we're going for a drive."

A few minutes later, Trevor stopped at a viewpoint overlooking the North Saskatchewan River. The moon peeked out from behind a small cloud and illuminated the riffles of flowing water.

"Oh, so pretty," Hayley said. "I didn't realize your farm was so close to the river." She looked around. Darkness hid most of the details, but bushes of various heights reached for the sky beside the graveled area. "What kind of shrubs are those? They look familiar."

"Saskatoons. We used to pick buckets of the berries here in early summer. I'd help Mom clean them, and we'd freeze a bunch. Of course, she'd make a Saskatoon berry pie or two. Good times."

"Your family did a lot together, didn't they? You still do." She could hear her own wistfulness.

Trevor's seatbelt clicked.

Hayley raised her hand. "Wait. Maybe we should keep our seatbelts fastened." His brow furrowed, and she reached over to smooth those lines away. "Because, you know, I can't keep my hands off you."

"Good point." He grinned and re-fastened the restraint. "I think that goes both ways, darlin'. So, now that we're properly confined, how about you tell me what's bothering you."

Hayley swallowed hard. "My parents. I've always been a disappointment to them, especially my mother, but now my father seems to have taken her side. He used to stand up for me sometimes."

"What do you mean?"

"I told them I didn't plan to return to Toronto." She clasped her cold hands in her lap. "That didn't go over well. My father accused me of being a quitter." And pregnant. She trembled, unable to speak those words. "I prayed for them, but it still hurts. I don't know what else to do."

Trevor's seatbelt clicked and he slid closer. "I promise I'll be good, but I need to hold you. All right?"

Hayley nodded, released hers, and scooted close to his side. "How can I make them understand?"

Trevor sat quietly for a moment, his eyes closed. Was he praying? A little thrill shot through Hayley. God really could change people.

Then he lifted her chin, and his eyes connected with hers. "You can't. Only God can change people's hearts."

Hayley gasped. "I had the same thought, right before you said it. God spoke through you. Wow. I needed that reminder. I can't change the way my parents feel, but I can keep loving and praying for them. I should ask your parents to pray. I think they have a direct line to God."

"Good idea. They're definitely well-practiced in prayer." Trevor chuckled dryly. "I gave them plenty of reasons."

Hayley leaned her head against Trevor's shoulder. "Thank you for understanding."

Contented silence filled the vehicle for several moments, until Trevor cleared his throat and coughed a little, as though he was nervous. Hayley looked up and noticed a line between his eyebrows. "What's wrong?"

"What are they going to think of me?"

28

Wednesday morning, Hayley pushed the couch back into place and shut off the vacuum. Lugging the machine around the large farmhouse took a lot of effort. How had Laureen managed, even before she broke her arm? *Thank you, Lord Jesus, for letting me help her.*

Earlier, Hayley had pulled cereal bowls from the cupboard and placed them on the scarred table. Laureen usually set the table because she said it made her feel useful. But today, she'd admitted she didn't feel steady enough to handle dishes.

Laureen's chin had trembled as she groped for the table and sank onto her chair. "I don't mean to grumble. But I'm used to serving, not being served." She'd patted Hayley's hand. "I am thankful for you, my dear. Please forgive my rotten mood."

Laureen's dizzy spells seemed to be getting worse. A twinge of apprehension wriggled through Hayley's mind. How could she not worry when the woman she loved like a mother grew less steady with each passing day?

"Hayley, do you have a minute?" Laureen gripped the doorway dividing the living room from the kitchen.

"Sure. Do I have time to put away the vacuum cleaner first?" At Laureen's nod, Hayley picked up the machine and carried it to the broom closet.

When she entered the kitchen, Franklin and Laureen sat shoulder to shoulder as though supporting one another.

"What's wrong?"

The old couple shared a long look before Laureen spoke. "You know my videostagmography, the 'dizzy test' appointment is this afternoon. Franklin was going to drive me, but plans have changed. His cardiologist had a cancellation and wants him to come in today. He wants to run some tests and said Franklin shouldn't drive. The cardiologist is at Royal University Hospital, and my test is at St. Paul's. To make matters worse, Franklin's appointment is at two, and mine is at two-thirty. We need your help, Hayley."

Hayley had driven to the mall at the edge of the city for groceries and other supplies, but that was as far as she'd dared. How could they expect her to drive right through downtown Saskatoon?

"You'll be fine, missy." Franklin winked. "While we're lounging in our respective waiting rooms, you should have time to visit Trevor, maybe steal him away for a cup of coffee."

The tightness in Hayley's throat melted away. Coffee with Trevor would be a sweet reward for stepping so far outside her comfort zone. She smiled, and hoped her lips didn't tremble. "I'll do it. As you keep reminding me, God's got this."

The responsibility of transporting these precious people terrified her. What if she froze at the wheel? What if she got lost? All kinds of terrible scenarios ran through her mind. *Please, dear Lord, give me courage. I need to overcome this fear. For all of us.*

~*~

Trevor stood behind the counter and wrote up an order for custom-made leather bike gear for a forty-something couple. His mouth quirked upward as he wrote in the special requests. "Lady" on the woman's jacket sleeve, and "Duke" on the man's. Pretty cheesy, but it was what they wanted.

The man watched Trevor write. "Yep. Comin' up on our twentieth anniversary, so we figured we'd check this off our bucket list. Plannin' to ride right across this great country this summer on our Honda Goldwing."

"Twenty years, eh? Congratulations." He looked forward to twenty years with Hayley. And then another twenty, and another…

The man slid his arm around his wife's waist and tugged her closer. "Thanks, man. Hasn't always been easy, but this lady's sure worth the effort."

The stout, rather plain-faced woman's smile lit her face and made her look almost beautiful. "Are you married?"

Trevor shook his head. "Not yet, but I hope to change that soon."

"Sweet."

Trevor smiled as he finished the order, collected their deposit, and walked the couple to the door. "I'll give you a call when your order arrives. Thanks for coming in." He opened the door for them, and as they exited, a figure across the street caught his eye. His jaw clenched, and he blinked. He looked again, and the person was gone. Trevor rubbed his jaw as he headed for the back room.

Something about the guy reminded him of his old foster dad, Larry Kirby. But he'd heard that Kirby had left Saskatchewan. Gone to the Maritimes.

Trevor smacked his palm against the workbench. That creep better not show his face, or he would finally get what he deserved.

Like you got what you deserved?

Trevor gritted his teeth. Sure, God had forgiven him and everything he'd done. And he was grateful. But he could never forgive Larry Kirby. Trevor had vowed a long time ago to kill the dirt bag, and given the opportunity, he would.

God wouldn't expect him to break a vow, would He? Trevor sighed. Yeah, God probably would. "Forgive as He has forgiven you." Max's voice echoed in his head. But in this case, God asked too much.

Trevor put on his safety glasses, clamped a rusty fender onto the work bench, and began to grind away the oxidation. Sparks and grit flew. After several minutes, Trevor shut off the grinder and wiped the fender. Clean metal gleamed under the fluorescent lights. The transformation pricked his conscience and made him wince. He hoped God wouldn't have to use a grinder on him, to clean off his rust of hate. Trevor jumped when Ryan slapped him on the back.

"Hey, T, you might want to check your phone. It just sang a real pretty love song to me." He struck a pose with his back arched and a hand over his heart and sang about a man loving a woman.

Hayley's ringtone. Trevor grinned, slugged his friend's arm, and strode to the locked closet where they stored their personal items. He scrolled through the messages. Concern replaced excitement. Hayley hated to drive in the city, even though she'd been working at overcoming her fear. And why did his dad need to see a cardiologist? Then he recalled the times his dad seemed unable to catch his breath.

After she dropped off his parents, Hayley wanted to take him out for coffee. That would perk up his day. Trevor groaned at his unintentional pun. He typed his response. *Yes, come. Busy, but I will make time for you. U R worth it.* His finger hovered over a silly heart emoticon. Nope. Not even for Hayley. He grinned and pushed SEND.

~*~

Hayley slowed the minivan as they neared the approach to the Yellowhead Highway. Light traffic, clear blue skies, and a divided highway awaited her. Nothing to worry about. She willed her shoulders to relax and switched on the right-turn signal.

"Doin' fine, missy." Franklin's gravelly voice reassured her. "You've got this."

"And God's got me. Right." The first time she'd driven this route, it had seemed terribly long. Today, it was too short. Her entire back tensed as vehicles raced by them, some swerving in and out of her lane.

A large box van pulled right in front of her. Hayley stomped on the brake. Franklin lurched forward, and Laureen gasped from the back seat. Hayley glanced in the rear view mirror. Traffic sped toward them. She pressed the accelerator and regained speed as a semi-trailer unit swung around them. "I'm so sorry. I thought that guy was going to hit us." She looked in the mirror at Laureen. "Are you all right?"

"We're fine."

But Laureen looked paler than usual. Hayley gripped the steering wheel, her knuckles white. The dashboard clock read one-thirty. Plenty of time to deliver both to their appointments, as long as she didn't cause any accidents. *Please, Jesus, I need You.*

The Yellowhead merged into Idylwyld Drive, and the four-lane road narrowed. More traffic, too many pedestrians, and stoplights at nearly every intersection.

Hayley's neck muscles began to ache as she tried to keep track of everything. "Which way?"

"You want the easy way or the faster way?"

"Easy."

"Figured as much." He chuckled. "Stay on Idylwyld to 25th Street, take a left, and follow it to the university gates. No problem."

A few minutes later, Hayley parked the car in front of the hospital, and Franklin opened his door.

"I know my way from here, and you need to get my wife to her appointment. I'll call you when I'm ready to go."

Franklin slid open the back door and leaned in. He cupped Laureen's wrinkled cheek, kissed her on the forehead and then settled on her lips. "See you later, sweetheart."

Hayley melted a little; she blinked rapidly to clear her vision.

Laureen moved to the front passenger seat and Hayley drove back into the traffic on 25th. One delivered, one to go. At the first red light, Hayley glanced at Laureen. "Should I go back the way I came, or is there an easier way?"

"Probably best to stay on this street to Idylwyld." Laureen patted Hayley's arm. "You're doing great. I'm proud of you."

Her warm voice settled into Hayley's soul. Maybe she *could* drive without fear. A horn blared behind her, and Hayley jumped. How long had the light been green? Heat rushed to her face as she accelerated. "Sorry."

"Just relax, dear. You're doing fine." Laureen sounded a lot more confident than Hayley felt.

She followed Laureen's calm directions and maneuvered the minivan between merging vehicles onto 22nd Street West.

"Good girl. After a few blocks, you'll want to get into the left lane. Avenue H is coming up, and we need to turn south there. The hospital is just down the road a few blocks."

Hayley turned onto the two-lane road and cringed. Vehicles were parked on both sides of the narrow road, making the minivan feel like a bus. She slowed, her jaw tight, and the minivan crept to their destination. Hayley parked in the loading area and slumped against the seat back.

"You did it." Laureen's smile eased some of Hayley's tension. The older woman's lack of color increased it again.

"Let me help you inside, OK?"

Laureen sighed. "Yes, please. I'm pretty woozy today. Guess this is a good day for my dizzy test." She leaned her head against the seat back. "In fact, maybe you should find a wheelchair. Should be some just inside the door."

Moments later, Laureen sat in a wheelchair and was about to be whisked away by a plump, friendly volunteer. "Don't worry, miss, we'll take good care of your mother."

Hayley opened her mouth to correct the woman, but Laureen caught her attention with a wink. Hayley smiled wistfully. "Thank you."

Laureen held up her free hand. "I'll call you when

I'm ready, but don't cut your time with Trevor short. I can wait." She blew Hayley a kiss. "And don't worry. God's got this too."

Hayley swiped her sleeve across her eyes as she returned to the minivan. Now she was on her own. She paused with the door open. No, that wasn't right. Her heavenly Father was with her. Watching over her, taking care of her.

"You've got this, and God's got you." Franklin's words echoed in her heart.

Yes, she could do this. Hayley studied Trevor's simple directions and then fastened her seatbelt.

Trevor promised he'd make time for her, no matter how busy he was. Well, she would brave city traffic for him, no matter how nervous she felt.

If that wasn't love, what was?

~*~

Ryan was warbling that silly love song again.

Trevor grabbed his chiming phone and scowled at Ryan. "Don't."

Several of the guys joined in with Ryan's singing.

Trevor shook his head, strode into the washroom, and shut the door against their good-natured teasing.

"On my way, leaving St. Paul's now." Her text was brief.

He couldn't wait to see her. Hold her. Kiss her. His woman. He addressed his reflection in the grimy mirror. "Calm down, man, it's just coffee. With the most gorgeous woman in the world, but still, just coffee in a public place."

It would take about fifteen minutes for Hayley to get there from St. Paul's Hospital, enough time to clean up and do some restocking. Business had been brisk, leaving little time to replace items sold. As he scrubbed his nails, Trevor considered his change of heart. Two weeks ago, he couldn't wait to leave, go to Toronto, and try to make a name for himself. Be a big shot in a big city. He cringed. *Thank You, Jesus, for saving me from myself.*

It was all God: Hayley's entrance into his life, Carlos and Max convincing him God loved him, and Nate Smith's warning to stay away from Lowrider. He hadn't heard anything in the news about the Toronto bike shop. Even if Smith had misled him for some reason, Trevor couldn't regret his decision. He was in the place he belonged.

Trevor checked the showroom displays, took note of missing items, and retrieved them from the storeroom. As he placed a large-sized helmet on the shelf, movement outside caught his eye. The back of his neck prickled. He glanced out the window.

A middle-aged man in baggy jeans, a bulky plaid jacket, and a ball cap glared back. The man made an obscene gesture, then turned and jogged across the street.

Chills raced up and down Trevor's spine, followed by intense heat. His jaw clenched, and his pulse pounded in his ears. He could never forget that face.

Larry Kirby.

29

Hayley turned off Faithfull Avenue and drove slowly down 45th Street until she spotted the sign for her destination, Easy Rider. Relief coursed through her as she pulled into a double-length parking spot just a couple doors down. *Thank You, Jesus.*

Trevor's workplace was a well-designed storefront with retro neon lights spelling out *Easy Rider Motorcycles*. Wire mesh was embedded into the glass of the full-length display window. On the other side of the glass, an old but beautifully restored motorcycle posed. Dark orange paint, fringed leather seat and saddlebags reminded her of something Trevor had said. Could this be his cherished, antique Indian motorcycle? If so, it was no wonder he took such pride in it.

She imagined a young Trevor working side by side with Franklin on a box of parts, and how they'd transformed those old, dirty pieces into this masterpiece. Amazing. Hayley looked up and met the gaze of a sandy-haired young man near the back of the showroom. His eyebrows lifted, and he disappeared through a doorway. Hayley pushed the door open and strolled into a bright but crowded store.

She barely got a chance to look around before Trevor strode into the showroom, and everything else faded. He opened his arms, and Hayley walked into his embrace. She wrapped her arms around his waist and clung to his strength, her cheek pressed against his broad chest. She didn't care if people stared.

Trevor's breath tickled her ear. "Let's get out of here, OK?"

"As long as you drive."

He chuckled and squeezed her closer before stepping back. "I'll grab my jacket and let Carlos know."

The young guy who'd stared at her blocked Trevor's path. "Hey, T, aren't you gonna introduce us to your lady?"

"As long as you remember she's taken." He pulled her to his side. "Guys, this is Hayley Blankenship. Hayley, these are the losers I work with." He indicated each one, beginning with the fellow who'd spoken. "Ryan O'Shea, who's also my new roommate, Jonesy…"

He rattled off several more names. Trevor had mentioned Ryan before, called him his friend. Ryan's friendly grin and the twinkle in his eyes made Hayley smile back.

Hayley waved her fingers from the protection of Trevor's encircling arm. "Hi, everyone."

A Latino man with sparkling dark eyes and a gray-streaked goatee entered the showroom, his hand extended. "I'm Carlos, Trevor's boss. I can't tell you how pleased I am to finally meet you, Miss Blankenship. Heard a lot about you."

Hayley smiled and took Carlos's hand. "Thank you. Please call me Hayley. It's nice to meet you. I've heard a lot about you, too—all good."

Carlos slapped Trevor on the shoulder. "All right, T-man, take this young lady out of here before I have to mop their drool off the floor."

At the coffee shop, Hayley cradled her half-empty cup of mocha cappuccino as she studied Trevor's face. The line between his eyebrows and the set of his jaw worried her. "What's wrong?"

"Nothing."

"Really? Then why do you look upset? Was it something I said?"

"Of course not. It's..." He shifted on the hard chair. "Remember the foster dad I told you about?"

"Larry Kirby."

Trevor nodded, his face grim. "He showed up outside the shop today."

"You're kidding. Did he see you?" A chill washed over Hayley.

"Yeah." Trevor growled. "I can't believe he came back. I was only a kid last time. If he tries anything now..."

Hayley reached toward him. "Trevor, you have to forgive that man. For your own sake."

"Not a chance, sweetheart. I made a vow a long time ago, and if I get the chance, I'll follow through."

No, her Trevor wouldn't. "You can't mean..."

Trevor clenched his fists and pounded the table. "Kirby caused the death of my foster sister. He doesn't deserve to live."

The hatred on his face turned Hayley's stomach. Bile rose in her throat, and she gagged. "Excuse me." She dashed to the washroom and barely made it into the stall in time. Everything came up, her cappuccino, her lunch, her hopes and dreams. Hayley knelt on the cold tile floor as tears streamed down her face. Her phone chimed. Hayley flushed the toilet, staggered to the sink, and rinsed her mouth and face. She leaned against the counter and checked the message. Laureen.

"Test went well. Franklin messaged he is still waiting. I will take a taxi to RUH. Meet us in Cardiology when you're ready. No rush."

A tiny seed of thankfulness germinated. Laureen's test had gone well. A good thing. Something to hold onto. Wasn't it? Something pricked her memory, but she couldn't pin it down. And Franklin's condition? Unsure. Then there was Trevor. Hayley's shoulders slumped. The man she loved had disappeared into a vortex of hate. She didn't want to know the rage-filled person waiting for her. *Jesus, what am I supposed to do now?*

~*~

Trevor shoved his untouched coffee to the side and buried his face in his hands. His fierce anger ebbed, washed away by a wave of regret. He'd never forget the look of horror on Hayley's face, her jade eyes wide and her lips parted and framed in white. In fact, her whole face had paled as she clutched her stomach, got up, and ran. Away from him and his rage. His chest burned as Hayley's words echoed. "You *have* to forgive that man, for your own sake." Truth pierced his soul. She was right. Hatred devoured him, and now it had injured Hayley too. He'd blown it. His dreams crumbled.

"Trevor." Hayley's tremulous voice, puffy eyes and downturned mouth spoke volumes.

Regret kicked him in the gut. He reached toward her. "I'm sorry. I didn't mean…"

"I'll drop you off at your work."

Trevor nodded, walked around Hayley to the coffee shop door, and opened it for her. She walked past him without speaking, her shoulders hunched.

Once inside the van, Trevor tried again. "Hayley, forgive me. Please."

She turned, eyes blazing. "Forgive? What do you know about forgiveness? I can't trust you right now. You're letting anger destroy you. Us."

Her words struck deep. Trevor couldn't think of a response, so he clamped his mouth shut.

Hayley cranked the key in the ignition and switched on the windshield wipers to deal with the light rain.

All the way back to the shop, the wipers seemed to whisper, "Forgive, forgive, forgive..." With each swipe, Trevor's mood darkened. Forgive Kirby? Not possible. He glanced at Hayley, whose total concentration centered on the road. The wall between them was palpable, and he'd do anything to break it down.

Except what she'd asked.

~*~

Hayley pulled over in front of Easy Rider and stopped. She didn't want to look at Trevor, but her head wasn't listening. Moisture glistened in his eyes and new lines were carved on his face. Her heart clenched, but her throat refused to allow words.

"Good-bye, Hayley."

Hayley nodded as tears blurred her vision. She swiped her coat sleeve across her face and closed her eyes until she heard the passenger door close. She sat with her head bowed for several minutes as she waited for her pulse to calm and her tears to dry. Waited for the old, familiar numbness to set in.

She found her way back to Royal University Hospital and maneuvered the minivan into a tight parking spot. Others headed toward a two-story tower in the middle of the parking structure, so Hayley followed them. She approached a round desk labeled *Information*.

The gray-haired woman at the desk smiled. "How may I help you?"

"Cardiology. Where will I find it?"

A few minutes later, Hayley found Laureen in the unit's waiting room.

"I didn't expect to see you for quite a while." Laureen peered at Hayley, and her brows rose in an inverted V. "What happened?"

Hayley shook her head as she sat beside Trevor's mother. Sometimes deflection was better than the truth. "How was your test?"

"My expected ordeal wasn't bad at all. The technician put a special mask over my eyes—it had cameras in it, or something—and then she put warm water in my ears. One side per test. It was supposed to create extreme vertigo, but I sailed through. I even feel less dizzy now. I am thankful."

Hayley forced a smile. "You must be relieved. But where's your husband?"

Laureen pressed her lips together and squeezed her eyes shut.

Alarm bells rang in Hayley's mind. "What's wrong with Franklin?"

Laureen took Hayley's hand in hers and began to trace circles on her palm. Just like Trevor had done on the plane when they'd first met. Pain ripped through her heart.

"Apparently he phoned his doctor without letting

me know. The episode after your visit from that young man scared him more than I realized. That's why he got the call this morning." She let go of Hayley's hand and dabbed at her eyes. "They did a scan of his heart, and when the results were read, they took him for an emergency angiogram. About twenty minutes ago. The orderly said it would take one or two hours." Laureen released a long, shuddering breath. "Hayley, will you pray with me? I need to pray."

Hayley froze. Could she pray? Her frustration was directed at Trevor, not God. She'd pray to comfort her friend. "Of course."

"Please, heavenly Father, heal Franklin. Guide the doctors to the best decisions to speed his recovery." Laureen gave a muffled sob. "I need him, Lord. But Your will be done."

Tears ran down Hayley's cheeks. Fear and pain closed her throat. She gulped back a moan and choked out, "Amen."

After several more heartbeats of silence, Laureen patted Hayley's arm. "Thank you, dear. Having you here means a lot to me. It'll be a long wait. Shall we see if the cafeteria serves drinkable coffee? Or have you had enough already?"

Hayley pictured her half-full cup back at the coffee shop. "Coffee sounds great." She started to rise. "Are you OK to walk, or should I find a wheelchair?"

Laureen waved her off. "I'm a little wobbly, but not as bad as before. If I could lean on you a bit…"

"Sure." Hayley helped Laureen rise and slid an arm around the older woman's waist. "I passed the cafeteria on my way here. It's not far."

Hayley helped Laureen to a table when they found the cafeteria. Then she grabbed a tray and retrieved two coffees, a couple small creamers, and two cinnamon rolls. "Here we go." Hayley unloaded the tray. "The coffee smells fresh, and the cinnamon buns looked too good to pass up."

"That does smell good. Thank you, dear." She took a careful sip. "Perfect. But I'll bet your cinnamon buns are better than these."

Hayley blushed with pleasure. This woman's graciousness brightened the worst day.

They nibbled the soft, gooey buns, and sipped coffee. Laureen looked more relaxed now as she shared humorous stories of life on the farm. Even difficulties became positive life lessons, and some of her animal tales made Hayley laugh out loud. Her gloom lifted.

"You and Trevor are going to the Good Friday service at Lydia's church, aren't you? It's just two days away."

Laureen's casual question made Hayley gasp, and she inhaled some coffee. When she caught her breath, her words stumbled. "I-I'm not sure. Certainly I want to come. But Trevor? I…don't know."

~*~

Trevor jerked when someone tapped on his shoulder. He shut off the welder and lifted his helmet.

"We got a problem." Carlos turned off the radio.

"I don't want to talk about it."

Carlos grimaced. "Not whatever put a burr under your saddle. Here. Now. There's a guy demanding to see you. And he's loaded. Don't-light-a-match drunk."

Could the day get any worse? Trevor took off his welding helmet and stood. "I'll take care of it."

Carlos pinned him with a glare. "Good. And then

you'd better shed whatever's bugging you. It's affecting the whole crew."

Yeah, he'd been a bear since Hayley had dropped him off. He'd shoved past Ryan when his friend had greeted him, strode to the workshop, and cranked the radio to its loudest. Then he'd buried himself in welding, welcomed the sparks that burned through his coveralls. He deserved to burn. "Sorry." He stopped mid-stride and turned to his boss. "Really. I am sorry. If it's all right with you, I'll take off after I deal with this guy."

"Might as well."

Carlos went back to his office, and guilt gut-punched Trevor. Carlos had done more for him than he could ever repay. Maybe he should have left for Toronto, after all. He wiped sweat from his face and headed to the noisy showroom. Whoever was doing all that swearing sounded terribly familiar. He stopped in the doorway, and the sudden silence reverberated.

His coworkers backed away, leaving the drunk in the center of the showroom.

Black rage enveloped Trevor. His fists clenched. His pulse pounded.

The man turned on him. "Well, well, Trevor Sinclair. I found you at last, you lousy, no-good, son of a…"

In two strides, Trevor crossed the room and lunged at the smaller man—but missed.

Kirby's face contorted, his skin purple and his eyes wild. He stumbled back, tripped, and shrieked as he fell.

Distaste curled Trevor's lips. He raised his foot to kick the waste of skin.

Max's deep, calm voice stalled him. "Don't lower

yourself to his level. You're better than that. Forgiven, remember? Take a step back."

In a daze, Trevor lowered his foot and obeyed.

"This isn't over!" Kirby scrambled to his feet and staggered toward the door. Halfway there, he swerved toward Trevor's Indian Chief.

Trevor tried to move, but strong hands held him back. "No!"

Kirby cackled as he rushed forward and shoved Trevor's priceless bike off its stand. It crashed against the display window, spreading erratic cracks the width of the glass. The bike slid to the floor, its right handlebar bent and the front fender crumpled. Larry Kirby turned, raised both fists, and shook them in a drunken victory dance. "*Now* it's over." He shoved the door open and staggered down the street.

"Why'd you hold me back?" Trevor yelled.

Ryan shrugged, palms up.

The other guys looked away. No one answered.

"Max. Where'd Max go?" How could the big man disappear so fast?

Ryan's brow furrowed. "You mean Carlos's friend?"

Trevor didn't even try to keep the sarcasm out of his tone. "Yeah, that Max."

"He was never here, man."

30

Hayley couldn't bear to talk about Trevor. But he should go to the Good Friday service. Maybe something there would pierce his unforgiving heart. *Oh, Jesus…*

Laureen patted Hayley's hand. "Not to worry. God will work it out."

Hayley tried to grab hold of that assurance, but the memory of Trevor's rage-twisted face snagged it away. She gathered their empty cups and plates. "Ready to go back to cardiology?"

"Oh, my. Yes. They may be done by now."

The two women had barely settled onto the hard, vinyl chairs in the waiting room when a man wearing green scrubs entered the room. "Mrs. Hiebert?" He glanced at a paper in his hand. "Laureen Hiebert?"

"I'm here." Laureen tried to stand, wobbled, and sat heavily.

The tired-looking young man sat beside her. "I'm Dr. Albrecht. I performed your husband's angiogram. Is this your daughter?"

"Close enough."

Dr. Albrecht's steady gaze seemed to carry a warning.

Hayley clasped her hands in her lap and wished she could pray.

"The angiogram showed severe blockage in two of Mr. Hiebert's arteries, ninety-five occlusion in one and ninety-two in the other. Dr. Sharma, head of our cardiac surgery department, has booked him for coronary bypass surgery tomorrow morning at ten. Because of Mr. Hiebert's high degree of occlusion, we'd prefer to keep him here until then."

Laureen's mouth opened and closed a few times. She rubbed her face and swallowed hard. "May…may I see him?"

"We're getting him settled into a room. I'll send an orderly to take you to him in a few minutes." He placed his hand on Laureen's shoulder. "You need to take care of yourself. Talk to your husband and then go home. He's in good hands. Trust me."

Laureen swiped at the tears dripping from her jaw. "Thank you, Doctor."

"You're welcome."

Dr. Albrecht walked away, and Hayley's composure left at the same time. She hunched forward, elbows on her knees, and sobbed. *This isn't fair, God. How are You going to make this good?*

A gentle hand stroked her back. Soothing, comforting. Hayley peeked to the side, and Laureen smiled through tears.

"God is in this, dear. Even when our feelings try to tell us otherwise. Think about it. From what the doctor said, Franklin could have had a heart attack at any time. But God prevented it, and now he's booked for surgery. Tomorrow." Laureen pulled a tissue from her pocket and wiped her face. "This is a gift from a loving Father."

How could Laureen be so calm? Her husband faced major surgery and could die at any minute, yet Laureen's faith didn't seem to waver. "How can you be sure God's in control? It feels like a train wreck to me."

"That's why we pay more attention to God's promises than our emotions." Laureen inhaled a long, shuddering sigh. "My emotions are pretty battered right now, but I know my Rock is solid. I can trust Him. Even with the ones I love the most." Laureen's hand went to her mouth. "Trevor. I've got to call my son."

~*~

Trevor ran his hands over the crumpled fender. Bent, but not torn. The handlebar too. A couple of the slender spokes were twisted, but he could handle it. It would take some work, but the bike was fixable. Then he noticed a stinging in his left hand and looked down. Blood dripped from the side of his hand where he'd brushed against the headlamp. Trevor groaned; his heart plummeted. Jagged glass and twisted metal were all that remained of the fixture he'd spent four months tracking down. How would he ever find another replacement? He flinched when a heavy hand grasped his shoulder.

Carlos cleared his throat. "Let me help you get your bike into the back. Good thing the mesh held the glass. Could have been worse."

Trevor's whole attention had been on his own troubles. As usual. He swallowed hard and pushed upright. "Look, man, I'm sorry. About all of this."

Carlos bent down and grabbed the back of the motorcycle. "Good. Now let's get this mess cleaned up. Then we'll talk."

A few minutes later, the two men faced each other across the desk. Carlos stroked his goatee while Trevor fidgeted.

"So that's the guy you told me about. And Sinclair, that's your birth name?" Carlos's desert-dry voice calmed Trevor enough to meet his gaze.

"Yeah. And yes, that was my foster dad. Impressive, eh?" His attention dropped to the floor. "I really regret what happened."

Carlos leaned back, his feet on the desk and his hands behind his head. "That's an awful lot of hatred to carry around. Especially for a guy who's been forgiven."

Guilt zinged, and Hayley's words echoed. *What do you know about forgiveness?* Not much, apparently.

"You're right. It's just…I've hated that man for so long, I don't know how to give it up." He slumped in the chair. "Hayley's right. I don't know anything about forgiveness."

"Ah, so that's what frosted your cornflakes. Tiff with the lady. Sounds like she's got you pegged. So what're you gonna do about it?"

"What can I do? I've totally blown it."

"In case you didn't hear me the first hundred times, God is the God of second chances, T-man. Repent. Give all your hatred to Jesus, who died to pay your penalty. Give Kirby to Him too. Let God be the judge. You are forgiven. Now step away. That's forgiveness."

Trevor hunched forward, hung his head, and concentrated on a tiny spring of hope. "God, I'm sorry. I would have killed the man if Max hadn't stopped me. Forgive me, and help me forgive." Tension seeped out of Trevor's body, replaced by a strange peace.

Carlos raised one eyebrow nearly to his receding hairline.

"What?"

"Max. You said Max stopped you."

"Yeah, it was weird. Ryan said he wasn't even there, but I heard him, and he grabbed me when I started to kick the dirty…Kirby."

"Interesting. Maybe your conscience sounds like Max now." Carlos stroked his beard. "Or perhaps Max is more than he appears."

"I don't get it."

"Don't need to. But I need to know if this is settled. How *are* you?"

Trevor nodded. "Good. Forgiven…again. At least by God. And the tight spring inside just relaxed. I'm free. Amazing." He paused, rubbed his chin. "But what about you, boss? Can you forgive me?"

Carlos slapped him on the shoulder. "Already done. Now you need to call your lady."

"I think I'd better try that in person. I'd like to take off, if you don't mind, after I apologize to the guys and clean up the mess."

"Sounds like a plan. Right now, I need to phone my insurance adjuster."

Trevor grabbed a broom and dustpan. "Thanks, boss. For everything."

Half an hour later, Trevor lugged what was left of the display stand out to the disposal bin behind the shop. He let the lid slam down on the evidence of his feud with Kirby. He closed the padlock and walked back into the shop, leaving his hatred behind, locked in God's mercy.

Trevor retrieved his jacket from the locker and pulled his phone out. He'd turned off the ringer after getting razzed by the guys, so he checked first for messages. No texts, but his mother had left a voicemail. He punched in his code and held the phone to his ear.

"Trevor, it's Mom."

The shakiness in her voice started an earthquake inside Trevor. His breath came hard as he strained to hear the rest of her message.

"I need to talk to you. We're heading home, so please come when you can. Just remember, I love you, and so does God. Hurry home, please."

Her muffled sob tore a gash in his heart. His mom, the rock of his family, sounded like she was falling apart.

Oh, God.

~*~

All the way back to the farm, Hayley's despondency deepened. While Laureen sat quietly, her head resting against the seat back, Hayley sank deeper, until she could no longer remember why she'd wanted to live. God didn't seem to care.

Once they were home, Hayley helped Laureen to the overstuffed chair, pulled the footstool close, and fetched Laureen's Bible and a cup of tea. Then she excused herself and climbed the stairs. The shakiness that had started on the drive home hit with full force. Hayley dropped onto the chair and put her head down on her arms. "God, I'm so mad at You. What in the world are You doing? Franklin and Laureen love You, and You're treating them like dirt. I thought You'd brought Trevor and me together, and now You've taken my dream away. Stomped on it. And me. I thought I could trust You. I want to, but this is too hard. Maybe You're not real. Or not good."

Dark whispers began. "That's right. God doesn't care. No one does."

She jerked upright. "Who's there?" She didn't see anyone.

The whispers continued, close to her ear. "It's no use. Life is an illusion. Give it up. You know how."

The pills. Hayley hadn't thought of them in weeks. Pain shot up her leg, straight to her heart, and she pushed her fist against her mouth to muffle a cry. The opiates she'd hidden were her only hope. She opened the bottom drawer and felt for the small bottle under a stack of papers. Her arm cramped, but she kept reaching until her fingers touched cold plastic. She pulled it out. Five pills.

One would ease her pain, two meant a long, deep sleep. The last time, three had almost freed her from her agony. Too bad her co-worker had picked that day to drop off some flowers.

There were five left. No more pain. The end.

Hayley held the bottle in the palm of her hand. *What have I got left to lose?*

Trevor? Already gone.

Franklin? He could die on the operating table, or before. Or after. Life was too fragile.

Laureen? She'd aced her test, but something still wasn't right. What was causing her dizziness?

Her parents? They didn't care, anyway.

Another whisper. "See? There's no one and nothing left. Go ahead. End it."

Hayley emptied the pills into her hand, and looked around for a glass of water. She'd left one on her nightstand, but now her Bible lay in its place. She picked up the Bible to hide it. But it slipped from her fingers and fell open onto the bed. Hayley reached to pick it up again, but the underlined words of Lamentations 3 caught her eye.

I remember my affliction and my wandering, the bitterness and the gall. I well remember them and my soul is downcast within me. Yet this I call to mind and therefore I have hope: Because of the Lord's great love we are not consumed, for his compassions never fail. They are new every morning; great is your faithfulness.

Hayley sank onto the bed. In her mind, she was back in her Toronto home. She'd shaved her long, highlighted hair so she'd look as ugly as she felt. Then she'd turned up her stereo and swallowed three pills. She just couldn't do life anymore. But she'd survived and God had something to do with that. So she'd searched her Bible for answers, and when she got to Lamentations 3, she'd found her life. Hayley read the words again, slowly, as though tasting each one. Bitterness and wandering. Described her then and now. But she'd found hope in God's unfailing love. She'd failed, but He hadn't.

What had happened to the hope she'd found back then? And now what was she thinking, to give into the dark voices so easily? She knew where to find the unfailing love she so desperately needed.

She slid off the bed onto her knees and buried her wet face in the crook of her arm. "Dear Jesus, I'm sorry. I let fear blind me to Your love and faithfulness. Forgive me, please. I do want to live. For You. Even if everything and everyone is taken away, I know You are faithful."

Tranquility settled into Hayley's soul as she knelt. She lifted her head and listened. No more dark whispers. A shaft of sunlight shone on her open Bible and illuminated the whole room.

Hayley stood, opened her hand, and stared. The pills were gone.

31

A frisson of panic hit Hayley. Had her skin somehow absorbed the pills? There wasn't even a trace of powder, but maybe she should wash her hands, just in case. She pushed to her feet, lost her balance, and plopped onto the bed beside her Bible. On its open pages lay the pill bottle. Hayley picked it up and counted—five pills. Hayley's hand moved to her chest as she inhaled deeply. *God, did You do that?* Warmth wrapped itself around her, and she swallowed hard. *Thank You. I don't understand it, but thank You.*

Now what should she do with the drugs? She no longer needed them for pain, and she certainly didn't want to hang onto the temptation to harm herself again. The law said they needed to go to a pharmacist. But who would take them? A name materialized in her mind. Max. She could ask Max, her guardian angel. Hayley smiled. That was how she thought of the burly farmhand ever since he'd protected her from Blake. She stuck the pill bottle into her jeans pocket.

A vehicle pulled up to the house, and Hayley recognized the engine's rumble. Trevor. But she couldn't deal with him. He and his mother needed privacy, anyway. Hayley tried to imagine Trevor's reaction to the news of his father's need for heart surgery. Pain squeezed her heart. Her anger toward him evaporated like fog in sunshine, and a fresh breeze of love swept her back onto her knees. *Dear Jesus, help him. Help them.* After several minutes, Hayley wiped her eyes and walked to the head of the stairs.

In the living room, Trevor knelt at his mother's feet, his face in her lap, and Laureen's hand rested on his head.

Hayley sank down on the top step. She couldn't intrude, but she couldn't tear herself away. Her arms ached to hold and comfort the man she loved. Oh, how she loved him. But he needed to be with his mother now.

~*~

Trevor heard a faint moan from the direction of the staircase and lifted his head. Hayley huddled on the top step, her cheeks wet and her eyes red and puffy. He swallowed hard. How much of her grief was his doing? He sighed.

His mother followed his gaze toward the stairs. "Hayley, dear, come on down. Please."

Hayley moved toward them.

Regret surged, and Trevor rose to his feet and met Hayley at the bottom of the staircase. "I'm sorry, Hayley. Sorry for holding onto anger, and sorry for lashing out at you. Can you forgive me? You were right. I didn't know what forgiveness meant."

Her face lifted, and her wide, jade eyes began to glow. "Really? You do now?"

"Yeah. At least, I'm learning." Trevor opened his arms, and Hayley stepped into them, wrapped her arms around his waist, and pressed her cheek against his chest. He held her close and breathed in the scent of her hair. He was home.

"Thank You, Jesus." Her whisper resonated in

Trevor's heart. Hayley lifted her head without moving away. "So what happened?"

"To help me understand?"

Hayley nodded, and Trevor sighed. "Too long a story for right now, but Carlos got through to me. He told me to give Kirby to God, step back, and let God be the judge. Made sense. Doesn't mean I'll ever condone what he did, but I decided to let God deal with him."

Hayley's hand came up and cupped Trevor's jaw. Its warmth seared him, and yet he shivered. He turned his head and kissed her palm. "I still need to tell Mom about this."

Hayley pulled back, a soft smile illuminating her face. "You'll add some joy to a dark day."

They walked to the couch across from Laureen and sat close together.

Laureen's lined face crinkled into a smile. "Looks like you two got things ironed out. I'm glad."

Trevor squeezed Hayley's hand. "Yeah, me too. A lot happened today, but through it all, I learned what it means to forgive someone."

Laureen's eyebrows lifted.

"Mom, Larry Kirby came by the shop today. Stuff happened I'm not proud of, but in the end, Carlos—and God—got through to me. I released Kirby to God, and I'm finally free."

"Praise God! Oh, honey, I'm so happy." Laureen clapped her hands, her face a wreath of joyful wrinkles. "You don't know how long I've been praying for this. God is good. I can't wait to tell…" She sighed as though deflated and leaned forward, her hands on the arms of the chair. "I want to hear all about it, but right now, I think I need to go lie down, if you don't mind. It's been a difficult day. Trevor, would you help me, please?"

Trevor jumped up. "Sure, Mom."

He put his arm around her waist and helped her to her feet. Together they moved into the master bedroom. Trevor guided her to the queen-sized bed and pulled back the covers. "There you go. Do you need Hayley to help you with anything?"

"I'm fine, honey. Just worn out. Wake me in time for supper, will you?" She held up a finger. "Oh, I forgot to ask Hayley to make biscuits to go with the soup from yesterday. Could you do that for me?"

Trevor quirked a half-smile. "Ask Hayley? Or do you want me to try to make biscuits?"

"Silly boy. Ask Hayley to make them." Laureen returned his smile. "I'm so glad God brought her to us. She's a wonder in the kitchen—and blesses our days with her sweetness."

Trevor pulled the blankets up and tucked them around her. "She's a sweet wonder, all right. But I'm the one who's blessed, Mom. God gave me you and Dad, and soon, hopefully, Hayley." Trevor kissed his mother's forehead. "Rest now. I'll wake you when supper's ready."

Her eyes closed, and Trevor gulped back a lump of gratitude. And a chunk of fear. *I don't deserve her, God, but thank You for making us a family. Take care of Mom and Dad, please. I still need them.*

Hayley was in the back entry, pulling on her mud boots. Pink bloomed on her face as she looked up. "I heard Max drive up, and I need to ask him something. I'll be right back."

"Wait." Trevor grabbed his boots. "I'll come with you. I've got some questions for him too, and we need to tell him about Dad."

Hayley's nose scrunched up as though she wanted to argue, but then she turned, opened the door, and shrugged. "All right. You might as well hear too."

"What? Hey, wait for me."

Hayley turned, and her paleness gut-punched him. She didn't speak, so he quickened his steps and caught her hand. She wrapped her fingers around his palm, and his tension eased. A little.

They found Max in the corral, filling the feed troughs with grain mix. He glanced up, nodded, and resumed his work.

Trevor grabbed the pail beside Max and emptied it into the second trough. "We need to talk to you."

Max straightened, set the empty bucket on the ground, and walked to the fence where Hayley waited. "All right. What can I do for you?"

Hayley rummaged in her pants pocket. "I need a favor." She pulled out a plastic pill container and handed it to Max. "Would you take this to a pharmacist for me? I don't want them around anymore, not even for one more night."

Max gave her a long look, nodded, and stuck the bottle into the pocket of his coat. "Consider it done." Then he turned to Trevor, and the light in Max's eyes sparked a shiver up and down Trevor's spine. "And what do you need?"

Trevor shuffled his feet, unable to tear his gaze from Max. The question he'd planned to ask, about his fight with Kirby, suddenly didn't matter anymore.

"My…my dad. He's in the hospital waiting for heart surgery tomorrow." Another shiver struck, and Trevor stared at Max. "You knew?"

The older man blinked, releasing Trevor. "Don't worry. I'll take care of things here for as long as I'm needed." He turned and walked into the barn.

Trevor and Hayley looked at each other, and he wondered if his expression looked as surprised as hers. "Well, I'm confused." He paused. "And not."

He turned toward the barn, but Max didn't reappear. Trevor touched Hayley's cheek. "Anything else you wanted to talk to him about?"

She shook her head, and smiled softly. "But you probably want to know about those pills."

"I admit, I'm curious." A memory flashed. "Are those the narcotics you mentioned when we met? The painkillers you'd worked hard to wean yourself off of?"

Hayley slipped her arm through the crook of his elbow and pulled him closer as they walked. "Yes. I'd forgotten I still had them, but after our fight and the news about your father…" Her voice trailed off.

Trevor stopped and cupped her cheeks with his hands. "You don't have to tell me. I love you, and I'm glad you got rid of them, but you don't owe me an explanation."

Her smile beamed, and the light in her eyes reminded Trevor of Max. "Maybe not, but I want to tell you. God is so amazing." The light dimmed. "The first part is hard, so bear with me."

She shared about her depression and the whispers that drove her to contemplate taking all the pills. Trevor's heart clenched, and he closed his eyes against the hopelessness in hers. Then, as she explained what followed, wonder filled him.

Trevor rested his chin on the top of Hayley's head and whispered, "Thank You, Jesus."

On the same dark, trouble-filled day, they'd both been granted miracles. He didn't deserve it, never could, but for some reason, God had stepped into his life. And Hayley's. Gratitude welled up and ran down his face. *God, I don't know what You're doing, but Hayley's right. You are amazing. I can't help but wonder what You'll do next.*

32

Early the next afternoon, Hayley completed her fifth circuit of the hospital's hallways and headed back to the lounge where Laureen and Trevor waited. Franklin had been wheeled into surgery two hours ago, and according to Dr. Sharma, he wouldn't be out for at least another four hours. If everything went well. *Please, God…*

Good thing Trevor had spent the night at the farm so he could drive them in this morning. No way she could have handled driving into the city after tossing and turning all night. Between concern for Trevor's parents and knowing he was two rooms away, sleep had refused to come.

Hayley's steps slowed as she neared the door to the cardiac unit lounge. She didn't want her nervousness to upset Laureen, but the hallways reminded Hayley too much of her own hospital stays. If only she hadn't checked online information about coronary bypass surgery. Her imagination had grabbed details of the brutal yet delicate surgery and created a gruesome merry-go-round of "what-ifs." At the door, Hayley peeked through the window.

Laureen's head lay on Trevor's shoulder. Both had their eyes closed. They could be sleeping, resting, or praying, none of which Hayley wanted to interrupt. She pivoted—and came face to face with Dave and Lydia Harris.

"Pastor Dave, Lydia, thank you for coming." She fell into Lydia's embrace, while Dave patted her back.

"We came as soon as we could," Dave said. "Thank you for letting us know."

Hayley gave Lydia one more squeeze and stepped back. "I'm sure Laureen would have phoned you, but the stress has exhausted her. I'm worried about her."

Lydia slid her arm around Hayley's waist and headed toward the lounge door. "Let's see if we can convince her to come to our house for a while. Have any of you had lunch? I thought you might like some homemade food, so I made beef stew—enough for several families, according to my husband. It's good comfort food."

"I didn't even realize it was lunchtime. My stomach's so tied in knots, I skipped breakfast. Laureen didn't eat much this morning, either."

Dave opened the door. "And Franklin's not expected to be out of surgery for a while yet?"

Hayley paused outside the room. "Not for at least four hours. But Laureen doesn't want to go back to the farm. She needs to stay close."

Lydia released her and entered the room.

Laureen and Trevor both looked up, and Laureen's weary expression disappeared under a broad smile.

"Lydia and Dave. My, what a blessing to see you today. Come, have a seat. Looks like we'll be here quite a while."

Lydia leaned down and wrapped Laureen in a gentle hug, while Dave shook Trevor's hand. "Good to see you again, Trevor. You have a lovely young woman and a proud mama here. I've heard good things about you from both of them."

"Thank you, sir. Hayley told me what a difference you've made in her life."

Hayley's tension drained, leaving her weak—and hungry. "Lydia invited us to their house for lunch. Beef stew."

Trevor's eyebrows lifted, and he looked at his mother. "Sounds good to me. What do you think, Mom? It's not far from here, right?"

"Fifteen minutes, tops," Dave said.

Laureen rubbed her mouth with her fingertips. "That sounds lovely. I don't know if I can eat, but I'm sure my son could make up for my lack of appetite."

At that moment, Trevor's stomach rumbled, and Hayley hid a grin behind her hand. His face turned a sweet shade of cotton candy pink. Hmm…maybe she was hungrier than she'd thought.

Laureen chuckled for the first time that day. "That settles it. We'll come. Thank you, dear friends. I'll let the nurse at the desk know where we'll be. Just in case."

~*~

Hayley helped Lydia clear the table after lunch while the coffee maker burbled. "That was delicious, Lydia."

Trevor leaned his chair back and rubbed his belly. "Sure was. Really hit the spot."

Laureen handed her empty bowl to Lydia. "Thank you, my friend. I didn't expect to be able to eat much, but the stew was *so* good…"

Dave pushed his chair back. "I'll get the coffee and then I'm taking charge of the cleanup. Feel free to take your coffees into the living room."

Hayley opened her mouth to protest, but Dave waggled his finger. "No, you've done enough. My turn."

A few minutes later, Trevor helped his mother ease onto the couch and settled beside her. Hayley scooted close to his other side, while Lydia claimed the mission-style rocker.

Laureen leaned her head back and closed her eyes. "Oh, my, this feels good. The chairs in the waiting room aren't bad, for the first hour or so." Then she straightened, and her hand covered her heart. "I wonder how Franklin is doing." She pulled out her phone. "No word," she said. "I guess that's a good sign."

"Yes, it is." Lydia clasped her hands. "Dave and I have been praying ever since Hayley called, as I'm sure you have been all along."

Laureen's smile flashed and disappeared. "Thank you."

Trevor's mouth twisted, not much more than a spasm, but Hayley understood. She'd worried more than prayed. She'd bet Trevor had too. Prayer, for them, wasn't the first line of defense yet. Unless *Please, God. Please, God* over and over counted.

Dave walked into the room, his large hands cradling a green mug. He lowered into the brown leather recliner. "I hope you know you're welcome to stay here as long as you want. I know the farm is your home, but it's quite a distance from the hospital. We have plenty of room, and our house is open to you."

Laureen blinked several times, looked at Trevor and then Hayley. "What do you think?"

Trevor shrugged. "I don't need a place. Mine is only ten minutes away. But I don't have a guest room since Ryan's living there. Thanks anyway. If you want to stay here, Mom, I'll go get some of your stuff from the farm. Maybe Hayley could help me."

Laureen leaned forward to meet Hayley's eyes. "Would you stay here with me? I'd hate to leave you alone in that big, old house."

Hayley smiled. "Of course. I'd love to." She checked the time and nudged Trevor. "Maybe we should go now. We've got at least two more hours of waiting, and we could be back by then."

Dave pulled the lever to raise the recliner's footrest. "Sounds good. We older folks will wait here, pray, and try to relax."

Lydia walked with them to the front door. "Before you go, I wanted to remind you of our Good Friday service tomorrow evening at seven, and invite you all to Daniel and Melody's afterwards." She addressed Trevor. "That's Will Jamison's mother and step-father. Hayley's friend Will plays our main character, Barabbas."

Trevor frowned, so Hayley answered. "I hope we can come—to both, but it depends on how Franklin is doing. Can we play it by ear?"

"Of course. OK, you kids drive safely, and we'll see you in a bit." Lydia stood in the open doorway as Hayley and Trevor descended the concrete stairs to the minivan.

Hayley walked to the passenger's side but halted when she heard the distinct ring of Laureen's cell phone.

Trevor froze, and all color drained from his face. His stricken gaze met Hayley's. "Mom's cell. Must be the hospital." He whirled and dashed up the steps two at a time.

Hayley stood rooted to the spot. *Please, God, please!* After a couple of extra-long minutes, Trevor came back outside. His sheepish grin triggered a wave of relief that left Hayley weak in the knees. She climbed into the car and slumped against the seat back while Trevor got in the other side.

He took several deep breaths before turning the key.

Hayley stroked Trevor's arm. "Not the hospital?"

"Nope. Mom's doctor's office. Wanted her to come in on Monday. She explained about Dad, said she'd get back to them."

"Thank You, God."

"For sure." He paused. "But I wonder about Mom's test results. Guess we'll have to wait."

Hayley couldn't muster the energy for conversation, and it seemed Trevor felt the same. Silence reigned in the minivan until they'd turned off Highway 16 onto the grid road leading to the Hiebert farm.

Trevor turned slightly toward Hayley. "So who's this Will Jamison guy? Anything I should know about?"

"He's a friend. More of an acquaintance." She paused. "Well, I did have a little crush on him a long time ago, but I knew he wasn't the one for me. In fact, he married my friend—*Look out!"*

Trevor jerked the steering wheel and swerved around a white-tail deer standing in the middle of the road. Gravel spit and flew. "Man! That was close. Nice buck, though. Did you see those antlers?"

Hayley stared, inhaled a shaky breath. She spoke slowly and precisely, as though to a child. "No. I did not notice any antlers. I was too busy watching my life flash in front of my eyes."

"Sorry. You OK now?"

"Yes, I guess so. Didn't really need that today, though."

Trevor let out a nervous chuckle. "Me, neither. But we didn't hit it—a good thing. And we stayed on the road. Even better. God must be watching out for us."

~*~

Two hours later, Trevor, Hayley and Laureen re-entered the cardiology waiting room. Laureen looked better, the lines around her mouth not as pronounced, so the break at the Harris home must have helped.

Hayley, however, couldn't settle. The antiseptic odors and bright florescent lights triggered an edginess and tightened her nerves. She jumped up, paced the room, caught Laureen's concerned scrutiny, and sat back down.

Trevor leaned over and rubbed the back of her neck. "Relax, sweetheart. Who's in control here?"

Hayley dropped her chin to give him better access to the tense muscles at the base of her skull. "God." His fingers found the right spot, and she moaned her gratitude. "Mm-mm, that's good." *Don't stop. Ever.*

The door swung wide. Backlit by the hallway lights, a person wearing scrubs stood in the doorway for a moment. He walked into the room. Above a rumpled mask, tired eyes sought out Trevor's mother. He crossed the room and sat beside Laureen.

Hayley forgot to breathe as she tried to read his expression.

33

Friday evening, Trevor drove onto the church property and surveyed the nearly full parking area. "Lydia wasn't kidding when she said we should arrive ahead of time. Looks like half an hour wasn't too early." He pulled up and stopped in front of the church doors. "I'll let you ladies out here, and I'll find you inside after I get parked. This should be a good break from the hospital, at least."

"Thank you, dear." Laureen unbuckled her seatbelt and opened the passenger door. "Hayley and I will wait by the doors. I just wish Franklin could be here with us."

Hayley took her arm. "But he insisted we should come, and he wants to hear all about it tomorrow, right?"

Laureen nodded, sighed. "God is *so* good."

Hayley and his mom disappeared inside the church. He drove to the far end of the lot, eased his vehicle between two SUVs, and hiked back to the building. Inside, he found his mom and Hayley talking to Lydia and a middle-aged couple.

Hayley must have been watching for him, because she waved him over, her eyes alight. "Trevor, come here. Meet Daniel and Melody Martens, Will's parents."

Trevor stuck out his hand to Daniel. "Pleased to meet you, sir. And thank you for the invitation."

He turned to Melody, but instead of taking his hand, she pulled him close for a hug. The lady was small, but her strength surprised him. "Handshakes don't work for me, I'm afraid. I'm happy to meet you, Trevor."

"You, too." Embarrassment made him mumble.

Laureen took his arm, saving him from further conversation. "We'd better find our seats, while there are still some available."

Melody grasped Hayley's hand. "Don't worry. We've saved places for you. But you're right, Laureen, we should go sit down."

"Hey, T-man, how's your dad?"

A hand clapped onto Trevor's shoulder, and he spun around. "Carlos. Glad you made it. Dad's surgery went well, and he got the breathing tube out this afternoon. First thing he said was, 'God is good.' That's my dad. And he's right."

The lady behind Carlos stepped forward and smiled. "Remember me?"

"Eva. Of course." He wouldn't mention how he remembered the angry ex-wife. From the sparkle in her eyes and the way she grinned up at Carlos, maybe she really had changed. Trevor tugged Hayley away from Melody. "This is my girlfriend, Hayley Blankenship."

Carlos raised one eyebrow and grinned while the two women exchanged greetings. "We'll talk to you guys later. Gotta find a couple seats."

Melody spoke up. "There may be enough room by us, if we hurry. And sit close together."

"Sounds good to me," Eva said, with a wink at Carlos.

~*~

At seven o-clock, the church lights dimmed and Pastor Dave walked onto the stage.

Trevor half-listened to the pastor's greeting as he studied the sparse set. Plywood or cardboard walls painted as blocks with barred windows indicated a jail cell. A shiver tickled the back of his neck. He'd meant to look up the Barabbas character in the Bible he'd unearthed in his room, but the events of the last couple days had distracted him. He wished he knew what was coming.

Everyone bowed their heads, so he ducked his as Pastor Dave prayed. Man, the guy could talk to God. Like He was right there. Trevor stifled a snort. Of course God was there. It was His place. He concentrated on Dave's words.

"Father God, we ask You to bless this little drama. May it bring glory to Your holy name, and may each person here attain a clearer understanding of Your amazing love and redemption through Jesus Christ. In His name, amen." Dave looked over the audience. "We don't pretend to know the whole story of Barabbas and his reactions, but this is a fictional account woven together with what we know about Jesus. One thing I ask. At the close of this evening, please leave quietly to allow yourselves and those around you to absorb the meaning of Good Friday. Thank you."

He walked offstage, and a spotlight lit a previously dark corner of the cell. A man, naked to the waist, crouched like a caged animal. His dark blond hair was matted, and dirty smudges covered his whole body. A clank sounded, and the man stood and turned.

Trevor stared at his back, covered with realistic, long, jagged scars, and marvelled at the makeup job.

A Roman guard stood at the doorway to the cell, his expression a grimace of disgust. "You! Barabbas. Get out here."

Barabbas stood like a fighter, his feet spread and fists clenched. Then he scowled. "I've got one more day. You can't…"

The guard opened the door and spat. "I'm not your executioner, you filthy, murderous animal. We both know you deserve to die, but you're free to go."

Barabbas's mouth fell open, and his hands hung loose. Then he scowled. "Not likely. Is this some kind of cruel trick? I know I'm slated for a cross tomorrow."

The guard stepped away from the doorway, leaving it wide open. "And you deserve to hang, but you've been released. That prophet from Nazareth, Jesus—he's taking your place."

Trevor could see himself in the guilty man, and he swallowed hard as the room went dark.

The spotlight switched on again and highlighted a narrow, stone road filled with people, some crying, others jeering. He could see the top of a crude, massive wooden cross as the one carrying it trudged up the road.

Barabbas, now washed and clothed, ran from person to person. "Who is this Jesus? What did He do? Why is He being crucified?"

One after another, they answered with a story of a wonder, how Jesus had touched their hearts and lives. A woman said he'd raised her dead brother. A man shouted that Jesus had healed his daughter. He'd cleansed lepers. Changed them all.

Time suspended as Trevor entered the scene. He could have been Barabbas. If not for Jesus…

The light shut off, and the pounding of a heavy

hammer and screams of pain echoed through the room.

Trevor recoiled with each strike. Then, as a shadow through a curtain, he saw the cross raised, its victim slumped. Trevor gulped back a sob. *Jesus. It should have been me.*

A beam of light illuminated Barabbas at center stage, his arms raised and his head thrown back. "I am guilty! He is not. It should have been me!"

Trevor flinched at every word. Grief turned liquid and dripped off his chin.

The light dimmed, and Pastor Dave's deep voice came from the darkness. "For God so loved the world, He gave His one and only Son, that whoever believes in Him shall not perish but have eternal life."

Around him, Trevor heard sniffles and more than a few sobs. As the room lights came on, Laureen handed him a tissue, and he wiped his face. He looked toward the darkened stage. And he knew, without a doubt. He was Barabbas.

~*~

Other than quietly spoken directions to the Martens's house, silence filled the Jeep until Laureen said, "How I wish Franklin could have joined us. It was amazing. I'm glad we went."

Hayley gathered her thoughts back from the crucifixion. "It hit hard—in a good way. Made me understand a little better what Jesus suffered. And why." She let out her breath in a shuddering sigh. "For me. For all of us."

Trevor pulled in front of a yellow bungalow. "Here we are. Gotta admit, I'm not sure how ready I am for a party right now."

Hayley leaned forward. "It's not really a party. Just Will and his wife, the Harrises and us. Melody said Will requested it. I can't wait for you to meet him—and his wife. She's been a special friend, even when I was at my worst."

Trevor turned off the engine but didn't move to get out. "All right. But we won't stay long, right?"

Laureen reached over and tousled his hair. "We'll leave the minute you say so. Agreed?"

"OK." He got out, went around the vehicle, and opened the passenger door for his mother and the back door for Hayley. He offered an arm to each of them, and Laureen set the careful pace to the house.

"I like this front porch." Laureen patted a thick column on the covered deck. "Very cozy. And the twig chairs make me want to sit back and relax out here—although it is a bit chilly."

Hayley grinned and looked behind them at the house across the street. "It's a lot like…oh, I guess that makes sense. The one over there was Daniel's house before he and Melody married."

Trevor pressed the doorbell, and the door swung open.

"Welcome, come on in." Melody reached for Laureen and pulled her into a hug. She released Laureen and motioned to Hayley and Trevor. "Please, make yourselves at home. Dave and Lydia will be a few minutes yet, but our son and daughter-in-law will be right over."

Trevor looked confused, so Hayley whispered, "They live across the street."

Daniel joined them in the small entry and held out his hands. "Let me take your coats. And help yourself to some coffee or hot cocoa and goodies. There's quite a variety, and I can assure you, they're all fantastic. I know, because I tried one of each." He winked.

Melody laughed. "My husband loves to sample my baking. And I love to let him."

As Laureen, Hayley, and Trevor handed their jackets to Daniel and Melody, Hayley heard steps on the porch. She grabbed Trevor's arm and pulled him to the side. "That must be Will and…"

The door opened, revealing Will and Nila, and Trevor's arm stiffened under Hayley's hand. She glanced up. His jaw dropped and his skin lost its color as he gaped.

"N-Nila? Nila Black? Is it really you?"

Nila stared back. "Trevor Sinclair?"

Hayley looked from one to the other. "You know each other?"

They didn't seem to hear her, and Will shrugged as he tugged Nila inside and shut the door.

Trevor swiped his arm across his eyes. "Nila." His voice trembled, and Hayley had to lean closer to hear him. "My favorite foster sister."

Hayley gasped as understanding dawned. *Oh, God…*

Nila's eyes sparkled with unshed tears, and she ran to Trevor's outstretched arms. "I can't believe this! I heard you were in jail."

He squeezed her tightly and wept until his shoulders shook.

"And I…I thought you were dead."

34

Trevor shuffled into his tiny kitchen Saturday morning and yawned as he filled the coffeemaker. He braced his arms against the counter as he relived last night's revelations. Nila—alive! He shook his head in wonder. After all these years of bitterness at her fate...God's timing couldn't have been more perfect. Right after Trevor let go of his hatred of Kirby, Nila showed up, not only alive, but happily married and glowing with impending motherhood. Incredible.

After Laureen, Dave, and Lydia had said their goodbyes, the two younger couples walked across the street to Will and Nila's. There they'd talked long into the night, sharing their brokenness and God's mercy. Trevor found out Will's scars weren't makeup when the couple explained how they'd met and how God had redeemed them both. Definitely amazing.

Trevor poured himself a cup of coffee, grabbed his Bible, and sat at the table. Last night's drama haunted him. Trevor flipped through several pages until he found the heading, "The Crowd Chooses Barabbas" in Matthew 27. Will's portrayal of the condemned man had triggered a searing need to know the whole story. He started reading at the beginning of the chapter.

Several minutes later, Trevor closed his Bible and wiped his face. "Amazing grace, how sweet the sound that saved a wretch like me..." His voice cracked, but he sang aloud anyway. Ryan had gone home to

Lumsden for Easter, so there was no one to hear him. Except Jesus. "I once was lost, but now am found; was blind, but now I see." *Thank You, Jesus.*

He wrapped his hands around his coffee mug and swallowed hard. The purple-gray mug reminded him of Larry Kirby's mottled face as he'd run from Trevor. Shame flooded him, and his shoulders sagged. He'd been forgiven by God, but what about Kirby? Trevor groaned. He didn't want to think about Kirby, not today. But the image wouldn't leave. "Do I *have* to ask his forgiveness, Lord? You know he won't give it. And even if I tell him I forgive him, he won't believe me."

He needs to hear it from you.

Really? Hadn't he done enough by releasing Kirby to God? He listened but didn't get a response. Fine. He'd give it a shot. He grabbed his phone and searched the internet. "Larry Kirby." Nothing. He'd tried. What more could he do?

Trust Me.

Yeah, OK. But Hayley and his mother were probably anxious to get to the hospital. He'd promised to pick them up from Dave and Lydia's by ten and it was already five after. He sent a quick text to Hayley. "Running late. Will be there in thirty minutes."

Thoughts of Hayley replaced Kirby's face as Trevor pictured her short auburn hair, full lips, and those sparkling jade eyes. Her creamy skin showed every blush, and her slender, feminine figure made his pulse race. But even more, Hayley's courage and faith drew him to her like a weld to steel. Yeah, he'd stick with her forever. If she'd have him.

He just had to figure out an impressive way to propose. Humming the old hymn, he headed to the shower.

~*~

As they exited the elevator closest to the ICU, Trevor pulled Hayley closer to his left side while his mother held his right arm. He held his head high and greeted everyone in the hallway with a smile. Life was good. Until they passed the room two doors before his father's. Trevor jerked when a loud, raspy voice howled, "I don't want to die!" He'd know that voice anywhere. He released his mother and Hayley. "Go on, see how Dad's doing. I have to take care of something."

His mom raised her eyebrows but didn't say anything.

Hayley clung to his arm, though. "What's the matter? Do you know him?"

"I do, and I need to talk to him alone. OK?"

Hayley studied him for a moment, then nodded. "I'll be with your mom and dad, then."

With a deep sigh, Trevor walked towards the other room.

A nurse stopped him. "I'm sorry, sir. Family only in this area. Are you related?"

"No, but I used to be his foster son."

"Well, according to our records, he doesn't have any family. But if you want to try to comfort him, please do. I doubt it matters at this point. I just need your name." He told her, and she wrote it down. "OK, Mr. Hiebert, you've got five minutes."

"He may not want to see me."

A string of curses poured from the wired and tubed form inside the room.

"He's been unconscious until today, and he was a

lot easier to deal with then. Go on in. If you dare." She turned back to her charts.

This morning I couldn't help but praise Your timing, Lord God. Not sure I like it now. But give me the right words to say, the ones he needs to hear, in Jesus's name.

Trevor steeled himself and walked into the room. The man on the bed was barely recognizable under the bandages and bruises. "Kirby?"

The man's eyes opened wide, and his lips trembled. "I'm…already dying. You're too late...Go away."

Trevor sat on the hard chair beside the bed. "What happened?"

"Tried to beat a train…after…you…I…lost." Kirby's voice trailed off.

"I'm sorry."

Kirby swore, gasping between words.

Trevor took a deep breath and leaned forward. "Look, man, I hated you for a long time, and it messed me up pretty badly, but Jesus died to save both of us. He loves you. You did some bad stuff. So did I. But I'm forgiven, and I've forgiven you. Because of Jesus. He paid the price for both of us."

A brace held the man's head immobile, but his glazed eyes turned toward Trevor. The darkness in them sent shivers down his spine.

"It's…too…late." Kirby's mouth moved soundlessly. Then he shuddered, gasped, and stilled. Alarms sounded, and several personnel hustled into the room.

"I'm sorry, sir. You have to leave. Now." A younger nurse brusquely pulled the curtains around Kirby's bed, shutting Trevor out.

Trevor moved out of their way, his heart heavy. *So*

what happened there, Lord? What good did that do?

He listened, but didn't hear an answer. He stood in the hallway for a moment, trying to regain his composure then walked into his father's room.

"There you are, son." Franklin's weak but cheerful voice greeted him. His dad was sitting up and looking awfully chipper in spite of the tubes and wires still attached.

"Hey, Dad, you look good. How do you feel?"

Franklin's eyes twinkled. "Like I've been halfway butchered. But I'm on the mend now, and I'm grateful."

Laureen patted Franklin's leg. "I'm thankful too. God's not done with us yet."

Hayley vacated her chair and moved to Trevor's side. When he looked at her, she tilted her head slightly and raised her eyebrows. He understood her unasked question and took her hand.

"Mom, Dad, I need to talk to Hayley for a few minutes. Do you mind?"

His mother's smile caressed him. "Go on, you two. I'm content to stay with my sweetheart."

"I'll be here when you get back." His dad winked and made a shooing motion.

Trevor led Hayley far down the hall, away from the room where someone called for a crash cart, and found a quiet corner. He pulled her close and inhaled the sweet, clean scent of her hair.

Hayley cupped his cheek with her hand. "Are you all right? What happened in there?"

Trevor leaned into her touch. "That was Kirby. He…he collided with a train after we fought." Regret and sorrow tangled into a lump in his throat. "I had to tell him about God's forgiveness…but he wouldn't listen." His arms tightened around Hayley. "And now, I think it may be too late."

~*~

Hayley traced the lines on Trevor's brow, but her touch couldn't erase them. "What do you mean, you *had* to talk to him? Did God tell you to?"

Trevor's lips twisted. "I think so. I sure got that impression, but now I don't know. I mean, what good did it do?"

Help me out here, Lord. Please. "So you obeyed, even though I'm sure it wasn't pleasant."

He grunted—in agreement, she assumed. Hayley lowered her voice to not much more than a whisper. "Did God tell you to change Larry Kirby? To save him?"

Trevor's head jerked up, dislodging Hayley's hand. After two agonized heartbeats, he moved his hand to the back of Hayley's head, lowered his face to meet hers, and spoke against her waiting mouth. "That's what I love about you. You get right to the heart of the problem—and my heart. Thank you."

Hayley slid her arms around his neck and pressed her lips against his. Mm-mm, citrusy. Part of her mind connected his taste to the health benefits of citrus fruit. *He must be good for me.* She smiled against his lips, but then he deepened the kiss, and all thought disappeared under a flood of sensation. Warmth, electricity, and need swirled together. Hayley moaned from somewhere under her ribcage. "More."

An alarm sounded down the hall, and Trevor broke contact, breathing hard.

Reality barged in, and heat rushed up Hayley's

neck. "Oh, my." She held her hands against her hot cheeks to cool them as she glanced around. No one seemed to be paying them any attention. Thankfully. She peeked up at Trevor. He looked a little overheated too, and that made her smile. Hayley took his hand, brought it to her lips, and kissed it. "Maybe we should go back to your father's room, hmm?"

Trevor sucked in a breath and straightened his spine. "Yeah, they're probably wondering what happened to us. You going to tell them?" He winked.

Hayley swatted his arm. "Not about kissing you." She sobered. "But about Larry Kirby—do you want to tell them?"

Trevor sighed. "I guess so. We don't always get a happy ending, do we?"

Hayley nibbled her lower lip for a moment. "No, not from our viewpoint, anyway. But we have to remember, God is in control. And leave it with Him. We could pray together for Larry Kirby. God knows his heart."

Trevor ran a finger down the side of her face, leaving tingles in its wake. "You're good for me, Red. Let's go see the folks, before you tempt me to kiss you again."

Hayley smiled. Another time, another place…she'd enjoy tempting Trevor Hiebert for the rest of her life.

She grasped his hand, and they walked toward Franklin's room.

But just as Trevor reached for the door handle, a nurse hurried toward them.

"Mr. Hiebert, wait!"

35

Hayley clutched Trevor's hand as the nurse drew near. Was something wrong with Franklin? Why else would she flag Trevor down?

"Mr. Hiebert, I'm glad I caught you."

Trevor slid his arm around Hayley and pulled her close to his side. She wasn't sure if he needed her strength or was offering his. Either way, she appreciated the gesture.

"Hello again." He glanced at the nurse's nametag. "Amanda. What can I do for you?"

The nurse shook her head, her eyes troubled. "Nothing, really. Larry Kirby passed away a few minutes ago. I thought you should know."

Hayley's hand flew to her mouth. *Oh, Lord…*

Trevor released a shuddering breath. "I see. Thank you for telling me." He frowned. "But wait a minute. Kirby did have family. He was married. To Delores."

"Let me check our records." The nurse hurried to the semi-circular desk and flipped several pages. Then she sat at the computer for a minute or two. When she returned, her expression told them she didn't have good news.

"Delores Kirby died two years ago of a drug overdose. I'm sorry." A bell sounded, and Amanda turned. "Excuse me, I have to go. I really am sorry." She rushed up the hallway to another room.

Hayley peered up at Trevor. Sorrow, relief, and

other expressions she couldn't decipher flitted across his face. "Are you all right?"

He looked at her without seeming to see her. "Yeah, I guess so." He rubbed his face. "I don't know what to think. Or do."

"Let's go see your parents. I know I could use a dose of your father's good humor."

"Me, too." Trevor pushed the door open, but stalled halfway into the room.

Hayley had to quick-step around him to avoid bumping into him. Then she too, stopped.

Franklin and Laureen huddled together on his bed, their heads close together.

Laureen glanced up at them, grabbed a tissue, and wiped her eyes. "Come in, you two." She smiled crookedly. "Don't mind us. We were just talking, praying, and praising God."

Franklin agreed with surprising vigor. "And now we need to talk to you."

Trevor pulled up a chair for Hayley and then sank into the one next to hers. Hayley steeled herself for their news.

"But first," Laureen said, "did you talk to the fellow in the other room? Who was it?"

Trevor clenched his jaw for a second before he responded. "Larry Kirby."

Laureen gasped. "What happened, son?"

Trevor inhaled a deep, shaky breath. "After our confrontation, he drove away. Drunk. Got hit by a train." He slumped forward, his head in his hands.

Hayley scooted her chair closer so she could rub his back. She yearned to hold and comfort him, but that would have to wait. *Dear Lord, help him get through this.*

Trevor spoke through his hands. "I told him I forgave him because God has forgiven me, but I don't think I got through to him. And now he's dead."

Laureen slid off the bed and stood in front of Trevor, her hand on his shoulder. "Oh, honey, I'm so proud of you."

He lifted his face, a perplexed frown scrunching his features. "What? Why?"

Hayley's heart swelled as Laureen poured grace onto her son through her tender touch and expression. *I want to be like her, Lord—wise and full of love.*

"Trevor." Laureen waited until he met her steady gaze. "Did you kill Larry Kirby? Did you make him get drunk and try to race a train? Are you responsible for *anything* he did?"

"No, of course not." He looked puzzled, but light re-entered his eyes. "No, I didn't."

"Did you obey when God sent you to him, in spite of the hurt he'd caused?"

Trevor nodded.

Laureen smiled through tears. "That is why I'm proud of you. One of the many reasons." She raised her face toward the ceiling. "Thank You, Lord, for the miracle You are working in this wonderful son of ours."

Hayley wiped under her eyes.

Trevor echoed her movement before he took his mother's hand. "I love you, Mom. And you too, Dad."

Franklin nodded. "Right back at you, son. I'm sorry for that fellow, but you did what you needed to. You did your part."

Laureen moved back to Franklin's side and settled onto his bed, carefully avoiding the attached lines. "Now, do you want to tell them, or shall I?"

"Go ahead."

Apprehension tightened Hayley's jaw, and she almost forgot to breathe.

Trevor leaned forward. "What?"

Laureen smiled, and Hayley's tension eased. The news couldn't be too terrible, not with that serene expression.

"You know we'd talked about moving into the city. Well, recent events…" She glanced around the hospital room. "We've prayed about it for quite a while, and now is the time for us to give up the farm. We need to be closer to medical care, and neither one of us is able to care for such a big house and farm work any longer."

Hayley slid down in her chair as her optimism dissolved. Where would she live? What would she do? What about *them?* She dared a peek at Trevor, but he was staring straight ahead as though seeing something she couldn't. He didn't look worried, though. Why should he? He already had a home and a job.

"I know this feels sudden to you both." Laureen continued as though she hadn't just ripped Hayley's fantasies apart. "But we've talked about it before. It will take some time to find the best home for us, and Hayley, I hope you'll help me with the search, since it will be on my shoulders for the most part."

Hayley's mind whirled. How could she hasten her own departure from the home of her dreams? But how could she not do everything possible to help these two beloved people, the ones who'd opened their hearts and home to her? "S-sure, I'll do whatever I can."

"Trev?" Franklin sounded tired, but he leaned forward to catch his son's gaze.

Trevor shook himself and then smiled. "Yeah,

makes sense. I should have expected this. Does complicate things a bit, but…" He stood and finally glanced Hayley's way. Barely. Why was he ignoring her now, when she needed his reassurance so much?

Trevor walked past her to the door. "Mom, could I talk to you for a minute? Alone?"

~*~

Late that night, Trevor paced his living room. The roller coaster events of the day had left him off balance; even taking his mom and Hayley out to his favorite Italian restaurant for dinner hadn't calmed him. Neither had the tender goodnight from Hayley when he'd dropped them off at the Harris place.

He dropped to his knees in front of his couch. "Lord God, I need You. Help me do this right. You've done a lot of amazing things in my life in a short time, but I need one more miracle." He rested his head on his clasped hands for several more minutes, until peace settled into his soul. "Thank You, Jesus."

Trevor's cell phone buzzed. He pushed *Talk*. "Hey, Ry, how're things in Lumsden?"

"Great. The whole family is here at my folks'—including my sister's four kids—so it's kinda crazy, but that's not why I called. Seen the news lately?"

"No, I've been busy." Understatement of the year. Trevor grimaced.

"Turn on your TV, channel ten."

"Now?"

"Yeah, hurry up."

Trevor pushed the button on the remote and punched in *10*. And stared. The camera zoomed in on Vince Starr, in handcuffs, being led out of an impressive two-story house.

The reporter's voice registered. "As part of the joint undercover operation by the RCMP and the FBI, Vince Starr, owner of Lowrider Cycles, was arrested today without incident at his home on the charges of drug smuggling and money laundering for a New York-based crime family. More arrests are expected in the coming week. Stay tuned..."

"Did you see it?" Ryan voice had gone up an octave. "That's who you were gonna work for, right?"

Trevor sank into his recliner. "Yeah."

Ryan lowered his voice. "Glad you didn't go, bud."

"Me, too." Trevor blew out a long breath. "Thanks for the heads up. And, uh…happy Easter." He disconnected, leaned forward, and whispered. "Thank You, God, for saving me from my selfish ambition. I would have been right in that mess if You hadn't stopped me." He paused, contemplated. "Thank You for saving me, period."

A name came to his mind: Nate Smith. The guy who'd looked him up, offered him a place to live, and then warned him to stay away. The questions he'd wrestled with fell into place like pieces to a puzzle. Smith had to have been involved in the undercover operation. No wonder he'd been able to find out so much about Trevor. "Thank You, God, for using Smith to protect me, too. Protect him now, for Jesus's sake."

His heart full, Trevor turned off the lights, locked the door, and headed to bed. Tomorrow was Easter, and he couldn't wait. A shiver of anticipation mixed with nervousness raced up and down his spine. Tomorrow would be a life changer, no matter how it turned out.

36

Easter Sunday morning, Hayley inspected her image in the full-length mirror. She'd decided to wear her favorite, a green silk dress, hoping it would boost her spirits and maybe impress the man she loved. The jade color matched her eyes, and the silk swirl around her knees felt luscious. She'd gained weight since the last time she'd worn it, and it felt good. She finally had curves again.

Trevor had called to make arrangements to drive her and Laureen to church, since Dave and Lydia always went early to pray together before the service. Trevor's offer of a ride was no surprise, but his tone of voice puzzled her. He'd sounded stressed…or something. She couldn't figure it out, and it worried her.

Hayley picked up her Bible and went upstairs to see if Laureen needed help. The older woman rarely complained, but she was anxious to get the cast off her arm. "Laureen?" Hayley knocked on the bedroom door. "Can I help you with anything?"

"Oh, yes, please." Laureen opened the door, and her hand went to her chest. "You look absolutely stunning, my dear."

Hayley's cheeks warmed. "You do, too. That royal blue looks fantastic on you. You're so beautiful."

Laureen turned around, exposing her back. "Thank you, but I can't zip it, and I really don't want to show up at church like this. Do you mind?"

Hayley pulled the zipper up. "How much longer until your cast comes off?"

"I'm not sure. At least another couple of weeks. Old bones don't heal as quickly, you know." Laureen faced Hayley. "I don't know what I would have done without you…" She leaned forward to kiss Hayley's cheek. "I love you."

The whisper shot straight to Hayley's heart, and moisture sprang to her eyes, threatening her composure—and makeup. "I love you, too."

The doorbell rang, and Laureen grinned. "I can't wait to watch my son's face when he sees you."

Hayley followed Laureen down the stairs and wished she could feel as confident.

Laureen went to the door and motioned for Hayley to stand in the center of the entry hall. "Right there, under the light. Ready?"

Hayley swallowed a lump of insecurity and nodded.

Laureen swung the door wide, and Hayley forgot to breathe. *Wow.* She'd never seen Trevor in a suit before, and he cleaned up good. No, not just good. Fantastic. Wonderful. Delicious. Her face burned.

Laureen chuckled. "Close your mouth, son, and come in."

Trevor shook his head and stepped inside. He looked from Hayley to Laureen and back again. "The two most beautiful women in the world." He lifted his face as though in prayer. "How did I deserve this?"

Laureen swatted his arm. "You didn't. We're evidence of God's grace." She grinned and mussed his hair.

"Mo-m."

Hayley smiled at his little-boy protest. Then Trevor came closer and took both her hands in his, and Hayley's smile dissolved as her lips quivered with anticipation. *Hurry up and kiss me.*

Laureen backed away. "I forgot my purse. I'll be right back."

Hayley heard footsteps going upstairs, and then she didn't hear anything but the pounding of her heart as Trevor lowered his head toward hers. He rested his forehead on hers, his minty breath caressing her face. "Happy Easter, beautiful lady. May I kiss you?"

She lifted her lips to his. "Yes, please, gorgeous man."

Too soon, footsteps intruded, and Laureen cleared her throat. "Ready to go?"

Trevor pulled back, breathing hard. "Um, sure, Mom. Let me help you with your coat."

Hayley pressed her fingers to her tingling lips, unable to speak. A tender thrill raced through her, as Trevor held Laureen's coat for her, fastened the buttons, and then kissed her cheek.

The sweetness of his gesture filled Hayley with a deep yearning. Would she ever enjoy that kind of relationship with a son of her own?

Trevor held out Hayley's dove gray coat. "My lady."

She smiled as she slipped her arms into the silk-lined sleeves. "Thank you, my lord."

Laureen fanned herself with her good hand and chuckled. "All right, you two, let's get to church. This is a Sunday for celebration."

Trevor sobered. "Yes, it is. For many reasons, and I have something to ask you."

Hayley's heart stuttered.

~*~

Trevor glanced over at Hayley as he stopped for a red light. She must have felt his gaze, because she turned and smiled.

"You OK with going out to the farm for a few minutes?"

Hayley looked down at her dress coat and heels. "Well, I'm not exactly dressed for a walk in the pasture, but you know I've missed the farm, even though we've only been gone a couple of days. And you've got me curious."

He grinned but refused to say anything more. His plan just might work. The light turned green, and Trevor accelerated. So did his pulse.

As he travelled the familiar highway, he ticked off the list in his mind. So far, so good. After church—and Pastor Dave's thought-provoking sermon on Jesus's resurrection—they'd enjoyed the ham feast Lydia and Hayley had prepared. Tick. Then, while helping clear the table, he'd asked Lydia if they'd give his mother a ride home from the hospital. She'd winked and agreed. Tick.

There was that glitch, a moment of panic, when they'd reached the ICU and found someone else in Franklin's bed. His mother had clutched his arm so hard, he'd probably have a bruise. But his dad had been moved into a regular room—another reason to rejoice. He'd never forget his mom's expression when they got to his dad's new room and found him sitting up, talking to his new roommate about Easter. And his dad's joyful smile when he spotted his wife.

Trevor glanced at Hayley again. Lord willing,

someday he'd have a marriage like theirs with the beauty sitting beside him.

After visiting with his father, Trevor had asked Hayley if she'd like to take a walk with him. He drove them to the Meewasin Trail, the paved walkway meandering beside the South Saskatchewan River as it flowed through the city. Tick.

Blue skies and warm, spring sunshine collaborated with his plans, and they'd walked hand in hand for nearly an hour, discussing fostering, farming, and other dreams. Where the trail led through a cluster of trees, he'd pulled Hayley into his embrace and tasted his favorite dessert—her lips. Until a jogger whooped as he ran by. Way to wreck a moment. Oh well, Trevor was anxious to get to the farm, anyway.

He slowed his Jeep as they neared the turnoff to the grid road. Would Max's efforts turn out the way he hoped? Had their walk given him enough time?

~*~

Hayley didn't know what to think. Trevor had been acting rather strange all day. She'd wondered if he'd planned to propose when he invited her to go for a walk, but it didn't happen. Now they were almost to the farm. Had Max gone somewhere else for Easter, so Trevor had to do the chores? They were both still wearing their Easter finery, but they could change into work clothes, if needed. She sighed quietly and hoped Trevor hadn't heard.

They drove into the farm yard, and he pulled close to the house. When he turned off the vehicle and removed his keys from the ignition, he dropped them. His ears turned red, and he mumbled something under his breath as he retrieved them. "Sorry. Here we are." Trevor got out and hurried around to her side to help her out. "My lady."

Hayley smiled. She could get used to such gallantry.

Trevor slid his arm around her waist and led her, not to the front door, but toward the barn. *What?*

As they reached the back corner of the house, a glow caught Hayley's attention. A few more steps, and she gasped. The gazebo was covered with hundreds of tiny white lights, and red cushions decorated its bench.

"Trevor?" Her voice quivered.

He smiled crookedly as he led her into the gleaming shelter. He gestured to the bench.

Hayley sat, her heart pounding. Could he hear it? She looked up at the man she loved.

He stood tall, his eyes hooded, his jaw firm, and a frisson of apprehension shivered through her.

Trevor sank to one knee, and her heart sang. He fumbled a bit as he pulled a small, heart-shaped box out of his jacket pocket.

Hayley couldn't hide her smile.

He cleared his throat, swallowed hard, and opened the box. Her breath caught. Inside lay the most gorgeous ring she'd ever seen, an emerald surrounded by sparkling diamonds.

"Hayley Blankenship, I love you. I know God, in His amazing mercy, brought you into my life, and I want to keep you here. For the rest of our lives. If you're willing. I want to live with you, have babies with you, maybe adopt some kids together, and grow old with you." He took a deep breath. "Will you marry me?"

She bounced on the cushion. "Yes! To all of it. Of

course I'll marry you. Today. Tomorrow. Whenever. I love you." She pulled on his extended arm. "Now come up here and kiss me. Please."

Trevor sat beside her, slid the ring onto her finger, and wrapped his arms around her. Finally, his lips claimed hers, and their hearts pounded in sync. He tasted so good. His arms felt so strong, so right. Then rational thought surrendered to wonder-filled, loving passion.

Sometime later, Hayley wasn't sure how long, they pulled apart, breathing hard. She caressed Trevor's forehead, down his face to his whiskery jawline. "I-I think we'd better set a date—the sooner, the better."

Trevor leaned into her touch. "I hoped you'd feel that way. But I thought weddings took a long time to organize."

Hayley snuggled deeper into his embrace. "I don't want a fancy wedding. You, me, Pastor Dave and Lydia, your parents…." A sigh escaped. "I guess we should invite my parents too."

Trevor's lips brushed her forehead as he whispered. "I already talked to your father. It was awkward at first, but he gave us his blessing. I promised to give them at least a week's notice."

Hayley's mouth fell open. "You're kidding. My dad? Blessing us? Wait a minute. Just how awkward was it?"

"God's got this, remember?"

He must. Gratitude and joy filled her until she thought she'd burst. "I love you, Trevor Hiebert. How soon can we get married?"

EPILOGUE

Two months later, Trevor and Hayley Hiebert snuggled in the backseat of a taxi as it whisked them to the airport.

Trevor kissed her nose. "Awfully nice of your folks to spring for a honeymoon in Hawaii."

Hayley pulled his mouth down to hers. "Mm-hm." Breathless minutes later, she shifted an inch or two away. "God's working there too. Mom hugged me—I'm still in shock. And Dad? I think you've got a fan, there, Mr. Hiebert."

"He must be a good judge of character."

Hayley laughed. "Obviously. It will be interesting, to say the least, if they do come visit us next Christmas."

Trevor covered a yawn. "I gotta say, that was the fastest—and slowest—two months of my life."

Hayley didn't bother to hide her yawn. "Agreed. Your mom was amazing. Moving, then our wedding—she breezed through it all as if she was half her age. Her Meniere's must be responding well to homeopathy. She told me she hasn't felt dizzy in weeks. And I love your folks' condo. The park behind them should help them adjust to the city."

"Yeah, Dad said he watches people now instead of cattle, and he's not sure there's much difference. Except cattle are more content."

Hayley rested her head on her husband's

shoulder. "No surprise there. They've got space, plenty of food, and fresh air—except when the manure pile thaws. And someone to take care of them."

Trevor nuzzled her hair. "Sounds like a good life, all right. Here's to farm life." He raised a pretend chalice.

Hayley followed suit. "And here's to a life filled with love, grace, endurance—like Pastor Dave said—and children. Lots of children."

"Hear, hear. Let's get started on that." He lifted her chin with one finger and whispered against her lips. "All of it."

Thank you

We appreciate you reading this White Rose Publishing title. For other inspirational stories, please visit our on-line bookstore at www.pelicanbookgroup.com.

For questions or more information, contact us at customer@pelicanbookgroup.com.

White Rose Publishing
Where Faith is the Cornerstone of Love™
an imprint of Pelican Book Group
www.PelicanBookGroup.com

Connect with Us
www.facebook.com/Pelicanbookgroup
www.twitter.com/pelicanbookgrp

To receive news and specials, subscribe to our bulletin
http://pelink.us/bulletin

May God's glory shine through
this inspirational work of fiction.

AMDG

You Can Help!

At Pelican Book Group it is our mission to entertain readers with fiction that uplifts the Gospel. It is our privilege to spend time with you awhile as you read our stories.

We believe you can help us to bring Christ into the lives of people across the globe. And you don't have to open your wallet or even leave your house!

Here are 3 simple things you can do to help us bring illuminating fiction™ to people everywhere.

1) If you enjoyed this book, write a positive review. Post it at online retailers and websites where readers gather. And share your review with us at reviews@pelicanbookgroup.com (this does give us permission to reprint your review in whole or in part.)

2) If you enjoyed this book, recommend it to a friend in person, at a book club or on social media.

3) If you have suggestions on how we can improve or expand our selection, let us know. We value your opinion. Use the contact form on our web site or e-mail us at customer@pelicanbookgroup.com

God Can Help!

Are you in need? The Almighty can do great things for you. Holy is His Name! He has mercy in every generation. He can lift up the lowly and accomplish all things. Reach out today.

Do not fear: I am with you; do not be anxious: I am your God. I will strengthen you, I will help you, I will uphold you with my victorious right hand.

~Isaiah 41:10 (NAB)

We pray daily, and we especially pray for everyone connected to Pelican Book Group—that includes you! If you have a specific need, we welcome the opportunity to pray for you. Share your needs or praise reports at http://pelink.us/pray4us

Free Book Offer

We're looking for booklovers like you to partner with us! Join our team of influencers today and receive at least one free eBook per month. Maybe more!